DEADLINES AR...

A Sam Monroe Mystery

By
Anne Macdonald

* * * * *

*****

Dear Irma,
I hope you enjoy
my story.
Love,
Anne

Chapter 1

Why can't you be more like Donna?" Rick asked.

Sam had hoped that Rick would still be asleep and this continuing argument could wait until later. Besides, why should I want to be like Donna, she thought to herself.

"So, you're going into the office, even though it's the last day of our vacation together?" Rick asked. He was sitting up in bed, staring at the blanket rather than look at Sam.

"Hey, I'm sorry I woke you," Sam said. Sam moved across the bedroom to her closet to select a navy blue suit to wear to work.

"I thought you were going to quit this job like we discussed?"

Sam walked across the bedroom to her closet. She had decided to wear her navy blue suit to work today. A suit was always easier than trying to figure out multiple pieces, Sam thought, especially when you're running late. She knew that Rick would be angry if she went into the office rather than stay home with him but Jane had called a meeting and her attendance was required. They had had 7 wonderful days together without either one of them talking about work, could going into the office for an hour or two really matter.

"Look, it's a good job and it pays well and I like what I do. It helped us while you got your Ph.D.," Sam replied.

"Yes, it did, of course it did. Your Dad never fails to remind me. But now I'm making money and it would be great if you were around when I'm around."

"Look Donna did everything Tom asked of her, working at the bank so they would have benefits while he got himself established and did work for Tom after hours doing the books and look where it got her."

"Hey, Tom's a jerk. He should never have taken up with that part-time secretary. But once he got her pregnant, what else could he do?"

There were probably a lot of other choices Tom could have made but the one's he chose were not one's that want Sam to be more like Donna.

"I'll call you as soon as the meeting is over and we can make plans for the rest of day."

"Don't bother. I'm going to head over to the school to catch up on things."

"Well, the semester's done and your grades are in, what else do you need to do?"

"Research and writing. Remember, I need to get published. Plus you've ruined the whole vacation for me now." Rick said. "I'm going to take a shower. You won't be here when I get out so have a fun day at the office."

Sam rolled her eyes and continued dressing. Rick may be unhappy but it had been a great vacation and this was just a minor hiccup. Sam looked at herself in the bedroom mirror. Her blue suit, light colored silk shirt, dark brown hair and blue eyes were set off by her newly acquired tan. Her lack of make-up would hardly be noticed.

Sam arrived late and headed straight to the conference room without checking her messages or emails. Jane had called her directly on Sunday, she and Rick's last day in the Bahamas, and asked her to be at this 8am meeting on Monday morning. They had argued about this on the plane flight home and she thought Rick had understood that she needed to at this meeting. It wasn't like she asked him to leave early, they were already scheduled to fly back on Sunday night.

Now that she was in the conference room with all the other members of the personal banking team looking at the grim looks on the faces of those around her, she realized that this was not the meeting she anticipated. Sam quickly took a seat at the large conference room table.

Jane stood at the head of the conference room table and announced that they were all being laid off. They were all being laid off because the newly merged bank had two different personal banking units and they needed to condense these into just one. The merger of the two units was heavily in favor of the other team, a more traditional team than the one that Jane had put together, the team currently sitting around the table together, the team that included Sam. They were all being sent home after their individual severance meeting with Human Resources of course.

They all filed out of the conference room, gathering their schedule for their severance meeting from Brenda at the door and saying good-bye to Jane. Sam was amazed at how well everyone appeared to be handling this announcement, unless they all needed to process what just happened. She heard no angry complaints and so far everyone seemed resigned to their fates. Sam realized that her life would not be the same again. She had worked hard to get where she was and now she would be leaving the bank, just like Rick wanted her to do.

Her meeting time was scheduled for 11:30am and it wasn't even 9am yet. A set of empty boxes were in her office waiting to be filled. They had been delivered while everyone was at the meeting. Sam immediately called Rick but there was no answer. She was just about to dial his University number when Donna appeared at her door.

"Well, I just heard the news. You must be devastated." Donna said. Donna was leaning against the doorway to Sam's office with a look of concern on her face. Donna's red curly hair framed her fair, freckled face and her tight skirt and blouse set off her figure while heals made her seem taller than her 5'7" frame. A lot of men fell for the package and it was a well put together package.

"I'm really, really shocked at what's happening. We're all going to be sent home for good. I know that I'll be alright for a while but some of the team members are the sole breadwinners for their families. This is really going to hurt."

"Well, it's what happens in the banking world in a bad economy and during a merger. Look at me, I'm only a teller but I'm still employed and that's a good thing," Donna replied, dropping to a seat in front of Sam's desk. "So, will you get an MBA now?"

"I don't know, I haven't had much time to think about it."

"You should try working out more, now that you're unemployed." Donna said casually, without looking directly at Sam.

Sam could feel the prickly fingers of tension and anger running up her spine to the back of her head. She hoped that the heat spreading across her face did not show so Donna wouldn't have the satisfaction of knowing that she had hit one of Sam's hot buttons.

"I see," Sam replied, gritting her teeth. "Don't you get bored doing the same thing over and over again every day?"

"Pretty much the same as you do," Donna replied.

"Actually, Rick has wanted me to quit for a while. Now I'll have some time to write my novel and consider what I want to do next," Sam replied.

"Really, I thought that, well no matter, who knows what I thought. You two and your careers. Tom and his wife and kids and his career. Humph. You know, there is more to life than careers," Donna stood up from the chair in front of Sam's desk. "Well, at least I'm still employed. Have you told Rick yet?"

"No, I tried him at home but he didn't pick up. I was just about to call him at the University," Sam replied.

"Well, my break is nearly over so I better get back down to the floor before they miss me. And I'm sorry that you got laid off. Call me later tonight so we can talk."

Donna was gone from her office as quickly as she'd arrived. Sam stared after Donna wondering how they could have been best friends. Well, it wasn't that hard, they had had more in common 9 years ago than they do now. Sam had been more ambitious and Donna more of a home body back then. Now they were almost completely opposite.

Sam called Rick at the University but got no answer. Rick could easily still be walking to his office from their condo in the leather district of Boston or he could be meeting with another professor or even Arthur, the department chair. Rick had said that Arthur was concerned that Rick wasn't published yet and that publication was needed for tenure. She then called Rick's cell phone and left a quick message asking Rick to call her but didn't leave any details about what had happened at work. News like this would be best delivered in person, she thought.

Sam was packed before her meeting with the severance counselor. It was a very straight forward explanation of benefits and severance pay and they were done. The counselor was concerned that Sam wasn't more upset about everything. Sam explained that she was pretty sure she would be good for a while because they both worked and they had no children. The counselor said that that Sam was lucky; so many of the others had more pressing concerns, particularly those who had a spouse who did not work or wasn't working right now. Sam didn't feel lucky, she felt rootless.

Sam then stopped by to say good-bye to Jane and Brenda. Brenda was crying, mostly from saying good-bye to everyone. Jane asked that Sam keep in touch and let Jane know how she was doing and what she was doing next. She encouraged Sam to go for her MBA but Sam let her know she wasn't sure about that yet. Sam then said good-bye to some of her team members who were still packing. It had been an exhausting day and it was now only 2pm.

Sam and a mover gathered up the five boxes she was taking home with her. The mover got all the boxes into a cab, said good-bye to Sam and lumbered back into the office building to help the next one. The trip home was fast, especially for this time of day. The condo was in the leather district of Boston and Sam usually walked to her downtown office every day, relying on cabs only in bad weather and when she had too much stuff to carry. It was nice that she and Rick could rely on being carless and had access to a rental car a couple of times a month to do more extensive shopping or to get out of town for a weekend. The cab driver helped her unload her boxes onto the sidewalk and took off for the next paying customer.

Sam stood on the corner, about 100 feet from her front door which was in the center of the block and wondered how she was going to get everything up to her condo. She couldn't do five boxes by herself and she didn't want to leave any of the boxes to random passersby. While she contemplated how best to do this or if she could find someone who would stop and help her, she saw two neighbors, Kate and Ben, heading out of the building. Kate and Ben were inseparable when they were both home, and both were without significant others. Sam waved and yelled to get their attention. They both waved back and then reluctantly headed to the corner where Sam stood with her boxes.

"I was just laid off and I need some help getting my stuff up to the condo," Sam continued. "If you could just watch my stuff while I make trips to get it all inside the door, I'd be really greatful."

Kate and Ben exchanged an odd glance and then both looked at her. "Why don't you call up to your place and have Rick help you?" Kate asked.

"Rick's at the University catching up on some work. If you could help me get this stuff inside the door, I can take it from there," Sam replied.

"Ok, well I'll call Rick for you and have him come down," Kate replied. Kate dialed the number that Sam gave her and again there was no answer. Kate and Ben exchanged a cryptic look and both turned to Sam.

"It might be best for you to go up yourself. If you and Ben each take the boxes, I'll grab the door," Kate replied.

"Well, ok, if you're sure," Sam replied. Sam thought they were acting a bit weird but she was grateful for the help so decided to ignore the looks Kate and Ben were exchanging. She knew they didn't like Rick very much. They thought he was cold, unfeeling and should treat Sam better.

"I'll keep an eye on things and Ben can help you take boxes up to your place. That way it should only take a couple of trips." A cab stopped to see if Kate needed a ride. Things like that always happened to Kate and never, ever happened to Sam or Ben apparently. Everyone else in the city had to fight for a cab but they seemed to just show up for Kate. Sam and Ben picked up the boxes and headed for the front door. Kate opened the door and another neighbor held it open while Kate opened the locked interior door.

"You know, I think that Kate could get a cab in a rain storm and I can't even get one on a good day," Ben said as they entered the building. Kate just rolled her eyes.

Sam got her keys out while they rode the elevator to the 6th floor. It was a short walk from the elevator to the front door of Sam's condo and she quickly opened the door and put her boxes down just inside the door. She held the door while Ben put his next to hers Kate stood in the hallway and Ben quickly joined Kate.

"Thanks for all you help with these. I don't know what I would have done if you hadn't been there to help me," Sam said.

"Not a problem. Are you sure you are all set?" Kate asked.

"I think I can handle it from here," Sam replied.

"Look, we're having a late lunch at Cecilia's. Please feel free to join us if you need a break," Ben said and he pushed a reluctant Kate out the door. "I'm sure it's been a rough day so far."

Sam thanked them again and closed the door. It was a good invitation and she hadn't had any lunch yet. As she headed down the short hallway to the office cum guest room she noticed that the bedroom door was closed, which was unusual. She pushed it open and was surprised to find Rick pulling on his pants. She was even more surprised to see a young woman getting dressed, half-hidden by Rick. She looked at the bed and realized that they had just gotten out of the bed, her bed, her and Rick's bed. Her mind was racing as she stood frozen in place looking at them numbly.

"Isn't this a surprise," Rick said with a cold smile. "You're home awfully early for a work day."

"I've been laid off," Sam replied. "What's your excuse?"

"Well, I'm taking a break with Ariella here," Rick replied with a toss of his head towards the girl standing next to him. "She didn't have to go to work today."

Rick had stopped dressing and looked at Sam with his arms crossed across his chest. Ariella continued to dress without looking at Sam or at Rick.

"Ah, well, that explains it then," Sam said and then turned back towards the kitchen. She needed to sit down and have a cup of tea or something stronger.

"Well, now that you know about us you can pack your things and leave," Rick followed Sam back to the combined kitchen and living room.

"Leave? Why should I leave? This condo is in my name, yours doesn't appear anywhere on the mortgage," Sam replied. Her voice presented a quietness and control she wasn't feeling. She leaned on the counter next to the kitchen sink, hoping she looked casual but knowing that the counter was holding her up.

"What do you mean this isn't yours?" the young woman's voice piped up from behind Rick. Ariella had followed Rick without either of them noticing her.

Sam looked at Rick. Her mind noticed that he really was very, very handsome with dark hair, a trim body and finely chiseled face. She should have known he was cheating on her and lying too. The vacation must have been a fluke. Hell, the marriage now seemed like a fluke.

Rick stared at Sam, as if his staring would somehow change things or intimidate Sam into leaving.

"Rick has no ownership of this condo. The mortgage is in my name and my father's so until a judge makes us split the proceeds of a sale during a divorce settlement, I'm the one staying here and he's leaving," Sam replied. Again, her calm and composure surprised even her.

"Well," Rick sputtered. "If that's how you feel, I'll be out of here in an hour. I'll pack my bags and you'll never see me again."

"That's fine with me. I'll be getting the locks changed as soon as possible," Sam replied. The kettle whistled, needing her attention, and she poured the overly hot water into the teapot.

"I don't understand. I thought we were going to live here and she was going to leave," the young woman said.

"I guess that she's not going to go quietly," Rick replied to the young woman. "Her wealthy daddy purchased this place and froze me out."

"My wealthy daddy, as you refer to him, helped us out when we had no money and you wanted to work on your Ph.D. without being disturbed by minor things like making a living. That's what I did."

"Yeah, well, he never liked me anyway. How someone as brilliant as he is supposed to be could not understand my work, I'll never know. Go back to your precious, dysfunctional, obnoxious family," Rick yelled across the room as he turned and headed for the bedroom. "I'll pack a bag and be out of here."

The young woman, Ariella, turned and followed Rick. She stopped at the entrance to the hallway and turned to look at Sam. The confused look on her face said that nothing was as it had seemed up until now. This was not the Sam that Rick had described to her.

Sam didn't notice Ariella observing her as she picked up the phone and the phone book and started looking for a locksmith. Sam found that the local hardware store had a locksmith service and she made the call. When she hung up, Sam was surprised to find Ariella was sitting in one of the chairs at the breakfast bar, still watching Sam.

"I guess I should introduce myself. My name is Ariella Fantini," the young woman said.

"Well, I don't know what appropriate to say in a situation such as this. It's good to meet you doesn't seem appropriate," Sam responded, shaking the hand with Ariella had extended. It seemed impolite to not shake hands, even in these .

"Yes, this must be very uncomfortable. I'm sorry that you got laid off today. You have a very nice tan."

"Thanks, we just got back from vacation." Sam realized at that moment that Ariella didn't know they had been away together for a week. It didn't concern Sam much as she took in the look of shock on Ariella's face. They were saved from having to say more but Rick's entrance into the living area.

"I have everything I need for now. I'll send for the rest of my stuff," Rick said. He had two bags and a garment bag over his shoulder as walked across the living area to the front door. "Can you grab my shaving kit, it's on the bed," he said to Ariella.

"What do you mean you'll send for your stuff? Do you think that I'm going to put your stuff together for you?" Sam asked.

"Oh, come on. You've been laid off and now you're going to complain about helping me out. You've got the condo, at least for now. Putting my stuff together should be a piece of cake," he responded.

"Or I could just throw everything into the street," Sam replied. Her anger was causing her face to turn red under her tan.

"You wouldn't dare," Rick replied. His eyes had a cold, steely look that Sam did not like. "Besides, what else are you going to do?"

"Write a novel, which is more than you can do," Sam replied. Her anger was palpable. Ariella took in the spiteful exchange without even blinking.

"Oh, now you're going to pick on me," he replied. "Let's go," he said to Ariella.

"You know, that wasn't a very nice thing to say," Ariella said. "But I understand why you said it."

Ariella turned, hopped off the tall chair and headed across the living area to the hallway. She returned with the shaving kit and followed Rick through the door and out of the condo. The door shut behind the two of them and Sam was alone.

Sam spent a several minutes just staring at the closed door. Her reverie was broken by the sound of the buzzer letting her know that someone wanted to get in. At first she thought it was Rick and was going to ignore it but after a few more buzzes, she decided to answer. It was the locksmith and she buzzed him in. When he arrived at her door, she let him in and explained what she needed to have done. He worked swiftly and was done before she finished her tea. Sam thanked him and wrote a check for the work. It was a premium price but she was glad to pay it.

What she needed to do next was buy new, clean, unused sheets and bedding and probably towels. She put down her tea, picked up her purse and headed to a local, very expensive linen store and bought sheets, blanket, comforter and mattress cover, all new and all very extravagant, along with some lovely towels. As soon as she got home with her packages, she stripped the bed and put all new linens on it. She bagged up the old, used bedding and put it in a corner of the living room. Well, if he wants everything bagged up for him, this is a good start she thought. She'd be damned if she was going to wash the sheets.

Just as she was heading to the kitchen area to warm up her tea, there was a knock on the door. No buzzer indicated that it was someone with a key to the front door. If it was Rick, she was going to give him a piece of her mind. Sam looked through the peephole to find Kate and Ben waiting. She opened the door to let them in.

"So, how long have you known about this?" Sam asked.

"Since late January or so," Kate replied, brushing past Sam who still stood holding the door. "We didn't feel it was our place to tell you. We hoped you would come home early some day to find them. Which now you've done and now we can console you."

"Really, you put some thought into this plan," Sam replied. Ben was still standing in the hallway politely waiting to be invited in. Sam rolled her eyes and stepped aside to let Ben enter as well.

"Well, I see you have new linens on the bed. I would have bought a whole new bed," Kate said. She had walked to the bedroom and back into the kitchen, dining, living area. "Did you buy the linens down the street?"

"Yes, I thought I'd splurge before going to the poor house," Sam replied.

"Well, they're very pretty and they suit you," Kate replied. "What are you going to do now that you're unemployed?"

Kate and Ben took seats at the counter that separated the kitchen from the dining area and Sam started the kettle to make fresh tea. Kate was about 5'11" tall and looked a lot like model, which she had been once. She wore a long, fawn-colored coat over cream colored pants and a cream silk blouse. Her blond hair cascaded down over her shoulders. Ben was also about 5'11", wore a t-shirt and jeans with a jacket. His mousy brown hair, gray eyes and pale skin all made him the less noticeable of the two. He didn't look like an internist but then again, what does an internist really look like when not at work. His bland looks were his disguise when he was not at work. Few people knew or suspected he was a doctor and they usually just walked by him without looking twice. And Ben didn't seem to mind this much. He said it allowed him to relax more when not at work. Sam smelled food and was pretty sure she should eat soon. The smell of food was coming from a bag that Ben had put on the counter. The smell was divine and Sam realized that she hadn't had any food all day.

"So, did you bring some takeout?" Sam finally asked.

"Oh, some Chinese we picked up after the movie," Kate replied. "What do you have to drink?"

"I thought you were going to Cecilia's for a late lunch?" Sam asked.

"Well, it was a bit later than we expected after helping you with the boxes and all, so we decided to just go to the movie and grab some Chinese after. On the way back, we thought we'd check up on you and see how you were doing," Ben replied.

Sam checked the refrigerator for drinks and found half a bottle of white wine, some soda, juice and water and not much else. She made a note to go shopping in the morning. What she had wasn't much but it provided something to go with the Chinese. Ben had moved around the counter and was going through the cabinets looking for plates, glasses and silverware. Kate took the containers of food from the bag and opened each of the packages so they could each take what they wanted. They ate in silence and then Kate and Ben cleaned up after dinner while Sam sat at the counter and watched.

"Well, it's been fun," Kate said. "But I have some friends to meet for drinks. Ta, Ta." And with that Kate picked up her bag, put on her coat and sailed out the door. Ben and Sam just watched her leave.

"Well, I'm on the late shift in the emergency room tonight," Ben said. He too put on his coat, gave Sam a hug and headed out the door.

Alone, Sam poured herself the rest of the wine and sat at the counter, turning to look at the boxes by the door that she had brought home. She then broadened her view to look at her dining, living area.

It wasn't a large space and strangely did not feel empty without Rick. They hadn't spent much time together at home lately. She worked days and he worked afternoons and evenings. Sam had been running to one place or another after work and she had thought Rick was doing the same. Now that didn't seem to be the case. She hadn't anticipated him being with another woman, she thought he was working on writing, getting published and getting tenure. It's what she would be doing in his shoes.

Next she looked at the bookshelves they had installed across the back wall that begain at the door to the hallway and around the right side wall until it met the windows. A couch was placed in front of the bookshelves across the back wall. Across from the couch were two chairs and between the couch and two chairs was a coffee table. In the right-hand front corner, at the end of the bookshelves and in front of the windows was a cozy reading nook with a comfortable chair and a light for reading. Directly across from the door was a hallway that led to the 2 bedrooms and a bathroom. The master bedroom with a large, walk-in closet was on the right-hand side and across the hall, on the left-hand side, was a full bath and a smaller bedroom that they used as an office. It had a day bed that was used on the rare occasions they had guests and was there overflow storage space. It had been quite

16

crowded before Rick had an office at the University but now he didn't use this one nearly as much. The master bedroom and the right-hand side of the living room were on an outside wall and the windows brought in natural light.

Now that Sam was alone her lips started to quiver and her eyes filled with tears. This could easily be termed the worst day of her life. If there was ever going to be a worse day, she didn't want to know about it.

Sam had just plopped herself down on the couch when the phone rang. The caller identification told her that it was her older brother Andrew. She was surprised as they didn't talk on the phone much and certainly not during the work week. To have him call her on a Monday was unusual and a little startling, she wondered if he already know that Rick had left her. She picked up the phone and answered.

"Sis, I just heard that you'd been laid off. I wanted to call and let you know that you can call me if you need anything, just ask and it's yours," Andrew said.

"How did you hear that I got laid off?" Sam asked. She was wiping the tears from her eyes.

Andrew explained that he had heard the news from a friend who worked in the New York City office of her bank. Sam was surprised that the news had traveled so fast, even internally, since she was or had been part of a small, specialized unit that hadn't existed for very long. Andrew explained that this friend was in very senior management and had received an internal memorandum regarding this dissolving of her unit that hadn't been released to the entire company yet.

Sam then proceeded to tell Andrew about the rest of her day. By the time she had finished telling the story tears were running down her face again. She was surprised at how quickly the words flowed out of her. Her story may not have been too coherent but Andrew let her continue until she had worn herself out. He said that he would come to Boston on Friday night and they would get her place organized,

17

meaning packing up Rick's things, on Saturday. He made her promise not to do anything until he got there. Sam thanked him and they hung up. Exhaustion crept over her and she had gathered up enough energy to head into the bedroom when her mother called.

She ended up repeating everything, including all the details of the morning layoff, finding Rick in bed with the other woman and Andrew coming to town to help her over the weekend. Her sobbing again made the story less than coherent but her mother didn't ask any questions, just made sympathetic noises, letting Sam talk until she was done. They hung up with the promise of speaking again the next day. She decided that it would take too much energy to get undressed and crawled into bed with all of her clothes on.

Chapter 2

When the alarm went as usual at 7am, Sam reached over, picked up the clock and threw it against the wall. She watched it break into a multitude of pieces, some of which bounced back on the bed due to the force behind her throw. Well, she thought, I won't need that old clock anymore. If Rick needed an alarm clock he could go out and buy one. After a few minutes of fuming, she realized her anger could get quite expensive, especially if she continued to break things while she was unemployed and living off her severance pay. That meant that the dishes and glasses were safe for the moment. The thought of the amount of money she had spent on sheets, bedding and towels made her groan.

Since she was awake, and was now less likely to break anything, she decided to get up take a shower, wash her hair and have some coffee. She stripped off her clothes and left them on the floor, a luxury but no one but she was going to trip over them, and headed to the bathroom to take a shower. Her mood was alternately angry and weepy. Her head was muddled with all the things she needed to do and nothing was making much sense. A long shower usually helped her think through her problems and come to some resolution but that wasn't happening today. Her thoughts were leaping around all the events of the previous day.

Once out of the shower and back in the bedroom, she saw that she had four phone messages. She listened to a message from her father, one from her mother, one from Rick's mother in upstate New York and one from Donna. Bad news travels fast she though as she dressed for the day. She decided to have some breakfast before answering her messages, particularly the one from Rick's mother. The phone rang several times while she cleaned up the kitchen from the previous night's Chinese dinner; she'd never even put the leftovers in the refrigerator. Better to talk to with everyone on a full stomach, she thought, as she ate her breakfast and watched the morning news.

She started with her father, who recommended a divorce lawyer and said he would also be down over the weekend. His trip from Long Island would just be a quick trip and he would need to return. Sam and her Dad were not always close, but intentions were good even if he wasn't the best and warmest father. He had never liked her choice of husband and was most likely secretly cheering the separation but he acted caring and concerned on the phone and she couldn't fault him for that. Plus it would be interesting to see whether or not he brought Vittoria along. Vittoria, the latest step-mother, was younger than her father, actually not much older than her sister Angela, and didn't always like spending time with her step-children. Of course, it was hard to blame her, the step-children were usually laying bets about how long this marriage would last and hadn't spent a lot of time getting to know Vittoria. They had long since decided that getting to know their step-mothers was a waste of their time, since the step-mothers seemed to be on a revolving door. Vittoria had lasted 5 years now, and showed more staying power than Sam or her brothers Jonathan and Andrew and sister Angela had even thought this one would last.

Sam then called her mother and was able to get through the conversation without sobbing, which reassured her mother. Her mother asked her to come down to Florida to stay for a while and Sam had let her know that she would think about it. She loved her mother and step-father but she wasn't sure she wanted to visit right now when there was so much to do here.

Sam's next call was to Rick's mother. She wasn't looking forward to this conversation but felt she would rather than handle this now than dread it all day. It was better to get it out of the way and move on. She liked Rick's mother but knew that a separate from her favorite and only son was going to be difficult. Rick's mother was sympathetic but not overly so. Mrs. Sampson hoped that Sam and Rick would be able to patch things up and that they would stay in touch with one another but did not want any details and seemed to know that Rick and she had separated. It was a friendly if very cool conversation.

Sam then called Donna at bank. Donna was on a break and was able to take her call right away.

"Wow, I can't believe what happened to you yesterday," Donna said.

"What do you mean? You know I was laid off," Sam asked.

"Well, Rick of course. I let him stay at my place last night. He had nowhere else to go and didn't want to stay at Ariella's since she lives with other students from the University. I can't believe you let one of the great ones get away," Donna continued.

"The great ones! What's so good about him?."

"Oh, Sam, don't you see. You can't keep a guy like that by working all the time. I still can't believe that you would devote so much time to work when your Dad could support you," Donna replied.

"Really, well that didn't stop Tom from leaving you," Sam said. It was a low blow but Donna was making her angry by not taking her side. If she didn't know better, she thought Donna sounded almost gleeful. There was a long pause before Donna spoke again.

"Well, I guess I should get back to work," Donna replied and then hung up without waiting for a response from Sam. Sam wanted to apologize and decided she would call Donna that night to do so.

Next she called Andrew to see if he would be staying with her or at a hotel. If he was thinking of staying with her, she would really need to clean up the office cum guest room cum storage space. He had never stayed at the condo before so she anticipated that he would stay at a hotel and was not surprised when he confirmed that was his plan. Sam was relieved to find that she would not need to clean quite yet. Andrew lived and worked in New York City and didn't have much time to spend with his siblings or father. He occasionally visited his mother in

Ohio, but that was mostly holidays, particularly Christmas. He'd only come to Boston twice since she was married so his visits had been minimal so far. A hotel would work out just great

Angela, her sister, called next. It was a quick conversation as Angela was calling from work and her job for the fashion design firm was very hectic. Sam and Angela didn't talk much because Angela had two young daughters, ages 9 and 7, a husband, Mario, who traveled to Europe frequently to cover soccer games as a former soccer star and commentator.

"So, I hear you and Rick have finally split up?" Angela asked, over the phone.

"Yes, we did," Sam replied.

"May I ask what caused the split?" Angela responded.

"You can, but I think you may have already heard from Andrew, Dad and my Mom what has happened," Sam replied.

"Yes, I did hear from all of them except your Mom. What I'd like to hear is from you," Angela replied.

"Well, there isn't much to tell. I was laid off yesterday morning and got home earlier than normal with all my junk from work and found Rick in bed with one of his students," Sam said, quickly so it wouldn't hurt so much.

"In your bed?" Angela asked quietly.

"Oh yes, we really don't have any other bed here except ours. And then he had the audacity to be surly to me and to insist that he should be the one to stay in the condo. I just can't believe it," Sam was close to tears now, her lower lip quivering. She was thankful that her big sister couldn't see her now.

"Well, I wish I could come up with Andrew this weekend but I can't, Allie has a dance recital and Marco's out of town on business. Otherwise, you know I would be there," Angela said, sounding a bit misty herself.

"That's OK; I think it would be too much for me if it were more than Andrew and Dad. As it is, I'm not sure what to do with Andrew," Sam replied.

"I'm sure you two will think of something. I thought Dad was coming up too?"

"Well, he said he was coming, but he said it was a quick trip so I'm not sure how much I'll see him or how long he'll stay. I don't know if Vittoria is coming or not," Sam replied.

"Ah, yes, Vittoria. She has certainly had more staying power than I thought she would have. I'm sure it will be good to have them all there with you. At least your Mom is not joining in. Well, I have to get to my next meeting. I'll call you on Sunday night so Allie can tell you all about the recital," Angela rang off quickly, already late for her next meeting.

Sam wanted to cry, again. Instead she attacked her apartment. She had new sheets on the bed, but a lot of junk in the house. It would feel great to start putting Rick's stuff together to get it out of the apartment. That thought made her pause for a second. She realized that she already knew, in her heart or her brain, that she and Rick would not be getting back together. It was all over and as emotional as she was, she was still sure that it was really all over and she was pretty sure she didn't want to get back together.

Just as she was about to get to work, there was a knock on her door. Since there had been no buzzer telling her someone wanted to be let in, she assumed it was Kate or Ben or possibly someone else from their building. A quick look through the peephole let her know that it was the young woman, Ariella, who had been with Rick the previous day.

She considered not opening the door and pretending to not be home but curiosity got the better of her.

"I'm sure you don't remember this, but my name is Ariella, Ariella Fantini," the young woman said to Sam, while standing in the hallway. "I want let you know how embarrassed I am by what happened yesterday. I have never been comfortable coming into your home and I want to apologize for my behavior," she said.

"Ariella, that's a pretty name. I don't think I've ever heard it before," Sam said. They were still standing in the doorway as Sam had not invited her in. And Sam was sure she didn't want to invite this young woman into her home.

"Thank you," Ariella replied.

There was a long pause while neither of them spoke. Since Ariella didn't appear to be leaving, Sam relented and invited her into the condo.

"Well, I'm glad to hear that you have never done anything like this before," Sam said.

"Thank you," Ariella replied. She walked over and took a seat at the kitchen counter.

"Well, is there anything I can get you? Water? Coffee?" Sam said. What she was thinking was why was this woman in her home and what did she really want, particularly since she didn't seem very talkative.

Ariella accepted a glass of water. She told Sam that was trying to clear things up, at least a little. Ariella had never meant to steal anyone's husband and had certainly never meant to intrude on Sam's privacy by being there yesterday. It was Rick who felt that they could use the condo without any interruptions. Ariella shared an apartment with four other students and there was no privacy, someone was always coming or going and since Rick was a professor at the University where they were all students, her place wasn't really a comfortable option for them. Ariella let Sam know that the two of them, Ariella and Rick that is, were going to rent an apartment together. Ariella didn't really like having Rick stay with Donna.

"Really, you know Donna?" Sam asked

"Oh yes, we've been out with Donna a few times," Ariella replied. "They seem to be really good friends."

Well that a startling bit of news. Donna had certainly never said anything to Sam about Rick and Ariella. Donna obviously knew more than she let on this morning.

"Yes, I can certainly see why you would not want Rick to stay with Donna for too long," Sam replied.

"Well, I'm sure this has all been quite a whirlwind for you. I'm so sorry that you were laid off too. What will you do next?"

"Well, believe it or not, I'm going to take some time to figure out what I want to do next. I'm really going to write a novel. I have some severance money and I can afford to take a few months off before I need to make some money again."

"Well, that's nice. Thank you for your hospitality this morning. I do need to run and get back to campus," Ariella said. She then jumped off the kitchen stool, placed her glass in the sink and left.

Sam was not sure what to think of this whole, unexpected meeting. She was surprised to find that she sort of like Ariella, who reminded Sam of herself when she first met Rick. She hoped Ariella was smart enough to stay in school to finish her Ph.D. Sam looked at the clock and realized it was already noon. She didn't want to answer any more phone calls or spend any more time in the condo so she grabbed her bag and headed out to visit a bookstore. This would be sure to distract her for a while.

Sam muddled through the rest of Wednesday, Thursday and Friday morning, shifting stuff around the apartment but not making much of a dent or many decisions. Her Dad, Philip, and Vittoria arrived in time for lunch on Friday. Philip and Vittoria needed to return to Long Island on Saturday morning for a small dinner party so their stay would be short. After a nice lunch at a local restaurant, Vittoria and Philip got to work on separating out Rick's books and boxing them up. This consisted of Vittoria reading off each title, Sam deciding if it was to stay or not and Philip putting the book in a box for Philip, a box of books to be donated or moving the books to be kept to the designated 'keep' portion of the bookcase. Sam had successfully moved her stuff from work into the office, creating space for Rick's stuff to be stacked by the door.

Andrew arrived on Friday night early enough for a late dinner with Sam, Philip and Vittoria. They caught up a bit on Andrew's life, which was easier than talking about Sam's life. His stories of life in investment banking were entertaining. After dinner, Philip and Vittoria said good-bye since they were leaving early Saturday morning and headed back to their room at the hotel. Sam and Andrew stopped at the hotel bar for a nightcap and to make plans for meeting the next morning. They grudgingly agreed that Vittoria had some staying power. They parted with plans to meet the next morning at Sam's place to start cleaning out Rick's things.

Sam returned to her condo, had a quick conversation with her mother, who was now calling every night to check on her, and then cried herself to sleep. It had been a long week and she was emotionally and mentally exhausted. After years of having a somewhat distant relationship with her family, they seemed to be suffocating her. She appreciated her Dad and Vittoria dropping in for an afternoon and they had been very helpful without expecting much from Sam. Andrew coming up from New York City and her mother calling every day as well as having Kate and Ben checking on her at unusual moments, even though she didn't really know them very well, was more human contacted than she wanted right now.

Chapter 3

The Saturday clean-up went pretty well. Andrew was unemotional about the entire process, which made it go a lot faster. He took care of bagging up all of Rick's remaining clothes and toiletry items without any help from Sam. Sam watched from the door, like a moth drawn to the flame. She didn't want to stop Andrew and she didn't want to touch any of Rick's things but she couldn't stop hovering either.

"Why don't you go and pack up his laptop," Andrew suggested, when he couldn't take the silent staring any longer.

"OK, I guess I can do that," Sam replied, biting her fingernails and leaning against the door jamb.

She didn't move until Andrew stopped what he was doing and looked at her. With a sigh, she headed off to the office/guest room to pack up the laptop and any files that might be hanging around. There were a number of flash drives and CD's on the desk that Sam knew were not hers, so she threw them into the laptop bag. Rick had moved a lot of his files to the University as soon as he got an office. He said it was easier to organize things in his office there. Sam had taken care of all of the finances, taxes and correspondence for the two of them so she kept those files to review at another time. She finished up with the desk, zipped up the case and put it in the hallway with the other items to be picked up or sent to Rick.

She was about to check on Andrew when there was a knock on her door. Sam looked through the peephole, saw it was Kate and Ben, and opened the door. They were heading out for a late breakfast and were there to invite Sam and Andrew to join them. Andrew came out of the bedroom to see who was there and Sam introduced him to Kate and Ben. Sam thanked them and let them know that she and Andrew had

27

already had breakfast. They smiled, said they were happy to meet Sam's brother and headed off to the elevator.

Andrew asked a few questions about them both and Sam answered as best she could. Until Tuesday Sam had really only known them in passing. They had made small talk when they ran into each other on the elevator and greeted one another when they ran into one another around the neighborhood. What little she knew about them she had learned mostly in the past 3 days or had gathered from their small talk. She told Andrew that Kate and Ben had been more or less keeping an eye on her since Tuesday. Andrew noted that it was nice of them to stop by and that they seemed to be decent people, although breakfast at noon did seem a bit more New York than Boston.

Andrew continued to pack clothing and went through the laundry basket for additional clothing of Rick's while Sam went back to tackle and separate the remaining stuff in the office. She kept her tennis racket but put Rick's out for collection. After some thought, she decided to keep her wedding dress, at least for now.

When she couldn't deal with anything else in the office, she joined Andrew in the bedroom. They discussed how to best get the items to Rick. After some discussion, they decided to have Andrew call Rick's cell phone and arrange to ship the items to any address that Rick provided.

Andrew's first call was not answered and several follow-up calls and voice mail messages were not answered that afternoon. They decided that if they didn't hear from him by Sunday morning, they would rent a storage space to store everything until Rick was ready to claim it. It would get the items away from Sam and out of the condo but they would be stored and accessible in a neutral, non-confrontational location.

The day went by swiftly and before they knew it, it was time for dinner. They decided to go out to dinner, particularly since there was little food in the house to eat or from which to create a dinner. Sam was not known for her cooking skills but she could make a mean macaroni and cheese. Andrew liked to eat out, wasn't always appreciative of a home cooked meal and was not impressed with macaroni and cheese in any form. Sam made a mental note to go food shopping as soon as Andrew left.

Sam and Andrew headed to a restaurant that had recently opened, had received great reviews and cost a fortune. Sam was pretty sure she didn't have anything appropriate to wear to this type of restaurant and tried to talk Andrew to a local pizza place. With one look, he won and she lost. He told her that since this wasn't a date, jeans, a nice t-shirt and jacket with boots or sandals would suffice. With the closet pretty well cleaned out, it was easy to find the clothes he mentioned and Sam did just that while Andrew headed back to the hotel to take a shower and change.

Sam wasn't very surprised to see Kate at the same restaurant. It was new and very hip to be seen there. Kate was seated with a handsome, well dressed older man. They were a noticeable presence even in the crowded restaurant. Kate smiled and made a small gesture in their direction to let Sam and Andrew know that she saw them but wasn't inviting them over to join her and her friend.

Dinner was magnificent and Andrew paid for both of them. It made her feel like someone liked her, even if it was only her brother. She looked around the restaurant and noted at all the different kinds of relationships; family, friendship, romantic, even some business looking relationships all taking place at the restaurant. She felt both included and left out at the same time. She was no longer part of a couple but she was certainly part of a family. It felt somehow less lonely than she thought it would feel.

"So, what was that sigh all about," Andrew asked her as he disconnected from the call on his cell-phone.

"Oh nothing, just thinking about life and relationships and observing the other people here tonight," she smiled. "When will you be leaving?"

"I have a flight around 4pm tomorrow but I'm going to make it earlier. That was just Rick I was talking to and he has agreed to be there at 1pm tomorrow to pick up his stuff. I had a call from work and I need to get back and deal with a tough client. Will you be ok without me?"

"Well, I've survived since Tuesday so I suspect I'll be ok. I need to do a lot of thinking."

"What will you do when Rick comes by tomorrow to pick up his boxes?"

"I'm going to ask Donna to meet him and go off somewhere by myself. I think it will be better that way."

"I agree, you shouldn't be there and you shouldn't be there by yourself. You think Donna will be available?" Andrew asked.

"Actually, yeah, I called her after you left. I didn't ask her to do anything but she let me know that she and Rick will be able to handle it. I suspect that Ariella and most likely some students will be there to help as well." Sam responded a little sarcastically. "Did I tell her that Ariella wants me to be comfortable with this, uh, arrangement."

"Yes, you did tell me about your conversation with Ariella. It will be best for you to not be there and it sounds like Rick has all the help he needs. Well, now that that's settled, I'll be off early in the morning so this is good-bye, at least until next weekend," Andrew responded.

"Next weekend? You'll be back next weekend?" Sam looked at Andrew quizzically.

"Jonathan's wedding," Andrew responded.

"Oh my god, I forgot all about the wedding," Sam responded. "Well, I guess I have to go, don't I. Yikes, I'll be all alone with my family."

"You are one of the bridesmaids so, yes, you have to be there. Plus everyone will want to gossip about what happened and Jonathan would be devastated if you didn't show up," Andrew responded, hardly able to suppress a grin.

"Oh, right, Jonathan. He's been paying so much attention to me throughout this whole thing. He hasn't even called me once," Sam replied. "What are you so happy about?"

"I thought your family was suffocating you? Besides, Jonathan is busy with wedding matters. Actually, I'm not sure anyone has told him about you yet," Andrew replied. "I won't be the major topic of conversation. You know everyone thinks I'll outgrow being gay but it's hard to outgrow being laid off and coming home to find your husband in bed with one of his students."

"Very funny," Sam said, wrinkling her nose at the thought of seeing her family all together. "You do have a point. I will be the center of attention and you can do whatever you want."

"You'll be there with bells on. You won't let them see you in any way other than strong and graceful. Besides what would Jonathan tell Hyacinth if you didn't show up? Besides, it will pass in a flash," Andrew winked at her.

"Well, this is the funniest I've seen you be in a long time," Sam replied. "You winked at me and you haven't done that since we were kids. And you do have a point about Cinthy, she is very nice but she's young and comes from the perfect family. She will have a hard time with all of this." Suddenly Sam was having a hard time suppressing her laughter. It all seemed so ridiculous.

"Well, maybe we need to have a light moment. You've been so serious since I got here. I thought my life was bad, but you seem to have taken all the sting out of my rather petty problems."

Sam smiled back. She doubted that Andrew's problems were petty and trite but he hadn't been one to talk much about them since his mother and step-father had had such a hard time coming to terms with is life choices. Even their Dad wasn't too keen on this direction for his eldest son.

Sam had had so much fun with Andrew when they were younger before he had become so serious about his education and his career. His decision to come out of the closet had been very hard on his parents. He had spent so many years trying hard to not reveal anything to anyone that he had almost killed himself so he finally had to tell them. He received so much negative feedback from his family that he became quite depressed and then his lover at the time left him. Andrew was still not his old happy go lucky self, but he was showing some of his old humor.

Andrew paid for dinner. As they were heading out, Kate caught her eye and gave her a wink and wave. Sam smiled and gave a small wave in return. Outside Andrew kissed her on the forehead and put her into a cab home. He waved at her from the sidewalk and was gone. Sam was so tired that she just went to bed when she got home, although she did take off her clothes this time. She knew there were messages on the answering machine, but she would deal with them in the morning.

Sam's new alarm went off promptly at 7am. Her dreams had been so vivid that she thought she was awake already and reliving the same day over again, like Groundhog Day.

Donna arrived promptly at 9am and sent Sam on her way. When Sam finally arrived home at 5pm, Donna and all the boxes were gone and there was a note on the counter asking her to check for more files around the office. She threw the note away and pulled out the take out she had brought home for dinner. Sam had spent the day walking around the Back Bay window shopping, checking out new books at the bookstore and picking up some groceries along with some take out. It had been an exhausting day and she was glad to be home and free of Rick's stuff.

Chapter 4

Her goal had been to point out why she just didn't have time or the desire to get divorced right now, but agreed to meet with the lawyer her father had found for her and get the divorce proceedings moving forward. She did point out that Rick hadn't been doing much to move the divorce forward as well, so it seemed just easier to let this process take its own course to its own conclusion.

She and Rick certainly did not have the attachment of children to keep them together. While they had both wanted children, and had even tried the medical route, nothing had worked out and they had remained childless. Surprisingly, Sam thought, Rick hadn't accidentally had a child with someone It was Thursday night and Sam didn't have much more to pack for the engagement party weekend at her Dad's place on Long Island. She decided that anything else she needed to do, she could do in the morning and it was time to get some sleep. It had been a long, long week.

In the morning she went out to pick up her car for the weekend from the spot reserved just for members of the car sharing club. For this trip she had requested a Honda Civic, mostly for its economical driving and practicality with gas mileage. She returned to her building, packed up the car and headed down the Mass Pike to 395 South. The drive was smooth and she caught the ferry to Long Island from New Haven, Connecticut. Once she landed on the island she still had another hour or two to drive to her Dad's place, depending on traffic, but she wasn't in a rush and it was a pleasant drive.

Sam stepped out of the cool, comfortable car and into the hot, humid spring day on Long Island and her father's estate. The party bustle was under way at the main house. Trucks were beeping as they backed into the yard where the engagement party would take place, arms were raised and lots of swearing and swerving were going on as the tent, flower, catering and bar vendors all jockeyed for space. It was Friday morning and there were party events on Friday night and Saturday night. Sam pulled her car into the parking area reserved for family, got out and put on her sun-glasses and a hat. Sweat immediately began to collect on the back of her neck and the afternoon sun almost blinded her. It was looking like it would be a long, hot weekend.

Her father's factotum and all around good guy, Desmond, walked across the gravel path to greet her. He was smiling, shading his eyes from the sun with his left hand while completely ignoring all the chaos taking place just down the back of the house.

"It looks like preparations for the engagement party are getting a bit crazy," Sam said by way of greeting Desmond.

Desmond had started working for her father as a body-guard when Philip's life had been threatened 5 years ago. The threats had to do with some of Philip's patents and new business deals. What had started as a body guard job had morphed into a personal assistant position and Desmond had stayed. Now he was a part of their family. He still had an Irish lilt to his voice, a well-toned body that he kept up even though he was no longer in the military and no longer directly involved in security. He had an ability of knowing just about everything about everyone with his easy manner and relaxed attitude.

"Oh that, that's just for the big part tomorrow night. You should see the inside for tonight's more personal family only dinner," He responded with a roll of his eyes and gave her a hug. "My, it's been too long since you were last here. And look at you all by yourself and looking quite fit and trim as well.''

"Apparently separation and unemployment do wonders for me," Sam smiled.

"And a week in the Bahamas probably didn't hurt either," Desmond said.

"Don't remind me," Sam winced.

"Hmm, not enough time between the vacation and the separation? Sorry to bring it up so soon. The tan looks good on you though."

"Thanks, the tan has faded a bit but not all the way. As for the other stuff, let's talk about it another time," Sam said.
"
"Right, we'll have to talk about all the gory details later." Desmond responded with the wink of an eye and a brilliant smile. If nothing else, he could make her smile.

"So, you and Angela and the two angels will be staying in the guest house. You are the first to arrive, I believe, and you will have your choice of the bedrooms. We have a woman from the village name Ruby who will be coming in to cook and clean for you while you are here." He referred to all the local people as being from the village, which sounded quaint but really they were maids and cooks for hire at the local estates and not friendly locals willing to pitch in at the mansion for the laird, as she suspected Desmond was used to in his native Ireland, or was he from Scotland, she couldn't remember.

"That sounds wonderful. Anything else I should know? Like who will be here for dinner this evening?"

"Ah yes, it's 'just family' this evening so that includes the groom's immediate family, including your mother and Joe, along with Honey and her latest. On the bride's side there will the bride's immediate family, two parents, Hyacinth and two siblings. Your mother, Joe, Honey and the latest will be staying in the main house with the brides' family and Jonathan. You, Andrew, Angela, Marco and the girls will be here in the guest house. Drinks will be outside in one of the tents and dinner will be served in the dining room. The caterer has taken over the kitchen and the dining room and Angus is seeing red," Desmond replied.

"Ah yes, Angus won't like having others in his kitchen. And on Saturday what will we be doing? Sam asked.

"All the family I just mentioned, plus some aunts, uncles, cousins and some neighbors and friends. It's going to be a strange weekend," Desmond replied, his smile becoming more forced as he spoke.

The both looked up as another car arrived. "Well, it looks like Angela and the girls are here. Let me help her get settled in. Do you need any help with luggage?"

"No, no, I'm fine. I'm travelling light. Please help Angela and the girls." Sam waved to her older half-sister who was trying to organize two girls, 5 and 7, while juggling luggage, toys and wave, all at the same time. Sam waved back and headed off to the guest house while Desmond headed off to help Angela and the two girls.

Sam had decided not to over pack. If she needed something she didn't have, she would get away to town to pick them up. It sounded like it might be good to get away. Most everything she would need revolved around parties so she had mostly party clothes, with a pair of jeans, a skirt and some t-shirts thrown in. It would be fun to stay with Angela and the girls, really, but a short trip to town alone would be soothing.

Her goal was to pick the bedroom on the first floor with the white curtains and the nice view of the hot tub and the woods behind the hot tub. This would allow Angela and her girls the run of the upstairs while Sam would have her own bathroom. So she was surprised to find Andrew was already there and had claimed the downstairs bedroom before her. He was unpacking all his very carefully folded shirts and underwear as she came into the bedroom.

"Oh, I'm sorry, I thought I was the first to arrive," she said to Andrew from the doorway.

"I thought it would be prudent to arrive early and claim the downstairs bedroom so that all you girls could share the upstairs," Andrew replied quickly. "Especially since Dad wants us all to be together this weekend."

"Oh, I see. He won't let you stay in town, so you're forced to stay with us. You could stay up at the main house, you know."

"Then I'd be with all the parents and here I get my own bathroom."

"My idea exactly. I was hoping to get this bedroom, I thought you would be staying in the big house," Sam replied.

"Sorry to disappoint."

"But I thought you liked the girls?"

"I do, but not necessarily in the bedroom next door." It wasn't so much that he minded Angela and Sam and the girls but he liked the that the two young girls would just take over and he would have no peace and quiet, which was most likely true.

Andrew and Sam's discussion was interrupted by Jonathan, who arrived to cheer them all up with his with bad jokes and the blissful cheer of one in love and the center of attention. Andrew's whole demeanor changed from bland investment banker to handsome yacht boat racer at the sight of Jonathan. Nobody could stand solemn in the face of Jonathan's obvious giddiness. Jonathan's smile was contagious and soon Sam was smiling as well. She put her bag down in the kitchen to give her brother a hug.

"Well, how is the groom to be handling all this," Sam asked.

"I couldn't be better. I'm just so excited and so is Hyacinth. We think that we'll survive this weekend and Dad's orchestration of our engagement party. Well, to be fair, Dad and her parents. Plus, we've decided we'll do a party this summer in Vermont with our own friends and of course our siblings too," Jonathan replied. "By the way, did you know Honey is here too, with a new one in tow."

"Yes, I heard from Desmond. I can't believe wife #4 is here. I didn't think she liked any of us?" Andrew replied.

"She didn't, which makes it even more interesting. Sorry your Mom and step-Dad won't be here," Jonathan replied. He got his words out just in time.

"Auntie Sam, you're going to stay upstairs with us. Isn't that wonderful? We can stay up all night and talk," Allie and Andie were speaking over each other and had obviously been talking about their plans for a while.

"Uncle Andrew you can stay down here, it's ok with us," Allie said so that Andrew wouldn't feel left out. Andrew just lifted an eyebrow as he stood in the bedroom door observing everyone in the kitchen. He loved his nieces but it was hard to compete with a girl's night upstairs. He'd just have to suffer through it.

"And we've decided we're going to call your mother Grandma because she doesn't have any grandchildren and we don't have a grandmother," Andie said to Sam and Jonathan.

"And we are going to stay up with you all night and talk about the good old days, just like you do," Allie announced.

"How do you know you're Mom and Aunt Sam want to stay up all night talking? They're getting old and need their beauty sleep too," Andrew asked.

"Oh, you guys always stay up. You did it last summer when we were all here and we tried to stay up but we couldn't. We're older now and we know we can do it this year, can't we Andie," said Allie with much authority in her voice.

"Yes, we are staying up and you can't stop us," Andie replied defiantly.

And with that the two girls picked up their bags and sailed through the kitchen door down the hallway and turned right to head up the stairs. "Aren't you coming," they entreated on their way up the stairs.

"Whew, now I'm really glad to be staying downstairs," Andrew said and turned back into the bedroom to continue unpacking.

Sam and Angela looked at each other, rolled their eyes and laughed.

"So, when will Marco be arriving," Jonathan asked Angela.

"He'll be here Saturday night. He doesn't want to miss the party but he's doing some soccer commentary in Italy this week and won't get back until then.

"Well, I'll just leave your luggage here and the boys can help you get it upstairs," Desmond said as he left through the kitchen door. Someone was calling his name while horns were beeping and vendors were swearing at one another. Andrew, Angela, Sam and Jonathan watched him walk across the lawn back to main house.

"Amazing he's lasted as long as he has," Andrew said.

"Well, it helps that he likes us," Jonathan replied.

"Us?" Angela asked.

"He must like something or someone or he wouldn't still be here," Sam said.

"Very true," Andrew said. "He must like Dad."

"Great, well we have lots of things to do and not much time to do it in. Let's get these bags upstairs and get you all ready for the party. The sooner you get over there the happier I'll be," Jonathan said as he grabbed two bags and headed up the stairs.

"How long are you guys staying for?" Andrew asked as he grabbed two bags and followed Jonathan. "These bags feel like they are packed for a month."

"Wait until you have kids of your own and a husband on the road," was all Angela could say.

Angela and Sam followed, with their hands full as well. At the top of the stairs they ran into Andie and Allie, who were busy figuring out who should have which bedroom. They had determined that they should take the room with the two twin beds and that their mother and father should have the room next to them while Sam was across the hall. Sam suggested that since the room across the hall was larger, their mother and father might like that one and Sam could sleep next to the girls. The girls reluctantly agreed.

The house was a Cape Cod style with a kitchen, living room, dining room and bedroom on their first floor and 3 bedrooms, sitting room and a bathroom on the second floor. It had been built originally as a home for the estate manager but now that most owners had mostly day help, it had been converted to a guest house for visitors.

They unpacked, changed into their lawn party outfits and headed up to the big house to meet everyone for the cocktail party and dinner. The girls skipped ahead, excited to see their grandmother, grandfather, Vittoria and their various step-grandparents and to generally be the center of attention.

The big house was a mansion with a wonderful, deep-set backyard and a front that rolled towards the ocean. None of them had ever lived in such a house when they were growing up, and none of them had grown up with their father, so none of them considered it to be home. They all visited, Angela most frequently as a break from the city, Andrew to get away occasionally with Sam and Jonathan less frequently.

Jonathan had a nice life in Vermont, teaching Philosophy and History at a small liberal arts college. His fiancée, Hyacinth, also taught at the same college and she and Jonathan had developed a very nice life together. They were close to Hyacinth's family. They all wondered how their father had talked everyone to having the engagement party on Long Island rather than in Vermont. Philip had paid for and hosted large weddings for both Angela and Sam as well but the father of the bride role is not the same as the father of the groom role. They would have to see where the wedding would actually take place.

The family party was relaxing, casual and small enough for everyone to interact with and get to know one another. The Saturday night engagement party, on the other hand, was a far more raucous affair. The four siblings, all got drunk during the very long party. Even Marco, who arrived a bit earlier than anticipated, was surprised by his wife, her sister and two brothers. Marco took over caring for his two daughters and getting them to bed in time to care for his wife when she stumbles in with Sam and Andrew.

When Sam wakes on Sunday morning, she finds that fog is hanging over the house and the grounds which does nothing to quell the fog in her head. She smells coffee brewing and hears bacon sizzling in the downstairs kitchen where Ruby has started breakfast for them all. She listens for a moment and doesn't hear anyone else moving around. Andie and Allie seem to be sound asleep, for once, and Marco is snoring in the bedroom across the hall, or maybe its Angela, they both had more than enough to drink.

Sam takes a shower before heading downstairs to check out breakfast. There she finds Andrew, yawning, drinking coffee and reading the paper along with Ruby who is putting the finishing touches on a wonderful breakfast of bacon, scrambled egg and French toast with fresh coffee, fresh squeezed orange juice and fresh fruit.

"Ahh, to live like this every day," Sam said as she headed for the coffee.

"It's the life we were born to," Andrew replied.

"Huh, maybe you were but I don't remember too many breakfasts like this when I was growing up," Sam said.

"Yeah, yeah, just ruin the fantasy for me," Andrew responded.

Sam smiled at Andrew and grabbed part of the paper from him. It was the New York Times, which Andrew loved and Sam rarely read, except when visiting. Ruby brought a plate each of eggs and bacon to Sam and to Andrew. She placed the platter of cut fruit in the center of the table with a serving utensil and poured them each a glass of juice.

"So, I see Desmond didn't corner you last night," Sam said without looking up.

"Oh, was that his plan?" Andrew asked.

"Well, as far as any of us could tell, he was staking you out like a gangster staking out a bank he was about to rob," Sam replied, trying hard not to smile too much.

"It's over and it's about time he learned that. It was fun while it lasted but I never had any long term intentions," Andrew replied. "Are the two little darlings up and about yet?"

"No, they seemed dead to the world, along with Angela and Marco," Sam said.

"Well, well, I think we finally tired out the little darlings. It's pretty hard to do, you now," Andrew said.

"Yes, Dad said that you've been spending more time with Angela and the girls."

"Did he? Well we both live in the city so it's sort of naturally come together. Marco has not been around much so I've been helping out with the girls. I guess you and he have been talking more lately?"

"He's been calling me about getting this divorce moving forward. He thinks I'm stalling, which I guess I am in a way," Sam replied. "Of course, it hasn't even been two weeks yet."

Andrew let her know that both her father and her mother wanted to talk to her this morning before she left for Boston. Sam hoped to get

42

out without having this conversation. But as they were talking, Sam saw her parents walking together across the lawn together, something she could only remember seeing her parents do a few times. Once she watched them walk along a beach during a childhood vacation. Philip and Miranda, which is how she thought of them these days rather than as Mom and Dad, had not spent much time alone together even when they were married and seeing them together like this seemed both natural and oddly out of place. When she was younger there had always something going on, which is probably what led to their divorce, and most likely contributed to all of Philip's divorces.

"I spy with my little eye," Andrew said over the top of his newspaper. He then grabbed his coffee and headed off to his bedroom off the kitchen.

"Chicken," Sam yelled behind him as her parents opened the door off of the kitchen.

Ruby smiled at Philip and Miranda and took her leave as well, leaving Sam alone with her parents.

"Your father and I want to talk to you," her mother said. Her mother was seated at the kitchen table while Philip poured himself a cup of coffee and stood next to the kitchen counter. Sam put her fork down and moved her breakfast plate away from her. It wasn't often that her parents came together to talk to her. Actually the last time they had talked with her together was just before her wedding to Rick.

Philip and Miranda talked to Sam about the need to move on with her own life. That getting a divorce would allow her to break free from the past. Sam assured them both that she had no intention of letting Rick back into her life in any capacity. She may not have hired a divorce attorney yet, but her intention was to divorce Rick. Her hesitation about divorcing had nothing to do with any desire to get back together with Rick but actually had a lot to do with her desire to not have to deal with Rick. And she didn't want to have to move out of the condo just yet. Enough things had happened to her in the past two weeks, she didn't need to move or to get divorced immediately.

43

Philip and Miranda seemed somewhat relieved and reassured about Sam's intention during their conversation. They had tried to talk her out of marrying Rick right after her college graduation. They had wanted her to wait until Rick finished his Ph.D. or until she was at least 25 but Sam had had other ideas.

Sam hadn't spent much time thinking about what to do next beyond her desire to write a novel and avoiding having to move for as long as possible. Like most parents, they were concerned about their daughter and wanted what they considered to be the best for her. Her plans to not find a job right away, not get divorced right away and write a novel weren't giving her parents any feelings of confidence.

Sam appreciated all of the concerns her parents raised. She and Rick certainly did not have the attachment of children to keep them together. While they had both wanted children, and had even tried the medical route, nothing had worked out and they had remained childless.

Andrew, who most likely had heard everything being discussed since his room was right off of the kitchen, started moving around and making noises. Miranda looked at her watch and decided that it was time to see how Joe was doing with the packing and headed off to the big house. Sensing the conversation in the kitchen was over, Andrew opened the door to his bedroom with enough time to say good-bye to Miranda and give her a kiss. Miranda asked to be remembered to Vivian and Mark the next time Andrew talked to his mother and step-father. Philip decided to stay for a few more minutes to talk with both Andrew and Sam.

Philip said good-bye to Andrew. He had been happier than they would ever know to have all 4 of his children and his 2 grand-daughters together under the same roof, more or less, for the past weekend. He knew he had not spent nearly enough time with his children when they were growing up and he wasn't as hands-on a grandfather, but he did enjoy having them all there. He asked Andrew and Sam to be sure to stop by and say good-bye to Vittoria and her mother, who had both enjoyed having everyone around this weekend.

Angela wandered downstairs in her pajamas, yawning and stretching. Sam always admired and was a little jealous of Angela's tall, lithe, athletic looking figure and her naturally blonde hair along with her ability to make everyone feel relaxed in almost any situation. Angela certainly took after her late mother, who had died at about the age Angela was today.

Sam herself was of average height, a little pudgy and had naturally dull brown hair that she spiced up with a darker brown coloring. Sam's best natural feature was her curly hair, which Angela always admired. Sam had dropped 10 pounds in the past two weeks and while it didn't really show in any measurable way, at least not yet, she had felt thinner.

Andie and Allie swiftly followed their mother down the stairs. While Angela had been woken by the smell of coffee, the 2 girls had definitely been woken up by the smell of food. Angela made a beeline for the coffee while the girls sat down at the kitchen table and started in on the fruit and Ruby returned to the kitchen to finish breakfast.

"Did I hear Grandmother Miranda's voice?" Angela asked.

"Yes, she and grandfather came to talk to me," Sam responded.

"How did that go Sam?" Angela asked.

"Oh, they seem to think that I'm moving too slowly on the divorce and that I've totally lost my mind for wanting to take a few months off to write a novel. I should be banking my severance pay for a rainy day and finding a new job as soon as possible. Of course, everything they said makes sense but I think that now is my rainy day and I'm going to use this time to do what I want to do," Sam replied.

"Good for you," Marco replied, walking into the kitchen.

After a few minutes of conversation, mostly about how everyone was getting home, Sam went upstairs to finish packing. Once packed, Sam brought her bags downstairs. She decided to leave her things in the living room and go up to the big house to say good-bye to everyone. Desmond had already had her car moved closer to the guest house. All of the family cars had been moved to make room for guests the night before.

Andrew had rented a car to drive out to Long Island but he was taking the train back and letting Angela, Marco and the two girls drive back together. A taxi was at the house waiting for him so he had left with Philip to head over and say good-bye to everyone.

When Sam arrived, Vittoria was in the large front hall of the main house with her elderly mother, saying good-bye to Andrew. Miranda and Joe, Philip, Vittoria's mother, Jonathan and Hyacinth were all there. Miranda was feeling a bit sad saying good-bye to bother her children, Sam and Jonathan, knowing she would most likely not see either of her children or Angela and the girls, or even Andrew until Christmas. It would be a long day of driving, flying and driving again before they would be home in Orlando.

Chapter 5

The unexpected buzz of her front door caused Sam's heart to race. She had been staring at her closet, quietly contemplating what to take with her to Florida for a November weekend with her mother and step-father. She had already decided what to wear to New York to meet with her new agent, but she wanted to make sure she had a warmer and less formal wardrobe for the Florida visit.

More importantly, she wanted to make sure her mother didn't see the need to take her shopping before the party. Their tastes were way too dissimilar and Sam knew she would come out looking like Dorothy in the Wizard of Oz, or something equally cute and adorable and totally not age appropriate, if her mother had the opportunity to dress her. Sam loved her mother, but her mother was having a hard time getting used to her children growing up and that caused a lot of friction, not just clothing choices.

Sam's first thought, when she heard the knock on the door, was that it must be someone from inside the building, Kate or Ben, or possibly even Donna, looking to be let in. They all had keys to the building but not to Sam's condo; Kate and Ben because they lived there and Donna because she used to come and water Sam's plants and check her mail when they were away. Now no one except Andrew had keys to her condo and she hadn't traveled anywhere in the past 6 months to need her plants watered or mail check.

She was a little surprised to find the buzzer going off since Kate was totally wrapped up in her new beau; Ben was working nights at the hospital this week and Donna and she were not seeing eye to eye lately. Sam didn't need anyone to pick up mail or water plants for a four day trip so she decided to just go and tell everyone about it when she got home.

Sam decided to call out and find out who was there before walking to the door. When she heard Ariella's voice through the door she was even more surprised. The sound of Ariella's voice brought Sam back to the day 6 months previously she had been laid off from work and come home unexpectedly early to find Rick and Ariella in bed together. Ariella's voice never bothered her when they had one of their writing meetings with Arthur at the University's English department, but it did when she heard it suddenly at her own door.

To be fair, during the past 6 months she and Ariella had developed their own rather tentative relationship around their writing. Arthur Churykian, the chairman of the English Department where Rick was an assistant professor, had been working to help both Sam and Ariella with their writing. Arthur was pushing the two of them to become colleagues.

She must still have a building key, Sam thought, probably Rick's building key. Well, she could only change the condo key; the building key would remain the same. She stepped back to think for a moment and was startled by a knock. Sam contemplated pretending she wasn't home for a moment but with a sigh and the knowledge that she would be up late packing, at least later than she anticipated, and the fact that she would see Ariella next week at their regular meeting, Sam decided to answer the door.

"Hi Sam, I hope you don't mind my dropping by like this. I only want a moment to talk?" Ariella asked quietly. Her usual exuberance seemed absent. "And I think I should return this building key to you."

"Ah, thanks, please come in. I was just packing." Sam replied, trying to be polite but not overly polite.

"Oh, I thought you were going to New York for just the day tomorrow," Ariella replied.

"I decided to continue on to Florida to see my mother and stepfather for a few days," Sam replied, and then added, "It's my mother's 60th birthday this weekend and some friends are having a birthday party for her," Sam said. "I can honestly say that I'm surprised to see you, I thought we had said we were getting together for coffee next week?"

"I know we agreed to meet next week but I'm hoping that you will hold something for me for a few days," Ariella said. "Do you have anything hot to drink, it's brutal out there tonight."

"Of course, I can make us some tea," Sam said.

"Tea would be great."

Sam moved to the kitchen to retrieve the mug of tea she had been drinking. She had just made a fresh pot of herbal and offered some from the teapot to Ariella. Ariella gratefully accepted a mug of tea and sat on one of the stools at the raised eating area that faced the kitchen space.

"What do mean by hold something?" Sam asked.

"Well, I have a flash drive and I was hoping you would hold onto it for me."

"Why would you want me to hold onto this for you?" Sam asked

"Well, I was hoping that you wouldn't mind. But if it's a problem, I'll find someplace else to store it."

"I'll be away for a few days and if you need it, you won't be able to get to it until I return. Wouldn't it be better if you left it with someone who will be around in case you need to get it before I return."

Sam's natural curiosity was to ask what was on the flash drive but she might regret knowing the answer. In their meeting earlier that afternoon, Ariella had implied that someone in the English Department was using some of her work as their own. Arthur had been reluctant to believe such a thing and had stopped that conversation. Sam wanted to proceed cautiously. Arthur had been instrumental in finding her an agent at a reputable publishing house for her romance novel and Ariella was a Ph.D. student, an assistant to Rick as well as Rick's lover. Sam wanted to make sure that she wasn't involved in whatever it was that was going on. She also didn't want anything to interfere with the divorce meetings that were scheduled to begin soon after her return from Florida.

"That's fine. I just wanted to ask, since you are so nice and have been supportive. I know what I said this morning shocked Professor Churykian and I'm not sure I trust anyone else with this," Ariella replied. Ariella looked very concerned and also very tired. "I'm sorry if I'm disturbing you."

"No no, you don't need to leave right away. I'm mostly packed now and just getting my thoughts together before meeting with my agent in the morning."

"Oh, right. Congratulations on selling your novel," Ariella replied.

"Thanks," Sam replied. "I'm surprised Arthur talked about it, he said he didn't want anyone to know yet. Sam and Arthur had a deal that they would not talk about anything personal regarding Sam with the divorce pending. Sam only visited Arthur when Rick was teaching in a classroom that was not in Baker Hall, the English Department building.

"Oh, he was telling Rick about it and some of us students happened to be in the conference room for a seminar."

"Well, I had already told Rick about writing the novel and finding a publisher but I don't think I told Rick that Arthur had helped me," Sam replied.

"Well, I wasn't really that close to the conversation so I'm not sure who told who what, just that your name came up and Rick was furious."

"Oh, Rick hadn't told you about selling the novel? Since I had told him, I just thought that you knew."

"No, Rick and I haven't had too much time to talk lately," Ariella replied.

Just then the phone rang and Sam answered it while Ariella sipped her tea. Donna was on the other end.

"Hey, are you doing anything special this weekend?" Donna asked Sam.

"Uh, no, I have no special plans. Just working on my novel and getting ready for an interview next week." Sam lied.

She didn't want Donna to know that she wouldn't be around this weekend. Sam knew that Donna and Rick were friends and she felt uncomfortable letting Donna into her place these days, particularly with divorce documents around. And if she didn't Donna in while she was home, she definitely didn't want Donna there when she wasn't home but she didn't want to explain that tonight. Sometimes it was exhausting dealing with Donna.

"Why, what did you have in mind this weekend?" Sam asked.

"Oh, not much, I thought we could catch a movie and some dinner together," Donna replied.

"Do you mind if I use the bathroom?" Ariella whispered to Sam.

"Please and I'll make some more tea," Sam replied with her hand over the phone.

"Are you alone?" Donna asked.

"Yes, quite alone," Sam lied again.

"Do you know that Arthur was talking about you today?" Donna asked.

Sam bit her tongue to stop herself from answering positively. "No, I didn't know that Arthur talked about me today. Why would he do that? And how would you know?"

"Well, apparently he helped you find an agent for your romance story," Donna said. There was a very heavy tone to the word 'romance' but Sam chose to not fall for the bait.

"Really, well he was very kind when I asked him for some advice," Sam said.

"Well, Rick was so embarrassed when Arthur talked about you in front of other faculty members that he left immediately. He feels that you are writing trash and not letting go of him. Really, I just don't know what your reasons are for interfering in his life," Donna continued. "And you should use a pseudonym so that you aren't besmirching his name.

"I'm not interfering in his life, I'm living mine," Sam said.

"Well, you could at least do it somewhere else," Donna said.

"Arthur is a good friend and I have no reason to not ask him for help. I've never visited Arthur when Rick is around and I don't plan on causing any problems for Rick," Sam said.

"Really, well that's wonderful. I'm sure that romance novels don't get as much attention as a true literary work, such as Rick is writing. Anyway, I thought I would stop by this evening," Donna indicated.

"Oh, Donna, it's getting late and I have an early interview tomorrow. It will be more fun to get together for drinks one night after work next week."

"Well, if you insist. It's really cold out there tonight anyway," Donna replied.

Donna ranted on for a few more minutes. Rick was living with another woman, not Donna, but Donna certainly acted as if she was the other woman, Sam thought. Donna rang off and Sam hung up the phone. She turned to head behind the kitchen counter but could see that Ariella had already poured the boiling water into the teapot.

Donna's words stung Sam. Donna's tendency to let Sam know how wonderful Rick was and what a wonderful masterpiece he would soon produce and compare that to how foolish Sam was being for writing just a romance novel hurt more than she wanted to admit. She felt betrayed but not quite ready to give up on their relationship. A true friend would be happy for her. Hell, Ariella was more excited than Donna and she had no reason to be happy for Sam.

Ariella and Sam talked for quite a while. The conversation revolved around Ariella's schoolwork and her Ph.D. dissertation. Sam sipped her tea and nodded occasionally. Sam recognized the intellectual snobbery of the Ph.D. student; she had lived with it long enough with Rick. Eventually, the conversation drifted off and Ariella left. Sam felt exhausted. Her editing would have to be put off until later, right now she needed to finish packing and arrange for an early morning cab to the airport.

Sam was nervous about her visit to her agent in New York City. This meeting was to discuss whether or not her agent was able to sell the idea of additional books from Sam. Things were moving quickly and she wasn't sure what was needed from her to complete an agreement for a series of books. She was both excited and concerned and wanted to make sure she didn't make any mistakes or sell herself short.

Other than Ariella, only her mother and step-father knew that she would be away for a few days. She hadn't had a chance to tell her Dad, her two brothers and her sister. She also hadn't told Arthur yet that she was negotiating a further contract and she should let him know when she returned. She would need more advice from him and also from an attorney. Hopefully, there was time to deal with all of this on her return.

Chapter 6

"You know doll, you've tightened up your final copy very nicely. Your main character's sense of humor is a nice touch too. I think this manuscript is going to be a good start for you," Stella Tibbetts said to Sam, Stella's newest romance writer in a stable of mid-list romance writers.

"Thanks, I really appreciate all your help and advice," Sam smiled at Stella but didn't offer any additional comments. "I still have some more updates to make to the final copy of the first one and I meant to have them all done for this morning."

"Hmm, you might need to learn how to accept a compliment better than that," Stella commented.

Stella had taken Sam under her wing a few months ago when Sam had pitched a story idea to her literary agency. She thought that this young woman in front of her had a lot more to offer and needed some encouragement to keep her going. Compliments like that and finalizing the divorce should help Sam become more focused on herself rather than on everything going on around her.

"I guess I have a lot on my mind, I didn't mean to overlook the compliment. A friend stopped by my place last night, unexpectedly, and I ended up getting side-tracked. Plus the contract you just offered me is very generous. I think I'm mostly in shock that I have a contract," Sam replied honestly.

"Well, you are awfully quiet for someone who is excited to have a contract to write 3 more romance novels," Stella said as Sam stared out the window. "I usually expect my clients to get very excited and jump up and down when I offer them a contract for 3 additional stories, especially my first time writers."

"Really Stella, I can't thank you and Brian enough for all you have done to help me. I think I'm just over-tired and a bit thrown off my routine."

"Would you like some coffee while we talk?"

"Yes, that would be great. I could use some caffeine."

Stella buzzed her secretary, Brian, and asked him to get them each a cup of coffee. Brian, as efficient as always, popped in with three mugs of coffee just the way they each liked it. He was fond of Sam and hoped that everything would work out for her. He also liked to participate in conversations with clients, when he liked the client. Sam and Stella had moved over to a large and comfortable sitting area that made up a part of Stella's office. Stella and Sam took seats across from each other to talk comfortably and Ben sat in a chair next to Stella. The wall of windows with its view of the city fascinated Sam.

Stella and Sam worked for a while on the final details for the publication of her first novel. There would be some final edits to make before the novel was sent to publication in 6 months time. It was a small romance novel and a first effort, so it would move along quickly. Stella then turned to an outline for the next novel and some concept ideas for the two that would follow. It was all exciting and mind-boggling to Sam. She felt as though she were walking through a dream and would soon wake up.

"So, how strange was it to have Ariella pop in like that?" Stella asked once they had finished their discussion.

"How did you know that it was Ariella?" Sam asked.

"Oh, just an educated guess," Stella replied. When Sam didn't respond, she added, "Besides, you just told me."

"Oh, right, I'm really not thinking clearly. I've seen Ariella a lot over the past few months at our writing meetings with Arthur. I think that the relationship between her and Rick has cooled off but I haven't asked any questions. Last night she wanted me to hold a flash drive for her but I declined since I would be away for a few days and she might need it before I got back. She has mentioned a few times that she felt someone was using her work as their own. I'm sympathetic but I just don't want to be involved."

"Has Ariella told anyone else about this?" Ben asked.

"Well, I've been there when she's mentioned it to Arthur and some of the others in our writing group but nothing much seems to have come of it. Not all of us are students at the University," Sam replied.

"Has Ariella been the one to contact you, rather than you contacting her?" Stella inquired.

"Yes, Ariella has initiated all of our get-together's. They have all been for coffee and some conversation," Sam replied. "Apparently Arthur told some members of the department about my selling my novel."

"And was one of those people Rick?" Stella inquired.

"Yes, according to Donna, Rick was there for the announcement."

"Ah, I adore my old friend Arthur but he does like to get his digs in while he can. You know he told me that he much prefers your writing to Rick's."

"I had no idea," Sam was truly astonished by this revelation. "Has he talked with you about student work being plagiarized?"

"No, he hasn't. So, how is the divorce going?"

"A lot slower than I first thought it would," Sam replied. "We'll be meeting with the attorney's to finalize a few things the week after I get back."

57

"So you don't think he's going to come back to you once he gets tired of Ariella?" Ben asked.

"Oh, I know he's not coming back to me, I don't want him. That part of my life seems to finally be over now. He's been controlling my life for too long. I can't believe I put up with it all these years. I'm ready to sell the condo, split the proceeds in some fashion and move on with my life. Now he's dragging his heals on signing the divorce papers because he feels he's entitled to more from the sale, even though his name is not on the mortgage. He also wants a percentage of my retirement money from the bank. He is being such a jerk."

"I thought your parents had made the down payment on the condo?"

"My Dad did and the mortgage is in his name and mine. Rick thinks he's going to wear me down, but he's not, and he's definitely not going to wear my Dad down. I may have to give him some money but I also helped him with all his school loans and supported us both while he was in graduate school so he could concentrate on his studies and then his dissertation."

"Good for you." Stella replied admiringly. "What are you going to do to celebrate completing your first novel?"

"I'm heading to Florida for my mother's birthday. It's a good way to get away from everything."

"How are things going with the family," Stella asked. It paid to know about her writers so she could troubleshoot issues and reflective plot lines. Plus she liked to hear stories and Sam's were usually pretty good.

"Well, they are all crazy, but my parents have been pretty good since I've filed for divorce. They're divorced themselves and don't really speak to each other. Both have made it pretty clear that they don't like Rick and haven't for a while now."

"Have you told Rick that you're going to Florida this weekend?"

"Actually, I haven't talked to him in weeks. We communicate through attorneys now," Sam responded.

"Ah well, that's too bad. I was wondering what his reaction would be like to your novel writing. I wish I had been there when Arthur dropped his bombshell. I've never met Rick but I don't think I would like him very much."

"Thanks. You are gloating more than I think even Arthur would. Are you suggesting I should this angst in my next story?" Sam smiled at Stella.

"You've got me," Stella smiled. "I'm glad to hear your going to take a short break before you start in on the next one."

"Thanks, I am too."

"When are you leaving?"

"I have a flight out of LaGuardia at 6pm tonight," Sam replied, looking at her watch. "Wow, it's almost 4pm."

You don't have much time," Stella checked her watch. "Brian, would you arrange for a car to get Sam to the airport?"

Stella moved quickly from the sitting area to her desk while Brian moved swiftly to his desk, cell phone already to his ear. Brian had it all arranged in a matter of moments and then came back into the office to help Sam with her luggage and push her swiftly towards the elevator.

"Is there anything else I can do for you,?" Stella asked as Sam was being pushed out of the office.

"No, I think I've got it all under control. I'll give you a call when I get back. And I'll have my attorney's review the contract before I sign it," Sam called back over her shoulder.

"You do that sweetie. Have a good time in Florida."

Sam left Stella in the office as she and Brian raced towards the elevator. They headed down, it was only 25 flights, and raced towards the parked black limo, pretty standard in NY these days. She said good-bye to Brian and got into the back seat while Brian and the driver put her luggage in the trunk.

Once back on the floor, Brian stepped into his boss' office for their post-client chat.

"She's looking really good," Brian started. "She's lost some weight, is dumping the husband and writing some pretty good stuff. I like her outline for the next story, too. I think you've got a winner there."

"I agree. She's come a long way in a few months. I hope things continue going well for her. That jerk did a real job on her self-esteem."

"I know. She should meet a nice guy somewhere who will take care of her and support her." Brian replied.

"How about you?" Stella smiled wickedly at Brian.

"You know that I'm looking for a pretty boy, myself." He replied coyly.

"Uh-huh, and I think she can probably take care of herself." Stella replied.

****

Sam made it to LaGuardia in time to catch her flight, but not by much. They were calling her name as she rounded the corner towards her gate. The ride from the city to the airport had been atrocious with stop and go traffic followed by checking in and getting through security.

Once on the plane she was able to relax. The next big hurdle would be when her mother and step-father met her at the airport and grilled her on her life for as long as she could take it. It would be a late night and she would be tired, but they would be excited to see her and their energy would pump her up.

It had been a long time since she had seen her mother and step-father by herself, without any other family members. As much as she loved her siblings and Angela's two girls, Allie and Andie, her mother's practice grandchildren, she would enjoy spending some time alone with her mother. The fact that Angela had two children, whom Miranda adored, was sometimes hard to handle. Sam did not begrudge the 'grandchildren' but sometimes it was good for her to not be around children. Sam and Rick had not had any children and while Sam wanted children, she didn't know if that was something that would happen to her. And, of course, it was nice to visit without Rick in tow, complaining constantly about everything.

Sam dozed off during the flight and woke up as they landed. It was a good, long nap that had refreshed her but not completely erased her tiredness. She made her way to luggage pick-up area where Miranda and Joe were waiting for her. Her mother and step-father were tan and relaxed while she knew that she looked pale and tired. It was a contrast that sometimes made her wonder why she was living in Boston.

"Samantha, my love, it's so good to see you," her mother squished her face between her hands, turning her back and forth. "I can't believe that you are finally here and all by yourself. It makes me so happy that you have finally gotten rid of that lead balloon you married."

Sam could see Joe rolling his eyes behind her mother, and then smiling and giving her a wink. He would never say anything like that about Rick, but he was most likely thinking something very similar.

"Mom, let's not talk about Rick this weekend. We aren't divorced yet and it's going to be tough enough dealing with him once I get back," Sam responded.

"What, your father hasn't gotten rid of that bozo yet?" Miranda continued, completely ignoring her daughter's request.

"Dad has lots of advice but his name is only on the mortgage, not on the marriage certificate," Sam responded.

Joe had moved over to the luggage carousal and pulled out her suitcase. It was somewhat easy to identify, since it was purple and battered from years of travel. He then moved Miranda and Sam off to the parking area.

"Miranda, let's wait until the morning to start the inquisition. Sam just got here and we don't want her leaving just yet," Joe stated quietly but firmly.

"Well, I guess you might be right," Miranda responded. "Sam, how did your meeting with the agent go today?"

Sam silently thanked Joe for moving them off of the divorce conversation as well as out of the airport to the car. She started in on the events of the day, which consisted of finishing off her first novel, with just a few more edits and getting a contract for three more stories. The excitement of this was more than enough to wipe away her remaining exhaustion.

Miranda and Joe had a lot planned for the next few days. There was Miranda's birthday party at the clubhouse of their over-55 community on Friday night, followed by lunch with her mother on Saturday and a get-together with some friends on Saturday night and Sunday brunch with even more friends. Sam was leaving late on Sunday night and would arrive back in Boston in the early hours of Monday morning. The agenda seemed very full but it would make the time pass quickly.

Friday started out bright and sunny. Sam had breakfast with her mother and step-father on their screened in patio. The temperature was a warm 65 degrees with bright sunshine and the promise of a warm and sunny day ahead. After breakfast Sam was high jacked by some of her mother's friends to decorate the clubhouse for her mother's birthday party. It was fun and since her mother's birthday was the impetus for Sam's visit, it felt appropriate. In the afternoon Miranda and her friends took Sam to a local dress shop to find her a nice dress for the party. As it turned out, the dress shopping provided her with a dress that was better than she anticipated.

Her mother had a lot of good, fun friends in Florida and they were all ready to celebrate her birthday. Miranda and Joe were in their element, talking with friends, joking and making everyone feel comfortable. Sam was surprised to find that she was enjoying herself too. She enjoyed watching her mother and Joe having fun and being relaxed with themselves. There were very few people her age at the party and even fewer who were single. Those who were single were certainly attracted to Sam, no matter their age or apparently their sex. Sam took it all in stride and entertained all who came her way with grace and charm, even if their bones creaked as they sidled up to her. She knew that she was going home and would not see many of these people again, at least not for a while.

The next morning dawned bright and sunny again and the three of them had breakfast out on the patio. This time Sam made breakfast while Miranda and Joe relaxed and recovered from the party.

"So, darling, I thought you and I might do some shopping today and have a nice lunch, just the two of us," Miranda suggested. "Then we are going to have dinner with some old friends. I hope that's ok with you."

"Of course, I'm here to do whatever you would like to do. It's been a long time since it was just you and I together. I'm sure we'll have a great time. Are we having dinner with someone I met last night?" Sam responded.

"Actually, we're having dinner with a couple who weren't able to join us last night. They are good friends but they had a competing event last night. They're bringing their son with them," Joe responded. "While the two of you are out, I'm going to get dinner started."

"That's wonderful, dear. Your steaks and ribs are the best, everyone says so," Miranda responded.

While they were all moving a bit slower than they had on Friday, it was a pleasant day for Sam and her mother. They spent the majority of the afternoon at lunch, chatting about all the changes in Sam's life in the past year. Miranda didn't want to ask too many probing questions but it was hard to restrain herself. She hadn't spent too much time along with Sam in the past 10 years and she wanted to give Sam the opportunity to lead the discussion.

Sam told her mother about how she felt about the six months, all the things that had happened to her and how that had changed her life. She was ready to move on with her own life now and didn't feel nearly as abandoned and alone as she had the day she found Rick and Ariella in bed together. And as much as she had loved her job, she no longer missed it or wanted to go back to it. Sam also talked about her changing relationship with Donna and how she missed their old friendship but the new Donna was not someone she cared to know anymore.

Miranda wondered if Donna might have always been like this and Sam just hadn't noticed. Sam pondered this for a moment and concluded that Donna had changed more than Sam had but before she could say anything, her mother moved on to a new topic, Sam.

Miranda talked about how she enjoyed this newer, less cynical Sam that was having lunch with her. Sam was taken back with this assessment of her by her mother. She hadn't thought that she was all that cynical but maybe there was some truth to this. She didn't feel nearly as angry as she had felt previously. In the last nine years of working and taking care of Rick, she had lost some of herself and her goals. Maybe her mother was noticing something about her that she hadn't put into thoughts or words yet.

Dinner that night was with the friends with a single son her age, as announced at breakfast. It was a nice time and again, Sam knew she would not see these people ever again or at least not for a year.

Because of that, she was a more open than she had ever been before about her upcoming divorce. At least that is what she thought when she looked back on this dinner. Miranda felt that Sam was doing all she could to make sure this nice young man never called her again. In Sam's shoes, she might do the same thing. Sam was already pretty sure that this nice young man was never going to call her, no matter what the conversation was about.

Sunday morning found them once again in warm, sunny weather. This time they all headed to brunch at a local country club where they met another set of Miranda and Joe's friends, with a single son her age. Sam did not anticipate anything different than the previous night's dinner and was surprised to find that she liked the young man she was obviously there to meet. He was also in the process of divorce and lived in Chicago. They talked a lot about living in the city and about winters vs. summer and a little bit about each of their divorces. All in all they had a good time and Sam and her new found friend exchanged email addresses and talked about becoming Facebook friends, although they both admitted that they each rarely checked out Facebook.

After brunch, Sam, her mother and step-father headed back to their home to pick up Samantha's things and head for the airport. The trip to the airport was fun and full of conversation. Miranda was going to be sad to see her daughter leave but she didn't want it to show too much. It was 6pm by the time they had Sam dropped off at the Orlando International Airport. Once they had seen Sam through the security gate Miranda and Joe headed back towards their car. They walked casually with Joe's arm draped across Miranda's shoulders. Miranda had a handkerchief and was wiping tears from her eyes.

"I thought you weren't going to cry," Joe said softly to Miranda.

"I didn't want to cry in front of Sam but I can't help it now that she's gone," Miranda replied. The sobs weren't as bad as Joe had expected.

"It was fun to have her here all by herself, wasn't it," Joe responded. "No Angela and children to distract you and certainly no Rick."

65

"Yes, most certainly no Rick. She has no idea how different she is now that he is out of her life," Miranda responded drying her eyes.

"Now we just need to find her a new guy," Joe said.

"No, I think she needs a break," Miranda responded. "I think it's time to find someone for Andrew."

"Really," Joe was surprised at this response since Andrew was Miranda's step-son. "I think that nice young man we had dinner with Saturday night would be perfect for Andrew."

"Joe, how dare you suggest such a thing. Suzie's son is not gay," Miranda responded vehemently.

"Right, just like Andrew is not gay," Joe replied.

This conversation had certainly stopped Miranda's tears. "Do you think Viv knows that her son is gay?"

"I have no idea. Viv and Marcus are certainly not ones to let anything out of the bag. It was good seeing them at Jonathan's engagement party but they were studiously ignoring Andrew and Desmond circling on another."

"True, very true. They could have had blinders on. Well, I guess we'll just have to wait and see what they all decide to do with their lives," Miranda responded. She had stopped crying and they were heading home to their more normal lives.

Chapter 7

Sam's flight from Orlando to Boston was uneventful. She was far more rested than when she had left on Thursday morning so she read and did some writing on the flight. She didn't bother to use the earphones to listen to music or watch a movie or TV. She could do all of that when she got home. For now, she used her time productively and worked on some editing she had promised Stella for the novel.

It was a cooler night than she anticipated after the heat and humidity of Orlando, Sam noticed as she exited the plane into the terminal at Logan International Airport. Not surprising for the time of year but it caused an unexpected shiver in her body as she headed across the waiting area towards the hallway that directed her to baggage claim. She had a fleece jacket on but it wasn't nearly warm enough.

The terminal was mostly deserted at this hour and the darkness outside the long glass windows caused the lights overhead to create a surreal feeling. Almost like being in a scene from the Twilight Zone, the eerie feeling of deserted boarding area, the passengers and the cleaning people the only ones occupying this strange world even though it was only 9:30pm. Sam nodded to the cleaning people who were idling in the hallway, watching all the passengers heading to the baggage area or directly out to find a ride or a cab.

Sam noted that her baggage would be arriving at baggage carousel 4 and she headed over to wait dutifully while the turnstile churned out some luggage. She and the others picked up their luggage and moved off to get their cars, a shuttle to a local hotel, catch a bus or take a cab home.

Sam stood at the cab stand and waited for a cab to take her to her condo in the Leather District of Boston. It had been a fun and exciting

3 days in Orlando with her mother and step-father and it felt like it had been an eternity since she had left Boston. She could no longer control her yawning.

After 15 minutes of waiting at the cab stand, she slipped into a cab that glided up in the cool darkness to whisk her back to her home and her waiting bed. She smiled at the driver, an older man, gave him the address and settled into the seat for the ride. There wouldn't be much traffic at this hour so she anticipated a swift ride home.

The cab driver glanced at her in his rearview mirror and then looked again. This look was a longer, more appraising look. Not that Sam noticed. She was focused on looking at the lights of the city as they headed out of the airport to the tolls and the tunnel into the city.

"Hey lady, do you know that you look just like the lady their looking for," he said as he put the car into drive and moved off away from the tolls.

"What lady?" Sam asked, taking a closer look at the driver. He had piqued her interest with his comment and his loud voice.

"You know, the lady," he responded, helpfully.

"No, I don't know," she replied casually, "I've been away for a few days."

"Where ya been?"

"To Orlando, to visit my mother and stepfather," Sam replied.

"In November. Are you nuts? It's still hurricane season and it hasn't even started snowing yet. You should be going in the winter when it's icy and cold here." Their eyes met in the rearview mirror. His large and hers quizzical.

"Well, I guess this news hasn't reached Miami yet." The cab driver yammered. "It's all over the local papers. They're looking for a woman who murdered her husband's girlfriend or mistress or whatever. And you look just like her."

"I look like the wife or the girlfriend?" Sam asked. She was getting a little nervous. This scenario sounded a little familiar. But if something had happened, she thought someone would have called her by now.

"The wife, of course. They've been showing her picture around the TV news. The picture looks a little heavier than you are and the hair is longer but otherwise it looks just like you," the cab driver responded.

Sam didn't know what to think now. She was more alert and concerned and wanted to call someone but didn't know who to try first. She decided to call Kate on her cell phone to see if she could get some confirmation of what the cab driver was telling her but Kate didn't answer. The cab driver pulled out of the Callahan tunnel and cut off another car getting into the Haymarket Square lane, causing screeching brakes and raised hands and fingers while slurs passed silently between the drivers.

"What happened to the mistress?" Sam asked.

"She's dead," he deadpanned.

"I got that part, how did she die?"

"Look lady, I'm not sure what's going on here. I'll get you home as fast as I can and then you can turn on the news and see for yourself," he replied while dodging more cars.

They rode in silence for a few moments while Sam fumbled with her cell phone. Funny, she hadn't checked it once while she was in Florida. They continued in silence, Sam wondering what was going on and the cab driver wondering if he had a murderer in his cab. He would have quite a few stories to tell after this. He desperately wanted to call into dispatch and let them know who he had in his cab. Instead he called in to let them know where he was dropping this fair off and to see if there was any fairs to the airport to make his return more profitable.

"What address did you say?" the cab driver asked her.

"It's that building just ahead on the corner," she leaned forward and pointed over his shoulder.

"You mean the one with all the cops around it?" he asked.

"Yeah, I mean that one," Sam responded quietly, dread filling her up and replacing the cool evening chill.

"Sheesh, lady, maybe you do look too much like the wife."

"Maybe I do," she replied.

The cab driver pulled up to the corner that had the least amount of activity. Sam handed him the cash and stepped out of the cab onto the sidewalk. There was sweat on her back that caused her to shiver as she stepped out into the cool night air. The cab driver walked around the cab, popped open the trunk, pulled her luggage out and placed them on the sidewalk. He noticed the cops eyeing Sam, jumped back into his cab without offering to help her with her luggage, turned to give her a wink and a wave and swiftly pulled into traffic on Beach Street. He would have a lot of stories to tell tonight but he definitely did not want to get stopped by the cops, it would ruin his evening haul.

Sam looked at the cops and the media swarming around the front door of her building. Her first reaction was to turn and run but there was nowhere to go. She noticed Kate and Ben standing with the cops on the corner along with some of her other neighbors. It took one of her neighbors a few seconds before she pointed out Sam to the cops and the media that were lighting up the neighborhood as well.

"Are you Samantha Monroe?" a cop asked her as he stepped quietly onto the curb behind her.

"Yes, yes I am," Sam replied. The cop had taken her by surprise and caused her to turn. It would be futile to lie or ignore them, she decided. Besides, where was she going to go with her luggage?

"Do you realize that we've been looking for you all day?" the shorter cop of the duo asked her.

"No, I didn't realize that. I've been away for a few days visiting my mother and step-father in Orlando," she replied, squinting against the lights that were now directed at her by several media crews, panic filling her heart.

"Get the detectives," the tall cop instructed the shorter one. The shorter cop grunted, looked like he was about to protest and then ambled through the door of her condo building. She and the tall cop continued to stand, silently, on the sidewalk in the chill. She had no idea if she was under arrest or not. It didn't look like the tall cop was going to let her go anywhere anyway. The short cop and another guy, not in a uniform, came out of the door and walked swiftly towards them.

"Mrs. Sampson?" the other guy asked. He was of average height, dark brown hair, grey eyes, no wedding band and he was in plain clothes. Rumpled but definitely not a uniform. Odd, she thought, I hardly ever look to see if someone is wearing a wedding band. She twisted her ring finger reflexively, noting that she had taken her wedding band off just a few weeks ago.

"Well, not exactly any more. We're ..., that is, ... Rick and I are about to get divorced," she stumbled over her words. "And my name's Monroe, Samantha Monroe, I never changed it.

"Really, that's what he said also," the detective replied.

"And when did you leave for Orlando?" another plain clothes guy in a trench coat asked her. This one was shorter, rotund with sandy brown hair and a twinkle in his eyes

"I left for New York on Thursday morning and then flew from New York to Orlando," she replied, stuttering and shivering. She was definitely scared and confused.

"Should we cuff her and take her in?" the shorter cop asked the plain clothes detective.

The first detective paused for a moment before replying, "No, no, I think we'll all go inside, away from the media, and talk about this."

Sam looked at the paper in the cops hand and saw a picture of herself. A part of her was impressed to see her picture in the paper and the other part of her was horrified at the image that had been used. It was from an English Department event several years ago and she looked awful. She was at her heaviest, with long stringy hair and a sour look on her face. She wondered where they could have gotten such a bad image of her and why that one had been used. Of course, she remembered, the only other picture taken of her recently had been at her brother's engagement party and it wasn't likely they had contacted her family yet.

With that the first detective took her by the arm and they headed for the front of her building. As they got closer to the front, the media were yelling questions at her, like why did she do it and why was she coming home now. At that moment Sam heard someone across the street call her name. She turned in time to have lots of flashbulbs go off in her face. The detective put up his hands to try and block some of the lights and questions and they swiftly entered her building.

The two cops followed quickly behind, one of them carrying her luggage. They all got on the elevator and headed up to the 5th floor. Sam noted that her door was open as they got off the elevator and cops were guarding her door. The detective nodded at them and they stepped aside to let everyone in. Inside her condo all the lights were on and more cops or maybe just people were milling around with rubber gloves on, checking on everything in her place. It was all very surreal and Sam was beginning to think she was watching a play or a movie. The people in gloves were laying dust all over the place, apparently taking finger prints from every surface. Others were looking through all the books, taking them out one at a time, opening them and then putting them back, not as evenly as she would like.

"Oh, that's good. Can you tell me what this is all about?" Sam asked.

"I take it you've been out of town for a few days. Can you prove that?" A female detective who had now joined the group asked her.

"Well, I guess I can. I have my boarding pass here and my itinerary from the airline. And you can talk to my mother and stepfather. I stayed with them." Sam felt a whole lot more nervous than she sounded. She couldn't believe she sounded as though she answered questions like this every day. The female detective jotted down a few notes on a pad of paper and then looked up the group gathered in front of her.

"Sam, where have you been," Kate and Ben were at her door, being held back by cops stationed there.

"If you don't mind, I'll conduct the questioning here," the detective stated calmly but authoritatively, not even looking up from his paperwork. Kate and Ben glared at the detective for a few moments and then stomped, loudly, down the hall.

"I'm Detective Peter O'Malley. We have a situation here and we're hoping that you can help us clear some of it up," he stated. "There's been a murder and you have become one of our prime suspects."

Sam looked at him mutely, not sure she even wanted to ask the most obvious question.

"Who was murdered?" she asked.

"Ariella Fantini," he replied.

"Really? When?"

"Friday night."

"Where?"

"She was found on the roof of a University building. Baker Hall. Do you know it?"

"How do you know it was murder?" Sam asked.

"Her throat was slit," he replied.

"Wow. What makes you think I did it?"

"We don't know that you did it, you are just one of our suspects."

"But my name and picture are on the front of the paper in your hands."

"I thought you didn't know anything about this?"

"I didn't until I looked at the paper you have in your hands," she replied. "And the cab driver kept saying that I looked a lot like someone the police were looking for. I thought he was mostly nuts."

"I see, and you had no prior information?"She looked up at him dumbly, not sure what to say. He made a few notes and tried hard not to look at her face.

"OK, let's start with where you were on Friday afternoon and evening."

"I was in Orlando for my mother's birthday," she replied. She told them about her mother's birthday party at the complex clubhouse, dinner Saturday night with friends and brunch on Sunday with even more friends. They let her continue uninterrupted, several of them taking notes. Detective O'Malley paused for a moment to make sure she was done.

"It would appear that you have quite a few witnesses to your whereabouts on Friday, Saturday and Sunday."

"There are even pictures." Sam replied. "I'm sure my mother can get them all together."

"I'm sure she can. Just to be sure, let's get some information so I can contact your parents. The detective here will take down the pertinent information," Det. Peter O'Malley waved to Darcy Kelvin and gave her some basic directions on what information to gather. Detectives O'Malley and Girard headed out to the hallway to talk quietly.

Sam gave Detective Kelvin quite a bit of information, probably more than she would ever want or need. She asked Sam not to contact her parents or anyone else on the list until after Detective Kelvin had completed her preliminary investigations. Sam agreed she would not contact anyone immediately Detective Kelvin then joined the other two detectives out in the hallway, where the three detectives had a heated conversation about what had led them to this dead-end.

"It looks like her soon to be ex-husband has handed us a load of bull," Detective O'Malley started. "I don't think this woman was involved in this murder at all."

"I have to agree with you," Detective Girard, the shorter, stout, sandy haired detective responded. "It does point to the ex-husband leading us down the wrong path."

"I don't necessarily agree that the husband was misleading us," Detective Kelvin, the female detective, responded. "He might really feel that she is the culprit and viewed his wife's actions as always being negative."

Detective O'Malley looked at her appraisingly. "As much as I would like to think that Professor Sampson and his friend were trying to be helpful, they have led us very much in the wrong direction and now we need to backtrack. A lot of time and energy has been wasted today on the wrong person."

"I agree with Darcy. He seemed so sincere and honest, though," Detective Girard replied.

"Whether or not it was deliberate, we'll now have to split up to investigate the original murder, investigate our two informants and talk to students and faculty who knew Ariella. And we'll have to re-review all of the other information we received about the murder as well. This one has disaster written all over it," Detective O'Malley said. "It's my fault, I'm the one who went with the wife and had to focus all of our energies on her, particularly since we thought she was missing."

"Thanks, Pete, but we also participated in the decision so you can't take all the blame for yourself," Raoul Girard replied.

"Darcy, would you let Mrs. Sampson, ah, Ms. Monroe, know that we'll be leaving now?" Pete O'Malley asked.

"Sure, you should know that she goes by Monroe, she never changed her name when she got married. We should make a note of that for the report."

The detectives talked some more in hushed but intense tone. Detective Kelvin then went back into the condo to tell everyone to wrap up and head out. They would take all of the evidence they had collected but since Sam was now less likely to be a suspect, they didn't need to continue collecting. The condo could be turned back over to Sam.

Darcy Kelvin apologized to Sam for the mess and told Sam that they would all be leaving now and she was free to stay and clean up. Sam thanked her, somewhat absently, as she looked around her place in shock. Darcy asked Sam if she were ok or if she needed them to call someone. Sam thanked her and said she would be fine. The police officers, detectives and forensics teams all left and Sam closed the door behind them.

Chapter 8

Misty Mustoe, investigative news reporter for Channel 8 in Boston, watched as the cops converged on the young woman exiting the cab. She recognized the woman from her picture as Samantha Sampson, the murder suspect. Misty positioned herself as close to the sidewalk as possible, jostling her way through the crowd of other reporters and by-standers. It helped that she was 6 ft. tall, had a gorgeous brown hair with red highlights and a deep resonating voice. Misty felt that these features all made people take notice of her, pay attention to what she says and give her space when she muscled through a crowd. The fact that she was pushy was what got most people's attention. It was a good thing that Misty wasn't terribly sensitive to people's reactions to her.

As the cops escorted the young woman with short, dark hair up the sidewalk to the front to the building, Misty and several other reporters yelled out. The goal was to get this young woman to look at the cameras and she did, along with most of the cops. They all yelled out questions like, are you guilty, where were you hiding and why did you kill her. The young woman just looked confused as the cops quickly hustled her in to the condo building.

"Damn, we should have stopped that cab driver to find out where he picked her up," Misty heard one of the other reporters say.

"Hey, I got the plate number of that cab," she heard another say more quietly beside her.

The second reporter pulled out his cell phone started dialing. He quickly confirmed the cab number and where the driver had picked up his ride. Misty's impression was that she had been picked up at the airport and that woman who had just been led into the building knew nothing of what had happened.

Misty made her way quickly back to news truck and joined Ron, her cameraman, in reviewing the video tape he had just shot. Ron had a great shot of Samantha's face looking like a deer in the headlights at the reporters yelling at her.

"Let's call Mal and see what he would like us to do next," Misty said.

Ron grabbed his cell phone and made the call. Mal, the news director, picked up on the first ring. He had been in the newsroom overseeing the 11pm news for the station and was waiting to interrupt the regularly scheduled broadcast if anything newsworthy happened.

"What you got for me," he said.

"We have some great footage of the suspect and the cops escorting her into the building," Misty replied.

"Anything else? You think she did it?" Mal asked.

"My gut says she didn't. She was dressed like she had just come back from someplace warm, Florida, California, something like that and she was pretty clueless about what's going on," Misty said.

"You think the tipster led us astray?" Mal asked.

"I think the tipster led a lot of us astray, including the cops," Misty replied. "The trail is cooling and they may have the wrong person."

"OK, I'll give you 90 seconds to summarize and then get out of there. Say she was unseasonably dressed," Mal said and hung up.

Ron had already picked up the camera and headed to the street, where there were fewer people and more light and his camera could pick up the activity at the front of the building. Misty stepped up to the front of the camera and looked over her shoulder at the front of the building. His shot started with Misty turning to the camera and beginning to speak. It was a little bit of a dark shot with her dark hair but it wasn't bad.

The news anchors, Frank and Sarah, noted the updated teleprompter in front of them. Sarah stopped her feel-good story about a birth at the zoo and announced the breaking news to their audience. Frank and Sarah then turned to Misty who summarized for those watching the news live what had just transpired. The tape previously made of Samantha Sampson being escorted from the cab into her condo building was shown in a small box. Frank thanked Misty for her update and they turned back to regular news programming.

"For those of you who just tuned in, we have just learned that the suspect in the Ariella Fantini murder case was picked up this evening at Logan Airport. She arrived on a flight that originated in Florida. We don't know yet what time her flight left Florida or when she may have flown to Florida. We will keep you updated as we get more news."

The shot then cut over to Sarah, the co-anchor, who made a comment about how sad this whole situation was and then continued with the zoo story. This was followed by sports and the weather. After they signed off, Mal asked both anchors to join him in the conference room.

In the conference room, he asked Frank and Sarah to take a seat and let them know that Misty and Ron were on their way back to the station and he wanted a quick word on the murder story before they all left for the evening. As soon as Misty and Ron arrived, Mal got down to business. It was late and they all wanted to get home.

"So, we led with the tip that the estranged wife might be the murderer and now it looks like our tipster was wrong. Misty, the tipster called you directly. What can you tell us about this person?" Mal asked.

"Derek is a friend from my home town. We've known each other since we were in middle school. We keep in touch occasionally but we don't hang out at all. I know that he was in the same graduate program at the University with Ariella and that he and Ariella were acquainted but I don't know much more," Misty replied.

79

"Do you know what led him to point to the wife?" Frank asked.

"No, not really. He said he had it on good authority that the Ariella and the wife hated each other and that the wife was extremely jealous," Misty said.

"Who's the good authority," Sarah asked.

"Derek got the information from the husband. I talked to the husband too. He was very, very convincing."

"Well, it appears that while he was convincing he may have had no idea where his wife actually was over the weekend. Can you get in touch with Derek and see what other information you can dig up. Like did he know the wife, what's the real relationship between the wife and the husband and what the relationship with Ariella was really like?"

"Which relationship?" Misty asked.

"Any relationship. It doesn't seem to cut and dried," Mal replied.

"I tried to reach Derek on the way back to the station but couldn't raise him on his cell phone and his roommate said that he hadn't seen Derek all day. They do keep different schedules but they usually see each other in the evenings," Misty replied.

"What's the roommate like?"

"Jimmy's also a student in the graduate program. He's finishing up his Ph.D. dissertation in History with a Literature focus while Derek has dropped out to work. Jimmy's fine but he did get caught up in a stalking situation with a female undergrad a few years ago. Otherwise he's clean."

"Stalking, that's not a good sign," Sarah said. They all nodded in agreement.

"Did he get a police record?"

"No, I think it only went as far as the campus police."

"Did he know Ariella as well?" Mal asked.

"Yes, I think he did. They were both working to finish their Ph.D.'s and they both started at the same time and they both knew Derek so, yes, I think they must have known one another."

"OK, Misty, see what you can find out from Derek and Jimmy, and try to interview the suspect tomorrow. Thank you everyone. I'll see you all again tomorrow at 3pm for our regular briefing for the evening news. Any information you get, let me know before the meeting," Mal said.

They all filed out of the conference room and headed out on their various trips home. Misty decided that she would stop at one or two bars on the way home that she knew Derek frequented or at least used to frequent. Ron decided to join her as it was still early, from his perspective, and he might be able to film something should anything come their way.

Chapter 9

Rick and Donna were watching the Sunday night TV news very closely. They were in Donna's apartment waiting to hear the announcement that Sam had been arrested for Ariella's murder. The news stations had been touting a surprise update about the murder and they wanted to find out what the update was all about.

The brief announcement that Sam had been out of town all weekend and was still a person of interest but not a suspect in the murder was a surprise to both of them. The news quickly moved on to other items after this brief announcement. It had been sensational while it lasted but it had quickly become old and stale when the wife was no longer the suspect.

They had both been interviewed by the police on Saturday, soon after Ariella's body had been found on the roof of Baker Hall on campus. The only person they both knew who might have had it in for Ariella was Sam, unless someone her father knew had been involved. At least that's what they told the police officer who had taken their statements.

"That's a shocker," Rick said while looking straight ahead at the blank TV screen. Donna had turned off the TV as soon as the announcer had outlined the fact that the suspected murderer was in fact no longer a suspect. The suspect, the news had flashed a tan Sam being escorted into the building by police, had been out of town at the time of the murder with a confirmed alibi and no possibility of having returned early or left late. The timing just wasn't there.

"It's ridiculous, how could she be out of town without our knowing anything about it. She told me she was going to be writing all weekend and didn't want to get together. I'm her best friend, she should have told me she was going away, she used to tell me everything," Donna and Rick locked eyes for a moment.

"Didn't you check to make sure that she was at home? That was something you were supposed to be doing?" Rick asked Donna.

"Well, I called a couple of times and she didn't answer. I figured she was writing and not answering the phone, again." Donna replied. "I never thought she would be out of town. She hasn't gone anywhere or done anything since she went to Long Island on Labor Day. And she hates her family, too."

"She doesn't exactly hate her family, they hate me and she defended me so her relationship with her family was a bit strained," Rick replied with unusual candor. "I bet things have gotten better now that we're not together. I'm surprised she didn't tell you that."

"But if not me, why didn't she tell Kate and Ben. She's been doing everything with them lately," Donna responded.

"How could she possibly write a romance novel? It will ruin my reputation at the University if this gets out. No one will take me seriously in the department if it actually gets published and everyone knows who wrote it," Rick said. "I hope she's smart enough to use her maiden name and keep me out of the whole thing."

"Well it looks like everyone knows about Sam and her novel now," Donna said.

"Yes," Rick replied. "Arthur always liked Sam more than me and I don't know why. He's giving me such a hard time about getting published that he's making me nervous. He's a major factor in my getting tenure," Rick responded.

"What's important now is what we're going to do now. Obviously the cops are going to be looking for a new murderer. And we implied that it was Sam." Donna said.

"Hard to say," Rick replied, staring at the silent TV.

"Is that all you have to say?" Donna asked. "I would think you would want to have more of a plan before the cops get here."

"Don't be sarcastic with me. It was all your idea to lead them to Sam," Rick replied.

There was a long moment of silence as the two considered their options. It had seemed so smooth and easy, convincing the police that Sam had been so rabidly jealous of Ariella that she might have been plotting to murder her for the past year. They had worked out a plan pointing the investigation towards Sam and that it would be such an open and shut case that they figured, in all the confusion, they and their white lies would get a bit lost.

They discussed their options and realized that the police would want to question them soon about their previous statements and they were both nervous about what might happen. They needed to come up with some plausible explanations for their previous statements that weren't contradictory and they needed to do so soon. There statements would need to be coordinated and not staged but resemble each other's particularly when they were questioned separately. They thought it was too late on a Sunday night for the police to contact them.

They were so intent in their conversation that the sound of the door buzzer made them both jump. They looked at one another and then at the door. The buzzer sounded again, two short, quick bursts. They briefly considered pretending that no one was there, but that did seem to make much sense, particularly since the lights were on. Rick motioned to Donna to be quiet while he tip-toed to the front door to look through the peephole into the hallway.

From the back, it looked to Donna as if his body deflated and he almost let out a groan. Rick saw Detective Girard, the humorous short detective. He paused for a second before opening the door, pulling together an attitude of astonishment at the turn of events.

"Why, Detective Girard. We just saw you on the TV news," Rick said.

"That was actually filmed a few hours ago, when Samantha Monroe returned from her trip," Detective Girard replied.

Rick and the detective looked at each other for a few moments without saying anything. Detective Girard spoke first.

"Good to see you Professor Sampson. I was actually stopping by to speak with Ms. Sussman. Would she happen to be home?"

"Ah, yes, she's right here. We were just watching the news together."

"I see," was all Detective Girard had to say as he stepped past Rick and into Donna's apartment.

"Detective Girard, how good to see you again," Donna said. "We were just talking about this turn of events in Ariella's murder. We had no idea that Sam was out of town."

"Apparently no one knew she was out of town, except her mother, step-father and literary agent," Detective Girard replied.

"Well, that really is a surprise," Donna replied. "Don't you agree Rick."

"Yes, yes I do agree that it's a surprise," Rick replied. He and Detective Girard were still standing while Donna was sitting on the couch.

"Do you mind if I ask a few questions?" Detective Girard asked.

"No, no not at all," Rick and Donna both replied.

"As it turns out, Sam Monroe was in Florida at the time of the murder. She was with enough different people that we believe she could not possibly have been involved in the murder of Ariella Fantini. Her mother, step-father and several guests at her mother's birthday party as well as other she spent time with can confirm her whereabouts."

Detective Girard waited a few moments to get a reaction from Rick and Donna. There were a few moments of silence while they thought about this new information.

"We were just talking about how we had no idea she was out of town. Are there other suspects in the murder?"

"Really, I thought you and Sam were very close?" Detective Girard asked Donna.

"Well, we were extremely close until recently. In the past few months we just haven't been as close as we once were, but I didn't think she would go away for several days without telling me," Donna replied.

"So, I'd like to get a sense of how you felt when you learned that Sam was no longer a suspect."

"Well, I, for one, am glad to find out that Sam couldn't have done it," Rick said.

"And why is that?"

"Well, I've known Sam a long time and while we have had our differences of late, I just can't believe that she would murder someone," Rick replied.

"Oh, I don't know. Remember how angry she's been of late. While I'm glad to hear that it wasn't her, I hope she finds peace with herself. Of course, Ariella has a very unsavory father so I'm wouldn't be at all surprised if someone related to her father's business was involved," Donna responded.

"That reminds me, have either of you ever met Ariella's father?" Detective Girard asked.

"Actually, I did meet him once. I didn't really know it at the time. It was a quick run-in while Ariella and I were out for a walk." Rick replied.

"Where was this walk you were taking?"

"Oh, it wasn't too far from campus, actually. We were heading to dinner somewhere and he just popped up in front of us."

"Really, so it was here in Boston?"

"Oh, yes. Ariella and I have never travelled outside of Boston together."

"And did he say anything?" Det. Girard asked.

"As far as I can remember Ariella introduced us and we shook hands and then headed our separate ways," Rick replied.

"Have you ever met Ariella's mother?"

"No, no, she lives in Italy I believe and her English isn't very good, according to Ariella."

"Ah well, her mother will be arriving in Boston tomorrow to identify her daughter's body and arrange for the funeral."

And Ms. Sussman, have you ever met Ariella's mother or father?"

"No, I have never met either of Ariella's parents," Donna shook her head as she spoke indicating that she had never met either of Ariella's parents.

"Thank you both. I'm sure we'll have more questions for you," Detective Girard said.

"Do you think her father will show up for the funeral?" Donna asked.

"Well we'll certainly keep an eye for him if he should show up," Detective Girard replied. "Dr. Sampson, will you be staying here for the forseeable future?"

"Uh, no. I'm staying at the Holiday Inn in Kenmore Square for a few days," Rick replied. "I just stopped by for dinner."

"Great, let me leave you each with my card. If you make any changes to your living situation or to your statement, you'll let me know. Dr. Sampson, Ms. Sussman, please call me with anything at all regarding this case. And, of course, call me if you are leaving town for any reason. Have a good night."

With that Detective Girard nodded to them both and left the apartment. Rick and Donna just looked at one another for a few moments.

"Well, I guess it's time for me to head back to the hotel," Rick said, picking up his coat and heading for the door.

"I had hoped that you would be able to stay tonight," Donna said.

"I think that under the circumstances I should head back to the hotel. What if someone is watching for me to leave?"

"Oh, it's always something with you. First it was Sam, then Ariella and now the murder. When will we be able to act like a couple?"

Rick really had nothing to say to this. He and Donna had known each other for years but only recently, since her divorce and his separation from Sam, and the souring of his relationship with Ariella, had they become physically close. He liked Donna as a friend, and he enjoyed their times together but he wasn't sure that he wanted to be tied that closely to her. For now he needed her and would continue with the relationship but once this was all done he would move on.

Chapter 10

"Honey, I think you need to come see this," Vittoria was in bed waiting for her husband, Philip, to finish getting ready and join her.

"I hope it's not another celebrity drug story," Philip called out from the bathroom. "There's really nothing I need to know about any celebrity."

Vittoria sighed. Sometimes the age difference between her and her much older husband did cause problems.

"Actually, it's about Sam," Vittoria called out. "She was wanted for murder but now she's been cleared."

"Sam, what could she possibly be doing on the news wanted for murder?" Philip replied, surprised and suddenly concerned about his younger daughter.

"Well, you know the young woman that her husband Rick left her for? Apparently she's been murdered and Sam was a suspect but she's been cleared because she was in Florida visiting with Miranda," Vittoria explained while turning up the news so that Philip could hear.

She looked up to see Philip standing in the in the bathroom door, toothbrush in hand and toothpaste foam dripping down one side of his mouth. He heard just the tail end of the news story repeating that Sam Monroe appeared to no longer be a serious suspect in the murder of Ariella Fantini.

"Would you hand me the phone," he said to Vittoria.

Vittoria tossed the cordless phone to him and then got up and grabbed her robe. "You call Sam and I'm going to see what I can find online."

Vittoria and Philip had been married for 6 years and the 35 year age difference didn't seem quite so obvious now, at least not when they were alone together. Physically Vittoria did not look much older than Sam and was about the same age as Angela. Philip, at 70, was still a vibrant man with dark hair that was peppered with gray and a short, compact body.

Philip made the call to Sam while Vittoria turned on the laptop in her office off of their bedroom. They hadn't heard anything about it on Long Island and it seemed to be considered a local case. They also had not been contacted by the police yet.

Meanwhile, Sam's older brother, Andrew, a lawyer in New York City, was getting ready for bed when a friend from Boston called with the news about Sam. He immediately called their sister Angela, who also lived in the city, to find out what she knew. Angela had heard nothing and it was now after 11pm and Sam's phone was busy so they both went online to learn more. Andrew then called Jonathan and woke he and Hyacinth with the news about Sam. They all agreed to wait until morning to let Miranda know what was happening.

It didn't really matter, since detectives had already visited Miranda and Joe to verify Sam's story about being in Florida for 3 days. While Andrew called Miranda, Angela tried to call their father, but got Vittoria instead who let him know that Philip had gotten through to Sam on the other line. Angela was relieved to find that someone was talking to Sam and that she was ok. She let Andrew and Jonathan know and then headed off to bed. It would be an early morning getting the girls up, ready and off to school.

Chapter 11

Miranda and Joe had enjoyed a leisurely late Sunday afternoon reading the paper and resting after a busy weekend. Around 7pm, as they were thinking about to head out for dinner, two plain clothes policemen showed up at their door to ask a few questions. What had seemed like it would take just a few minutes turned out to take several hours.

The detectives had wanted to first confirm Sam's whereabouts for the past few days. Once Miranda and Joe confirmed that she had been with them from Thursday night through early Sunday afternoon, the questioning had become more intense. After the police stepped out for a few minutes to consult with their superiors, they were told that Sam had been a suspect in the murder of an Ariella Fantini. There had been an intense search for Ariella in the Boston area. With the confirmation of Ariella's actual whereabouts, Sam could now be cleared since they could confirm and had friends and neighbors who could confirm that Sam was with them all weekend.

The detectives stayed with Miranda and Joe in case any other questions came from Boston. They monitored all calls to and from the house and would not let Miranda or Joe make any outgoing calls to Sam or anyone else. Once final confirmation was received that all was clear, they graciously apologized to Miranda and Joe for the inconvenience and were on their way.

As soon as the police left, Miranda called Sam on her home line, which was busy, and then on her cell phone, which was turned off. She and Joe concluded that Sam had never turned her cell phone back on after the flight. Miranda then called her ex-husband Philip and got Vittoria on the line. Vittoria was able to confirm that Philip was on the phone with Sam and that her friends Kate and Ben were with Sam in her condo. Miranda then called Andrew, who was more than a bit surprised to hear from his step-mother.

"Miranda, how good to hear from you," Andrew said pleasantly.

"Don't give me that. Did you know about Sam and about Ariella's murder?" Miranda asked.

"I found out about it about a half hour ago when a friend from Boston called me," Andrew replied. "Angela and I talked and Angela was going to call you in the morning to let you know."

"Well, some detectives just left here. They were confirming Sam's alibi," Miranda replied.

"I'm sorry Miranda, we hadn't thought they would contact you so we all agreed we'd let you know in the morning so you would get a good night's sleep."

"Since Sam was with us all weekend for my birthday, we are her alibi," Miranda replied.

"I'm glad Sam went down for your birthday. Did you have fun?"

"It was a great party and it was great having Sam here. We think we have someone to introduce you too. He's the son of some friends of ours. They wanted to fix him up with Sam but he wasn't interested because he's gay. Well, Joe and Sam think he's gay. I thought he would be a nice boy for Sam. I'm pretty sure his parents either don't know or are in denial. My god, I can't believe that this has happened and that I'm babbling like an idiot."

"Miranda, this is pretty awful. Of all the things to have happen. I always thought Rick was a rat."

"Do you think he did it?" Miranda asked

"I don't think he's capable. He can't even get published. OK, that was really awful of me to say. It's his lack of skill that's going to get him into trouble."

Andrew suggested that Miranda and Joe look at the local news outlets online to get more information. He told Miranda that the scene of Sam being escorted to her building was online, he'd already seen it. Miranda groaned and hung up. As soon as she hung up, Joe yelled out that she had to come see the Boston news online.

Andrew then called Sam and got through. Sam had promised her Dad and Andrew that she would call the next morning, once she had sorted through what the police had done to her condo as well as sorting through her thoughts about what had happened. Also, the police would be taking a more thorough statement from her so she would need to go to police headquarters. Andrew promised to relay this information to Angela and Jonathan.

Chapter 12

"Wow, can you believe this?" Kate said to Ben after the update about Sam was finished on the news. Kate and Ben were watching the news in Ben's apartment to see the latest on the murder case and Sam.

"Not really. First Sam didn't tell us that she was going away for the weekend and then Ariella is found murdered on the roof of a building at the University, we're questioned by the police, they institute a manhunt for Sam, Rick acts like he's the offended party and then we find out that Sam couldn't have been the murderer. I'm pretty sure she could never slit someone's throat," Ben replied.

"Never say never darling. I think she could have done it if she was angry enough. The fact that she actually liked that treacly little tart, well, that has always been a surprise to me," Kate responded.

"True, Sam should have been shut of all of them from the beginning. Now she's the center of attention," Ben replied.

They had had the advantage of being outside the building and seeing a rather stunned and surprised Sam get out of the cab, face both detectives and the media. Her look of total astonishment, plus her tan and her warm weather clothing, led them to believe that she had had no idea what was going on.

Everything had happened so quickly outside the building that they hadn't had a chance to talk with Sam. Their discussion continued with a review all of the events of the past two days. First the announcement of the murder, followed by a news item that they were looking for Sam, followed by a visit from the police and then an announcement on the news that Sam was a person of interest in the murder of Ariella, followed by tonight's revelation that Sam is about the only person who couldn't have done it.

When they hadn't been able to find Sam on Saturday and had no idea if she was missing or dead herself, they had become worried and certainly defensive of their friend. The fact that they had both been caught up in their own lives and had not spent much time with Sam lately had caused each of them some anxiety but nothing they couldn't overcome. Since Kate and Ben kept unusual schedules, Ben as a resident at a local hospital and Kate as a multiple divorcee who didn't need to work, they were the first to know about Rick and Ariella when they had frequently run into the pair coming in and out of the building at unusual times. They both liked Sam, even when they hadn't known her well, and neither liked Rick.

They had helped Sam haul her stuff from the street to her apartment the day Sam was laid off and they had been there to provide support after Sam found Rick and Ariella in bed together. They had been amazed and impressed by how well Sam had handled everything and had decided to be as supportive as possible of Sam. During the past six months they had become great pals, getting together for dinner and going to movies and generally being there for one another. Then both Kate and Ben had become involved with others and Sam had been so focused on her novel and her writing group that they had started to spend less and less time together.

"OK, I think it's time to go visit Sam. The worst that could happen is that the police are still there and don't let us in, again." Ben said, after a few moments of silence.

"I can't believe that they thought that Sam could have murdered Ariella," Kate said. "I'm pretty sure she and Ariella saw each other last week."

"Really, I don't think you told the police that," Ben responded.

"No, the police didn't ask anything like that when they questioned me. They just wanted to know where Sam was and was I hiding her or did I think her family was hiding her. What did they ask you?"

"Pretty much the same thing. They also asked if I thought that Sam was strong enough to bludgeon Ariella, slit her throat and then drag her up to the roof," Ben replied. "Of course, I wasn't supposed to tell anyone the details of the murder but I figure I can mention it to you. You just can't tell anyone else."

"Yikes, bludgeoned, her throat slit and then dragged to the roof. How awful for her family," Kate replied. "Of course I won't tell anyone. Besides it will all be public knowledge soon."

"Well, I think that her mother is dead and her father is Dominic Fantini, the mob guy who's on the run, so I'm not sure she had a stable, loving family life." Ben responded. "I wonder what she and Sam talked about."

"Well, they both wanted to be writers and they had both lived with Rick, maybe they were trading notes?" Kate replied.

"Yeah, just like I'm sure you trade notes with all the wives of your lovers?"

"Ha, ha, very funny. You know Sam is not like that. I'm not sure Ariella was really like that either. I'm not sure how or why she got hooked up with Rick."

"Are you sure her mother's dead? I think they just said she was coming to Boston to identify her daughter's body and arrange for the funeral."

"No, I'm not sure her mother is dead. I just I'd heard it somewhere. Well, I think the coast is clear now and we can stop by Sam's to see if there is anything she would like us to do," Ben said looking out his window at the last of the police cars to leave. The media had left some time ago to file the change to the story and to work on new motives and ideas.

Kate grabbed her coat and bag, Ben made sure to lock his door behind them and they headed up to Sam's place on the 6th floor. The elevator in their renovated factory building rattled all the way up. They knocked on Sam's door and waited for her to answer. They could hear her muffled voice talking behind the door and knew she must be on the phone.

"You know, I have no idea what we should say to her. What do you say to someone who was just found not guilty of murder?" Ben asked.

"I'm sure we'll think of something," Kate replied.

Sam let them in as soon as they arrived while she was talking to her father. Her condo was a mess, papers, books and food from the kitchen cabinets. The police had checked everything and put nothing back. Kate and Ben started to clean up, as best they could.

Chapter 13

"Jesus freakin' Christ, did you just hear that," Derek looked at his roommate Jimmy. "Sam couldn't have killed Ariella, she wasn't even in town."

They had been watching the news for the promised update on the murder of their friend and fellow student, Ariella Fantini. They both had known Ariella and liked her and had both been shocked when the police arrived at their apartment to question them about her murder. They had each been students of Rick Sampson's and both had met his wife Sam Monroe.

"I never believed Sam was the murderer anyway," Jimmy replied, eyeing his roommate. Derek was known to be argumentative just for the sake of argument.

"Yeah, and what did you base that on. Her innocent good looks?" Derek replied.

"No, the fact that she is a decent and caring person," Jimmy replied.

Derek made some non-committal noises from the couch but didn't pick a fight. Derek and Jimmy shared a relatively inexpensive apartment in Andrews Square and a love for literature and history. Derek had been a student of English literature and Jimmy was still a student of History and Literature. Derek had had to drop out to pursue an income. They had met at school and had decided they were compatible enough to live together. Mostly because they both needed a place to live and because they figured they could tolerate one another for a few years.

Other than that, they didn't have too much in common. Derek was the son of working class parents from Stamford, CT, and Jimmy the son of upper middle class parents from Westchester County, NY. Derek had to work for his rent while Jimmy could rely on his parents for financial help. Derek had a tendency to blame others when things didn't go his way. He complained that the professor's were working against him when they critiqued his work or when he got poor grades; his boss was at fault whenever things went wrong at work and it was always someone else's fault when he was unable to pay the rent. Jimmy worked hard for his grades, was respected by his professors both for working hard and for being able to handle the critiques of his work seriously and striving to improve. If not for the stalking incident, everything would be perfect.

"Oh, get real, how could you possibly know what Sam would or would not do. You only know her as the wife of our professor, or former wife, or whatever," Derek said to Jimmy, rolling his eyes to the ceiling.

"I've talked with her a lot lately and she's very nice. She doesn't seem to be at all jealous of her, er, Rick and Ariella," Jimmy replied.

"Where in the world have you seen her? Have you been stalking her like you did that undergrad," Derek sat up suddenly and looked directly at Jimmy.

Jimmy blushed and squirmed in his chair. He was very uncomfortable talking about the stalking incident. Plus he also realized that he may have said too much to Derek. He wasn't sure but Derek was friendly with Misty Mustoe and Misty had broken the story first, with a lot of personal details.

"She's been around the department talking with Arthur," Jimmy replied.

"What do you mean by she's been around the department?" Derek asked.

"Uh, well she's been in to see Arthur when I've been in the department and we've talked some," Jimmy replied.

"And why would she be visiting Arthur? Does Rick know?"

"Now that you say that, I don't think she's ever visited when Rick was around. Usually it's when Rick and most of the other faculty are not around, usually in the early morning when it's just Arthur and Nancy," Jimmy responded. "I think that Arthur has been helping her with some writing, but I don't know what it is. We've talked when she's been waiting for Arthur. Ariella was there once or twice as well and she and Sam were cordial. They even went out for coffee together when Arthur was called to the Chancellor's office unexpectedly."

"Did the police question you about Ariella?" Derek asked

"Yeah, but only briefly," Jimmy replied. "They also asked some questions about Sam, but not about Sam and Arthur."

Derek looked at Jimmy appraisingly. The story that Rick and Donna had given him about Sam and Ariella might not be all true. His statement to the police might need to be explained pretty soon. And Misty would certainly want an explanation. They both jumped when their silence was broken by the phone ringing.

"If it's for me, tell them you haven't seen me all day and don't know my schedule," Derek said quickly as Jimmy picked up the phone. Jimmy nodded his assent and listened intently to the speaker. It was Misty and she needed to talk to Derek pronto. Jimmy responded, as requested, with the information that Derek hadn't been around all day and he didn't know when Derek would be back. Jimmy listened for a few moments, said uh-huh a few times and finished with the agreement that he would leave a note for Derek to call when he returned.

"It was your friend Misty. She really, really wants to talk to you," Jimmy said to Derek.

"I bet she does," Derek replied.

Jimmy opened his mouth to say something and then closed it. Whatever Derek was into, Jimmy didn't want to know anything about it. It was bad enough that Ariella had been murdered so brutally but it seemed to him that Derek was somehow involved in this story that the news stations were telling. Ariella had been his friend and he knew that she would not want Jimmy telling too many details of the last few weeks.

"Crap, I gotta go. If anyone calls you don't know anything and you don't know where I am," Derek said. Derek was putting a few clothes in a bag, grabbing his leather jacket, and Jimmy certainly wondered how he could afford that when he couldn't pay his rent.

"Where are you going?"

"It's best if you don't know, then you can't tell anyone."

"Will you have your cell phone on you if I need to reach you?"

"Yeah, you can always leave me a message," Derek replied as he headed out the door.

Jimmy watched him go with a mingled sense of relief and fear. Jimmy was happy to have the place to himself for the next few days to think things through. On the other hand Derek seemed to know more than he was saying and none of it sounded good.

Chapter 14

Sam was on the phone with her father when she heard the knock on the door. While still talking she looked at Kate and Ben through the peephole in her door. She opened the door to let them in while and continued her conversation.

"Yes, Dad, I'll call you in the morning and let you know about anything new," Sam said into the phone while waving Kate and Ben into the apartment. She and her Dad concluded their conversation and Sam turned to her friends.

"So, how long did you guys know about this and why didn't you call my cell phone?" Sam asked.

"We found out about the murder yesterday but we didn't find out about you as a suspect until the police interviewed us today. Then everything just snowballed and the police told us not to contact you, particularly since they thought we were hiding you somewhere," Ben said.

"Then the media showed up in the afternoon, some police officers stayed all day and we couldn't really go anywhere or make any phone calls. The detectives told us not to contact you," Kate added, walking around the room and talking quickly. It was a bit unusual to see Kate so worked up, she was usually so calm, graceful and in control.

"It was just such a surprise to come home and find the cops and the media waiting for me," Sam replied. "And no one had warned me or anything. What do you mean they thought you were hiding me?"

"Well, since they couldn't find you and no one seemed to know where you were, they assumed we had hidden you away somewhere," Kate replied.

Ben, Kate and Sam then talked about the events of the past few days. Kate and Ben expressed their surprise about Sam going away without telling them. Sam pointed out that Kate was dating a new guy and Ben was working the night shift at the hospital so they would hardly know she was gone. Plus she had scheduled it at the last minute.

"And as I was packing, Ariella showed up," Sam said.

"Really, I don't think the police know that Ariella was with you on Wednesday night," Ben replied.

"Well, I have to go to the police station to make a statement tomorrow so I guess I'll tell them then," Sam replied.

Chapter 15

"Well, well, Mr. Jones, what do you think of this rather interesting turn of events?" Mr. Fantini asked. Mr. Fantini was sitting on the hotel room bed with the TV remote in his hand. He had muted the TV after the news broadcast regarding the murder of his daughter was aired. Mr. Jones was standing behind the small bar in the living room area of the hotel suite making each of them a drink. While once they would have had alcohol and a lot of it, they were both now drinking seltzer with lime. They were watching the news from Mr. Jones' hotel room.

Mr. Fantini and Mr. Jones had each arrived on Saturday night, after they had learned of Ariella's murder. Their rooms were not reserved under the names they currently used with one another. Mr. Fantini and Mr. Jones were not using their real names since they were wanted by the police in Boston as well as the Feds and possibly in several other countries. This arrangement suited them just fine. They had both been able to travel under assumed names without much bother for years. The former Mrs. Fantini would be arriving the next day and they wanted to be there to provide as much support as possible.

"It looks like the soon to be ex-wife wasn't the murderer. She doesn't look to be the type to commit a murder, at least not this type of murder," Mr. Jones replied.

Mr. Fantini did not respond right away. He contemplated the blank TV screen while he thought about the events of the past 24 hours. Ariella was his only daughter and she had been raised, mostly, away from the life he had led and for which he was now wanted. When she was very young and he and Gina were still together, Ariella had been the apple of his eye. He still remembered how Ariella had always been so happy to see him, she would run to the door to greet him with a smile and a hug. By the time Ariella was 7, he and Gina were getting divorced and

Gina was moving back to Italy taking Ariella with him. It wasn't long before Gina was remarried, to a business man in Italy and Ariella was going to private school. Her first private school was in Italy, close to her mother and step-gather, then in Switzerland and finally in New Hampshire. Mr. Fantini always kept in touch but he and Ariella had never achieved the closeness they had in the early years. Now she was gone and there would never be a chance to be close again.

"So, as far as we can tell, this Samantha Monroe is about the only person Ariella knew here in Boston who could not have killed her."

"That would be a correct assumption. Except we don't know everyone that Ariella knew," Mr. Jones replied.

Mr. Jones was far more secretive. He had started out as a bodyguard for Mr. Fantini and then had moved through the ranks of the organization. Over time they had developed first a trust and finally a friendship that transcended the organization. Mr. Jones had retired and now lived with his family on a large property in the West. He was certainly known to the authorities but not under the name Mr. Jones. He was a large man who was doing his best to remain in shape while he aged. He finished making the drinks and handed one to Mr. Fantini and kept one for himself. He settled into the chair across from Mr. Fantini, loosened the button of his sport coat and sipped his drink.

"Good point. She did know a lot of students at school but she was involved with this Professor and broke up his marriage or at least helped break up his marriage. And then she befriends the wife," Mr. Fantini continued. "I was very disappointed in her for taking up with a married man. I was a bit more proud of her for befriending the wife. But all in all, I felt that she was making some very poor decisions with her personal life.

"Still, she had an excellent academic record and it looked like she was going places with her writing. What do we know about her friend Jimmy?" Mr. Jones replied.

"Well, he is, or was, a good friend and may also have whatever information Ariella told me to look for. I'm inclined to think that she would have put her trust in Samantha Monroe rather than Jimmy Houser with this information. She had a lot of respect for Samantha and she knew that Samantha was outside the mainstream university structure."

"When did you talk to Ariella about this?"

"About what?"

"The information she wanted to have held somewhere, the professor, the wife, everything?" Mr. Jones asked.

"Ah, yes, we talked a few days ago. We talked at least once a week. I used a variety of ways to contact her that haven't been traced. Anyway, Ariella was concerned that someone was stealing her work, or attempting to steal her work, and she was looking for a place to hide it."

"And what makes you think it isn't with Ms. Monroe?"

"Ariella had told me that Sam didn't want to hold it because she was going away for a few days and didn't want Ariella to want it back quickly," Mr. Fantini replied.

"So apparently she hadn't told Ms. Monroe that it was a copy for safe-keeping?"

"No, she didn't."

"But she went to Ms. Monroe's apartment with it?"

"Yes, she did but she said she left with it as well."

How do you propose we contact Ms. Monroe?" Mr. Jones asked.

"I think we should visit her at her apartment."

"Not a bad plan, but I think that she might find it a bit unusual for us to just show up at her place to chat," Mr. Jones replied.

"True, very true," Mr. Fantini replied.

They talked for a long time that night and developed a plan to help them solve the murder of Ariella. This plan did rely at a minimum with having a conversation with Sam Monroe.

Chapter 16

Arthur Churykian, the Chairman of the English Department at the University, was watching the news at his home in Brookline. At 73, he was ready to no longer be the Chairman of the English department. He had agreed to stay on until the end of the academic year but now he felt that that was too far away. Now that this murder had taken place and the body was found on school property, the roof of the English department building to be precise, and with all the attention from the school administration, he was ready to retire.

He had been ready to retire a few years before, but his wife Ruth had died unexpectedly and he decided to stay on for a while longer while he figured out what to do next. It was a fun job and he was old enough to intimidate but not be a threat to the other faculty members, most of whom he'd hired anyway. But this murder was sick and disturbed; Ariella was a good student, a thoughtful person and had the potential to be a great writer. And now to have Samantha accused of the murder and found to be innocent all in 48 hours was more than he could understand. Samantha was not as good a writer as Ariella and was married to an asshole of a guy who just couldn't write, and who had traded Sam in for Ariella, but still that was stuff he had come to expect. He had not expected one of his students to be murdered. What a mess.

He turned the TV off and through the remote down in disgust. Just as he did so his phone rang. Arthur checked caller id and then answered the phone. It was Nancy, the secretary for the English Department.

"Hi Nancy, did you see the news?"

"Of course I did. It will be a crazy day tomorrow. Between students, their parents, the faculty, the police, the dean and everyone else we could possibly think of, I don't think we have any possible idea about how bad this will be," Nancy replied.

"You'll be there, won't you?" Arthur asked.

"Of course I will. You should have no concerns on my part," Nancy replied.

"I just wanted to make sure," Arthur replied.

"Will you still be having your dinner party on Wednesday night?"

"Yes, it will be my last one ever and I refuse to cancel it," Arthur replied.

"Well, you know my opinion," Nancy said.

With that they discussed a few items for the next day and hung up. It would be Monday morning soon enough. Arthur knew he should rest but his mind was too active to rest.

Chapter 17

The three detectives, O'Malley, Kelvin and Girard, were perplexed, concerned and a little embarrassed. They had believed the story of the wife, jilted and abandoned for a younger student, the estranged husband surprised and confused by what had happened and the friend to both of them assuring them that the wife was jealous and was obsessed by her soon to be ex. It had appeared so cut and dried; they would find and arrest the wife, continue their research and make the case and present all the evidence at the trial, along with forensics. The verdict would be guilty and they would all move on to their next cases. They had believed it so well that they had not looked closely at other possibilities.

The case was all over the news now and they looked like buffoons. If they didn't look like that now, they would once the TV news and the local newspapers dissected the story and reported on every aspect of the investigation or lack thereof. This would change how they would interact with the information that had already been gathered, any new information as well as everyone they had already interviewed. Time on the case was passing swiftly, the 48 hour window was already lost, and they now needed to move swiftly and accurately.

Everything would need to be kept tightly scrutinized internally without access to or interpretation by the media. The information provided by the husband and the so-called best friend was now highly suspect. All interviews would need to be reread and most everyone involved would need to be interviewed a second time. The wife's statement would prove to be very interesting. The detectives left the condo while the forensics team packed up their gear. The uniform cops would stay until they were all done and a female uniform would stay with the wife until everyone was gone.

The street was quiet and peaceful as O'Malley, Kelvin and Girard stepped out of the condo building. The reporter's had all left to file their reports and the bystanders had gone home. Detective O'Malley spotted the unmarked car with the two cops assigned to keep watch for the evening and probably the next few days. When Sam Monroe had arrived, the crowd had been thick on the street and it wouldn't take much for some yahoo to think he or she could take things into their own hands and do something foolish. Now it appeared that everything was calm and back to normal but that was a thin façade on an oily situation.

"Well, well, it looks like Wu and Martinelli are back together again," Detective O'Malley said.

"What makes you say that," Detective Kelvin said.

"They're in the unmarked car across the street, under the tree. They must have been assigned to keep an eye on things," O'Malley replied.

Kelvin and Girard looked in the same direction as O'Malley and noted the car and its occupants. They didn't want to draw too much unwanted attention to the two cops so quickly looked at one another again. A cell phone went off and Girard answered quickly, nodding and speaking softly to whoever was talking on the other end.

"Was that that your wife?" O'Malley asked Girard. They were all in the car headed back to the station and when Girard disconnected from his call.

"Yes, yes it was. She just wanted to know I'd be home. I let her know that I'll get the kids ready for school tomorrow," Girard said.

"When is she due?" Kelvin asked.

"In about 3 weeks and she's tired all the time now, what with four active boys to take care of and me coming and going at all hours of the day and night," Girard replied. "I sure hope it's a girl this time."

"You think a girl will be easier?" Kelvin asked.

"Well, my wife has always wanted to have a girl, so I hope it's a girl too. It will keep the boys in line."

"How in the world would a baby girl keep 4 boys in line?" Kelvin asked and no one replied. O'Malley gave her one of his 'do not do this' looks. Girard ignored them both form the back seat of the unmarked car.

Girard was 35 years old and had been married for 12 years. His boys were 11, 10, 9 and 7. He and his wife thought they were done with having any more kids and were surprised to find they were expecting number five.

Detective Peter O'Malley was 38, divorced and a little bit jealous. He wanted to have children. His ex-wife had convinced him to put it off until their lives were more stable. Then she left him for a lawyer and she and her new husband were expecting their first child.

Detective Darcy Kelvin was 33 and had a long-term partner. She and Sarah weren't sure whether or not to bring a child into this world or to adopt. It was a decision they were struggling with every day. Darcy watched Raoul handle four boys and one on the way with awe and respect. He made it look so easy and he didn't question the how's and why's of having and raising children too much, at least not with them. The rest of the trip back to the station was quiet, actually it was silent. It was after midnight and they had all been up and on the move on this case since 6am.

It was busy both outside and inside the station when the three detectives arrived, even though it was after midnight. Inside, their arrival was greeted with some comments from other detectives and officers about how they had the wrong person and why they didn't know better. They were also greeted with some knowing nods and smiles from those who were sympathetic to their situation.

It wasn't uncommon to follow the wrong lead, it happened to most detectives at some point in their career. They all knew that a crime not solved in the first 48 hours might never be solved. And without a weapon or any DNA evidence or even knowing the scene of the murder, it was going to be harder to pinpoint the murderer.

Ariella's body had been found on the roof of Baker Hall on the University campus at five on Saturday morning. Two members of a cleaning crew had gone up there for a smoke and literally stumbled over the body. It was very, very close to the door. At first they thought she was sleeping. It was still dark and there was no blood or messed up clothing or anything to make the cleaning crew think that anything like murder had taken place.

It was only when one of them bent down to wake her that he noticed that her throat had been slit. He had screamed and fallen back in shock. It was the other cleaning crew member who had made the call to the police from the roof. He had called 911 and spoken in rapid Spanish to the attendant. Once the attendant had calmed him down a bit, did he speak in English and let them know the location and what they had found. On the tape you could hear sobbing of the other crew member in the background. When they arrived, the campus police had found one crew member sitting next to the body holding the dead girl's hand while another was curled up in the fetal position sobbing quietly. They understood that both crew members had been taken to the hospital for observation.

The campus police were the first to arrive on the scene, followed by the Boston PD, then Medical Examiner and finally the detectives. All this happened while the sun slowly rose over Ariella's body and what had happened to it was slowly revealed.

Investigators determined that she had been killed elsewhere. There was no sexual assault and her clothes and body were clean of most any blood or anything else. Whoever had killed her was either very experienced or had spent a lot of time cleaning up after their deed.

Detective O'Malley had seen the body on the roof and knew how gruesome the murder had been. Kelvin and Girard had arrived after the body had been bagged and taken off of the roof. He would never fully understand how anyone could commit such a horrific act against another human being even though he investigated murders daily.

On Saturday morning, University personnel had been brought in to help identify the body since no other identification was present. A campus police officer initially recognized Ariella. It wasn't long before information was passed along to senior administrators at the University and the Chairman of the English Department, Arthur Churykian, where Ariella was a graduate student, and Arthur was able to confirm the identification. The usually robust 73 year old Department Chair looked pale and gray as he stood over the body of his student in the cold, steel gray morgue.

When the detectives had asked Arthur about any known family members, he had been able to let them know that Ariella's father was mob boss Dominic Fantini. Dominic Fantini was currently on the run from the FBI, the cops and the mob. Fantini had a lot of knowledge about the mob and information that the FBI, Boston politicians and police wanted to be kept secret and he was willing to remain silent and keep secrets for a price. That price included his continued freedom to travel unchecked. Many others felt they might be safer if he was just dead. There were those who would prefer to see Dominic Fantini in permanent custody in either prison or the witness protection program but Dominic wanted neither of these and so had negotiated his own alternative lifestyle.

The detectives search for next of kin had led them to Frederick 'Rick' Sampson, Ariella's boyfriend and roommate or at least he had been her roommate until very recently. They had interviewed Rick and had fallen for his theory that his estranged wife, Samantha Monroe-Sampson, was really jealous of Ariella and might have killed her. When they went to look for Sam they found her best friend, Donna Sussman, and heard a very similar story. They had quickly believed that not being able to find Samantha indicated her guilt.

It took them until late Sunday afternoon to get a judge to issue a warrant for a search of Sam's condo. In the interim, they were able to contact Sam's neighbors and friends, Kate Shuster and Ben Gunn, who had a very different story to tell. They had also tracked down a couple of students, Derek ?? Soper and Jimmy Houser, who knew Ariella and who had conflicting stories about Ariella's murder. Derek felt that Sam could have committed the murder and Jimmy felt the murder was committed by someone who Ariella believed was presenting her work as his or her own. Jimmy implied Ariella was about to reveal something nasty about someone in the English Department.

It had been easy to go along with the story that the husband and boyfriend, respectively, had told them about jealousy and rage. Once in Sam's condo, though, they knew the murder had not been committed there. And then the media had shown up asking questions about the murder and the suspects and the case quickly became one of containing information rather than investigation.

The Bureau Chief was waiting for them in the detective's squad room, even though it was after midnight. He greeted them all and asked them to sit down for a moment.

"I want to let you know that this case has now attracted the mayor's attention and therefore the Commissioner's attention. They are going to want action and a quick resolution," he said.

"Yes, sir," O'Malley replied for all of them.

"It's going to take a lot of attention and a lot of detail work. I think that the three of you are the best detectives I have for this case and you all have done a lot of work in the past 40 or so hours," he continued.

"Who wants us taken off of the case?" Kelvin asked.

"The Commissioner, of course," the Bureau Chief said. "And of course, Larrabee."

"Ah, Larrabee. He still looking to run for office?" O'Malley asked.

"Whether or not he is looking to run, he is tight with the Commissioner and he wants to clean the floor with your ass. He's still smarting and he is not your friend."

The Bureau Chief was a big bear of a man who looked intimidating no matter how he was dressed, in a uniform for a formal press conference or casually attired in chinos and a polo shirt on the golf course or as he appeared now in jeans and a t-shirt. He commanded their respect with the quiet, calm voice and respectful demeanor. He was a man of integrity who had distinguished himself on the streets and in the offices of the police department.

"Right, we'll start going over everything now," O'Malley replied. The incident with Larrabee coupled with finding the wrong suspect and the media glare still did not daunt O'Malley. He knew he could do the job and do it right.

"First, I want all three of you to go home and get some rest. We'll meet at 8am to go over next steps," the Chief said.

The three of them looked at one another, nodded to the chief and then headed for the door. The Bureau Chief wasn't moving and anything else would have been the direct violation of his order.

When O'Malley arrived at his desk a little before 7am, the Bureau Chief was visible in his glassed-in office. Dressed in a dark suit with a white shirt and dark tie but otherwise showing no signs that he had never left. Kelvin arrived soon after and both she and O'Malley went through everything on their desks that needed immediate attention but which was not a part of the Fantini case. Girard arrived closer to 8am, looking a bit disheveled but just as determined to get to work on this case. At precisely 8am, they all filed into the Chief's office. Larrabee watched everything from his desk. He was currently on the night shift but had stayed deliberately in case he was needed.

"Here's what I would like you to do," the Bureau Chief said. "Detectives O'Malley and Kelvin will re-interview everyone who has been interviewed already and will also talk with Miranda and Joe Johnson in Florida. They are Samantha Monroe's mother and step-father whom she was staying with in Florida this past weekend. Detective Girard, I would like you to stay at the station sifting through all the written records that have been collected so far and to review all forensic evidence as it arrives."

"Sir, I would like to be in the field as well," Girard said.

"I know you would, Detective Girard, but with your wife due in less than 3 weeks, I would like you to stay here. Also, Detective Larrabee will be at our disposal for anything you need during the night shift. I know that you would prefer to have someone else, but that's how it is going to be."

"Thank you, sir. I think I speak for all of us when I say that we will be able to work in those parameters," O'Malley said. Kelvin and Girard nodded their assent.

"Great. The four of us, along with Larrabee will meet at 8am each morning to review the case. And Officers Wu and Martinelli will keep an eye on Samantha Monroe's place. I'm concerned that some overzealous citizen may do something foolish."

"I thought her name was Samantha Sampson?" Girard asked.

"Actually, she never changed her name when she married; she just used her husband's name when it was convenient. Most everyone knows her as Sam Monroe," O'Malley replied.

"I guess I do need to review those files," Girard replied.

"Now, let's invite Larrabee in and get this show on the road," the Bureau Chief stood and waved to Larrabee, who swiftly joined them in his office.

While O'Malley and Kelvin were to re-interview Arthur Churykian, Rick Sampson, Donna Sussman, Derek and Jimmy along with

Miranda and Joe Johnson, Girard would be in the office during the day and available to take Sam's statement when she arrived along with any other statements from anyone coming into the station. Larrabee would be responsible for re-interviewing Kate Shuster and Ben Gunn when he came on duty at 4pm and then pick up with any material needing review at night. There were interview transcripts, Medical Examiner's report and any forensic tests to be reviewed and recommendations made. All media requests would go through the Public Relations and the Bureau Chief. From there they would decide their next steps.

Chapter 18

Kate and Ben left and Sam's mind was racing. It was 2am and she knew she wouldn't be able to sleep for a while, at least not until she calmed down and she didn't feel like she would calm down anytime soon. She wasn't sure that she would ever calm down. Ariella was dead, murdered and left on the roof. The fact that Sam would never see her again was unimaginable. Ariella was young and with a very promising future as a writer. And to be or more accurately have been considered the leading suspect in her murder seemed even more unbelievable.

Sam wasn't sure how to absorb this information or even what it would mean for her own life. She would definitely have to find out what one does when one is considered a murder suspect. She would call her divorce attorney in the morning for more information. The detectives had made it clear that she needed to go to the police station to make a statement tomorrow and she would do so. It was at least an action that made sense. While there, she would try to ask her questions, such as how does being a murder suspect affect her ability to get a job or get credit or, well, or do anything normal ever again.

The detectives and the cops and the investigating team had made more of a mess of her condo than one would have thought. They had been through everything in the house and not been very good about putting things back neatly. Sam decided to take a shower to calm down and to hopefully relax enough to get some sleep. It was always easier for Sam to think, make plans or even solve problems in the shower. After her shower, Sam popped into the kitchen to look for some food; she was starving now. She was speechless to find a dapper, older man sitting on a stool at her kitchen counter. Behind the dapper man was a much larger man in a leather jacket, arms across his chest, leaning against the kitchen counter. Her arrival had stopped their conversation.

Sam stood in the living area staring at the two strange men and unable to decide what to do next. How they had gotten into her place, why did they seem so calm and should she scream. The good news is that she was wearing a robe. Had she been totally naked, as she sometimes is when she pops into the kitchen for a snack before bed, she would still not have known what to do but at least she had a robe on. The two strange men were patiently waiting as if they were forgotten guests.

"Ms. Monroe, I'm happy that you didn't feel the need to run or faint," the dapper man said, smiling kindly. "I should introduce myself; I am Ariella's father, Dominic Fantini. And this is my associate, Mr. Jones. We are both very sorry for all you have been through, particularly this evening."

"Uh, thanks," Sam responded. "Is there something I can do for you?"

"Yes, I want you to help me find my daughter's murderer."

"While I'm very sorry about, um, Ariella's death, but I'm not sure that I can help. I didn't kill her, if that's what you're thinking," Sam replied, more than a bit stunned.

After a very long pause, she added "And I certainly don't know who killed Ariella."

"Well, we don't know who killed her either and we are looking for help. Even though I'm her father, I don't know that much about her day to day life. Of all the people she associated with, at least her life in higher education. The person that knew or knows most of the people around her and who couldn't have murdered her is you. Therefore I think that you are most likely able to help find the killer," Mr. Fantini said.

Again there was a long, silent pause while they contemplated one another. OK, he does make a logical argument, Sam thought, except for the knowing most people in Ariella's life, which was doubtful.

"Really," Sam replied. "I don't think I know that many people that she knew, other than my husband, of course, and a couple of the students and, well, the other professors. I'm rather stunned that you think I know that much about her life."

"Well, you see, that's certainly more than I know." Mr. Fantini seemed a bit concerned about her response, as if he didn't expect someone to not respond positively to his request. He drummed his fingers on her kitchen counter while the man behind him shifted his weight from his left leg to his right. "Plus, you have the advantage of being familiar with the higher education field and could ask questions that I will not be able to ask and talk to people that I will not be able to talk to. It seems that Ariella liked you quite a bit, even though I understand you weren't the best of friends. Of course, I mean after the initial incident where you found them in bed together."

"Really, well, yes, I agree that I most likely know more about the day to day operations of the University and the English department but I'm not really a trained investigator. And I really don't know many of the people that she knows , or knew." Sam said. "I really don't think that I can help you at all."

"Well for starters you know your husband plus you know several of the other faculty members. You also know the head of the English department and many of the same students that she was friendly with. Even though you didn't all associate together doesn't mean you didn't know them all," he replied quietly.

"Well, I don't know what to say, except to say that you seem to know more about what you need to ask these people than I do," Sam replied, while Mr. Jones smiled kindly at her. "I'm not sure what to say about your request except that I'm not a detective, I don't feel that I know that much about Ariella and I'm pretty sure that there has to be someone better qualified to help you than me."

"Well, I'm not inclined to call the police, at least not directly, and I don't think that a private detective would be as quick to get to the facts of the case as you will be," he replied, still with a very quiet voice.

They contemplated each other again silently. Sam thought about what to make of this request. She knew that Mr. Fantini was associated with the mob and had certainly appeared, well not willingly as a guest but had been featured or at least talked about on the news. She was fairly sure that he wasn't in any way going to harm or threaten her, although the man behind him did cause her some concern, since neither had yet been threatening in a physical way. She had no idea how they had gotten into her condo without her noticing and she suspected that they would be fairly quick to do so again.

"What if I do some inquiries for you and then we can see how it's going. If I'm not doing well, you will then able to move on to someone who is a bit better well-trained at this sort of thing," Sam responded.

"Who would you talk to in these inquiries?" Mr. Fantini asked.

"Hmm, well I guess I would start with the chair of the English Department," Sam replied.

"Good choice, what would you ask him?"

"I'm not sure. We've been chatting about my novel and I need to update him on what's going on with the agent and that kind of stuff. I could see what he has to say about Ariella. After that conversation, I can get back in touch with you and let you know what he said. From there, we can decide if you want me to continue," Sam said. It sounded good to Sam and it seemed to her that she would do one interview and prove she was no good at this and he would find someone else to investigate. That was reasonable, Sam thought, and would at least get these two men to leave her condo.

"How about talking with the detective?" Mr. Fantini asked. Sam thought about this for a moment before replying.

"Well, I do have to go in tomorrow to make a statement. I could ask some questions and see if they give me more information," Sam replied.

"How about asking him who he thinks the murderer is, now that we all know it's not you?" Mr. Fantini asked.

"Hmm, isn't that a bit too direct? Besides, why would they answer me?" Sam replied.

Both Mr. Fantini and Mr. Jones shrugged in rather non-committal ways.

"I'll think about asking that question after I talk to Arthur," Sam said.

"Thank you for at least trying to help me," Mr. Fantini said. "Mr. Jones and I will be in touch with you again."

"Um, how will you reach me?" Sam asked.

"Oh, I think it will be very similar to how I reached you this time," Mr. Fantini replied, a smile tugging at the corners of his mouth. "But if you should need to reach us, please call the number of this card and leave a message with the number to call you back. Once you provide your name, they will know what to do."

"Thanks," Sam said, taking the card from Mr. Jones.

"We'll arrange for a cleaning crew to come in," Mr. Jones said and he helped Mr. Fantini up from the stool and handed him a cane. "It will allow you time to work on these questions for Mr. Fantini."

Mr. Fantini and his bodyguard left through the backdoor behind her kitchen that led to a staircase rather than to the main hallway to the elevator. Sam hadn't noticed the cane until Mr. Jones picked it up. Possibly the weight loss was due to an accident. Sam wasn't sure what she had gotten herself into. First she's accused of murder and she's cleared and then she's asked to help solve the murder by the dead girl's father, who just happens to be a mob boss on the run. And they would arrange for some cleaning people to come in. She wasn't sure, but she felt that the night could not get any weirder.

Sam contemplated just leaving and heading back to Florida to stay with her mother and step-father but rejected that as a foolish, childish thing to do. Instead she headed off to bed. The shower had relaxed her and this strange meeting was certainly distracting her from her thoughts of the murder. After such a strange night, Sam decided to leave some lights on. She crawled into bed and was soon fast asleep, although her dreams were a bit odd.

Chapter 19

Even though Mr. Fantini had kept Sam up rather late talking, she was up bright and early, well if you consider 8am early which she did. Sam decided that she would talk to Arthur and report back to Mr. Fantini. It was the least she could do for a man who had lost his only child. At least she thought Ariella was his only child. The cleaning crew arrived promptly at 9am and were finished cleaning by 11:00am. She signed a document stating that they had been there but was not asked for payment. She suspected payment had already been made by Mr. Fantini or Mr. Jones or someone they knew.

As they had discussed, Arthur should have some advice for her on how to find out if someone had been stealing or plagiarizing Ariella's work. Sam decided to arrive a little after 10am; knowing that Rick would be at a seminar class from 11am - noon. She had been to Arthur's office at this time before so that would not be an issue. How to bring up the topic was more of an issue and she was still thinking about the best way to approach this.

It was a beautiful, if cool, November morning. The sun was bright, the sky was clear and the air was crisp but not freezing so Sam decided to walk to campus. A walk would be both refreshing and great exercise. She was determined to continue losing weight and getting in shape. She had definitely let herself go the past few years before she was laid off. Now she needed to think about getting back into the dating game.

Sam thought about her relationship with Arthur and how it had changed over the years. When she first knew Rick, he was in his first year as a graduate student in English with the goal of pursuing his Ph.D. and becoming a professor himself. She was in her senior year as a business student when they were invited to dinner at Arthur and Ruth's home in Brookline. It had been a big thing for Rick and he had wanted both himself and Sam to make good impressions. Rick and Sam had been dating for two years and were getting married as soon as Sam graduated in May.

Sam had immediately liked both Arthur and Ruth. She was the youngest person at the dinner and had sat next to Ruth, who was as kind as she could possibly be to a young woman. She had missed Ruth these last few years, since her death from breast cancer. Arthur had been devastated at the time and had only slowly started to recover. He had planned to retire and he and Ruth were going to travel around the world. He was going to devote himself to writing and teaching the occasional class. After Ruth's death, the Dean had convinced him that he should stay on as a full-time faculty member and Arthur's children agreed that this would be a good idea so Arthur agreed to chair the department. Both roles had kept him busy and kept him involved.

Her thoughts kept her company while she walked and she was soon on campus. Once she reached campus, she felt energized by all the students. She realized that they were not that much younger than her but their energy was engaging. It was a little too cool for students to be sitting under trees around campus but there were many walking swiftly between buildings and to and from the library. A few were attempting a game of Frisbee and others were standing around chatting and laughing.

Sam continued on to Baker Hall, where the English Department was housed. At the front of the building, next to the door was a makeshift memorial to Ariella with flowers and candles and people around. She had blocked out thoughts of Ariella until now. She stopped for moment to look at the memorial. The sun no longer seemed so bright and warm and Sam shivered as she looked on. It wasn't long before there were a few stares and whispers and she decided it was time to move on. Out of the corner of her eye she noticed that there were plain clothes men and women who were keeping an eye on the crowd. The University seemed to be handling this in a low-key but respectful manner. Sam nodded at the plain clothes person heading towards her and headed up the stairs of Baker Hall.

Once inside, she decided to walk up to the third floor. She quickly opened the door to the floor, nodded to Nancy, the department secretary, and headed briskly down the hall to Arthur's office. She didn't want to be stopped and questioned about anything, particularly about Ariella. The secretary was crying and two of the professors were attempting to comfort her. They all watched Sam as she passed, too confused to stop her and not quite ready to ask her any questions. They had all followed the news over the weekend and had seen Ariella both as suspect and vindicated.

Not many people were in the hallway as Sam made her way down the hall to Arthur's office. The outer door to the office space was open and Sam nodded to Arthur's assistant as she headed towards Arthur's office door. She could hear voices and assumed that it was one or more students in talking with Arthur. She was in the doorway before she realized that the people in the office were actually two of the detectives from the previous night, Detective O'Malley and Detective Kelvin.

The conversation stopped short as they all looked up to see Sam in the doorway. For a moment, Sam considered turning and leaving but on second thought she figured it would be better to stay and possibly talk to all three of them. It seemed to be an eternity before anyone spoke.

"Sam, my dear, we were just talking about you, and about the unfortunate happenings of this past weekend. How are you?" Arthur came around this desk and took Sam by the elbow and led her to the only free chair left in his office.

Sam realized that she was actually holding her breath and let her breath out in a deep sigh as she sat down. The two detectives followed all the movements in the office without speaking. Sam nodded to them but didn't really know what to say. Arthur took his seat again.

"Well, I think that one of us has to speak and it might as well be me," Arthur chimed in when no one else spoke.

"I'm fine," Sam responded.

"Really?" Arthur replied.

"Well, yes. I do want to talk to you when you have a free moment. I don't need to interrupt you and the detectives here." Sam started to get up.

"How rude of me, I should not have interrupted our interview," Arthur responded, nodding to the detectives. "It's just that you had such a look of shock on your face."

Sam thought for a moment before responding. Her plans were changed now that the detectives were in Arthur's office. She needed to think quickly about what to do with the detectives. She was sure she was ready to tell the detectives about Mr. Fantini but before she could think this through, she found herself talking.

"I came here to talk with Arthur about Ariella. I know that this will sound fantastic and unbelievable to you, but Mr. Fantini stopped by to talk to me last night and wants me to help find who killed Ariella. He seems to think her murder had something to do with Ariella's writing and the fact that she told her father that she thought someone was stealing her work," Sam said.

There was a long moment while everyone took this information in. Detective O'Malley was the first to speak. "You should have called us as soon as you could to let us know about Mr. Fantini. He's not only Ariella's father but he's on the FBI's most wanted list."

"I, well, it was just too much for me last night to really think about calling you, or anyone else for that matter," Sam replied. "Oh, and he had a bodyguard with him, Mr. Jones. He was very big and very quiet."

"So, why did you come to talk to Professor Churykian?" O'Malley asked.

"Um, well, Mr. Fantini thought that Arthur would be able to provide some insight into Ariella's work," Sam said.

Everyone turned and looked at Arthur, as if there would be something that he could say that would make sense of all of this.

"I have to say that everything I have heard so far in this investigation has talked about Ariella as a girlfriend, a husband stealer and as a victim. No one has asked me any questions that talked about Ariella in her own right," Arthur replied. "I can see where her father, no matter who he is, would want to find out more about her and why she was murdered. I'm a little surprised to hear the charge of plagiarism but it does happen. Did Mr. Fantini provide any reason for saying this?"

"He said that Ariella had told him this in a phone conversation within the last week. He didn't say when he talked to Ariella or any other details," Sam replied.

Detective's O'Malley and Kelvin were not at all surprised to hear about the plagiarism. It had been brought up by Jimmy as well as their boss, the Bureau Chief. It was definitely an unexplored reason for the murder that they overlooked until now and one which seemed to make sense.

"He also mentioned that Ariella kept a journal and he hasn't been able to find it," Sam said.

"How close was he with his daughter?" Detective Kelvin asked. "We thought they didn't really speak to one another."

"I don't know," Sam replied. "He talked as if they were somewhat close. At least close enough to talk on a regular basis."

The conversation about Ariella continued among the four of them. The detectives were trying to get a sense of what she had been like from both Arthur and Sam, two people who had spent time with Ariella in different ways and for different reasons. The detectives were definitely probing for information about any enemies of Ariella's or someone who might want to do her harm.

Arthur felt that Ariella was a talented writer of fiction, one of the most talented to come into the department in some time. He also felt that she wasn't making the most appropriate choices in her personal life, both in her relationship with Rick and with some of the students she had befriended in the program. Sam felt that Ariella had a lot of skills in fiction but didn't always know how to separate her personal life from her work. Arthur had seen Ariella's work drop off recently and felt that it was related to stress, although he wasn't sure what was causing the stress.

The detectives asked Arthur and Sam if they knew that Ariella was no longer living with Rick but had left the apartment that they shared and moved in with a friend. Neither Arthur nor Sam knew this. Sam expressed surprise since Ariella had visited her the previous Thursday night and had not mentioned nothing. Arthur let them know that Ariella had not let him know her change of residence.

"Speak of the devil, here's one of her friends now," Arthur said looking at the door to his office.

"Ah, sorry professor, I thought you would be alone," Derek replied. The number of people already in Arthur's office didn't seem to be a deterrent.

"Derek, how wonderful to see you. Why don't you join us? I think that you can provide us with some information about Ariella that we seem to be seeking," Arthur said.

"Yes, please do join us," Detective O'Malley said. "If you are Derek Soper that is."

Derek nodded in assent. He neither smiled nor looked very forthcoming with information but he did join everyone in Arthur's office.

"We've been attempting to get in touch with you," Detective Kelvin continued. "Have you received our messages?"

Derek explained that he had been devastated when he heard of Ariella's death from the detectives on Saturday when they had come to take his statement. He hadn't paid any attention to anything else until this morning, when he decided to come into the English department to see if a remembrance of Ariella was being organized. He also wanted to check in and see if his roommate Jimmy was around.

Sam had met Derek before and remembered that he had dropped out of the graduate program. She seemed to think that it had more to do with money than with skill or ability. Rick had thought that Derek was very talented, when he focused on the assignment, but generally got by without really trying his best. Detective Kelvin took Derek to an empty office to take his statement while Sam, Arthur and Detective O'Malley continued to talk.

"So, Mrs. uhh, Sam, Dominic Fantini, a known mobster, visited you while you were all alone last night and asked you if you would do some investigating of his daughter's murder and report back to him with anything you learn, is that correct?" Detective O'Malley summarized.

"Yes, basically, that's what we discussed. Except he wasn't alone, he had a bodyguard with him," Sam replied.

"Really, he had a bodyguard. And what was the bodyguard's name?"

"As I said, he was referred to as Mr. Jones with no first name."

"Ok, that's interesting. When you meet with Detective Girard later today, I'd like you to look at some mug shots to see if you can identify Mr. Jones for us. I'm sure that's not the name we know him by. If they stop by again, will you call me and let me know?" Detective O'Malley asked.

"As much as I'd like to, making a phone call didn't seem like something they wanted me to do. They were very intent on just talking. But I'll see what I can do. By the way, I have a funny feeling he is having my place watched," Sam said.

"Would it be ok to have us bug your place so that we can hear what is being said?" Detective O'Malley asked.

"That's fine with me, but if he's watching my apartment won't he see what's going on?" Sam asked.

"Possibly but I don't think he'd do anything. He'll be sure to have recorded only what he wants to have recorded, but he might slip up and provide some useful information," Det. O'Malley replied.

Sam thought about it over for a moment and decided that that would be acceptable. If nothing else, the cops may gather some useful information and the police might be more quickly alerted if something else happened. They agreed to have the technicians' access the apartment in a manner similar to the way in which Mr. Fantini had left early that morning.

"What did Mr. Fantini tell you to do so that you would get more information regarding Ariella?" Arthur asked.

"He left me a phone number and instructions on how to introduce myself to the person who answered so that the message would get to him. He also said he'd pop into my apartment to get an update in a few days," Sam replied.

Detective Kelvin returned to the office after finishing her interview with Derek. Derek said he had to leave and was quickly gone while they all discussed the situation. Arthur mentioned that he was having a department wide dinner on Wednesday night and Sam was certainly welcome to attend. She had attended before but never as a single person and she wasn't sure she wanted to go to the dinner with the English department faculty and students. It would be tough for several reasons. The first was that she would be going alone, the next was that

Ruth would not be there, which would be hard for her to face, and finally Rick would be there which might be even harder to handle.

Arthur noted that it was not going to be like a sit-down dinners he and Ruth used to host in the past, but it would be more of a cocktail party with servers walking around with trays of food. Arthur had hired a caterer and an event planner to pull this together in a relatively short time. This was the type of thing that Ruth handled so superbly in the past. One thing Arthur did know was he would have more time to spend with his guests and that his guests would be allowed to mingle better than at a sit-down dinner. Arthur very much enjoyed seeing faculty members mingle together and exchange ideas and it gave him great pleasure to provide a venue for doing so for the entire department.

Arthur encouraged Sam to attend. She could pump some of his guests for their thoughts on what might have happened. She was the jilted soon to be ex of Rick's who had been considered a suspect in the murder of Ariella, she would be a hit at the party and, in Arthur's opinion, people would flock to tell her things that wouldn't tell anyone else. This role would allow her to pump his guests for more information. Sam just wasn't sure what she should be gathering information, either here or at the party, but in the end she agreed to attend with some reservations. She wasn't sure what she would do if she was forced to talk with Rick. They now talked almost solely through their attorneys and they were scheduled to talk again in a week or so. With Ariella gone this could be an even more uncomfortable meeting.

Detective O'Malley reluctantly agreed to allow Sam to attend. He really didn't have any authority to stop her from attending, and he did feel that some people would talk more readily to her than to the detectives. They would make sure that police were nearby in case something unexpected happened.

Sam confirmed the date, time and expected dress for this party and decided to leave for home as it was already past 1pm and Rick would soon be back in the department. So she was more than surprised to step out of Arthur's office to find Rick waiting by the assistant's desk.

"Well, I wondered who was taking up so much of Arthur's time," Rick said.

"It's good to see you as well. My sympathies on Ariella's death. It must have been a great shock for you," Sam replied.

"Well, of course her death is a huge shock. Not that I'm aware of her comings and goings any more. Didn't you know that Ariella had moved out about a week ago? Since everyone is talking about how you were one of the last people to see her alive the night before you left, I would think the two of you talked gleefully about this," Rick said.

"No, Ariella never let on about the two of you separating. We actually didn't talk about you. We mostly talked about writing and her plans for the future," Sam replied.

"Well, she was concerned that someone was taking her stuff and that I wasn't sympathetic enough. Her father arranged for a new place for her to live."

"And when were you planning on telling us this bit of information," Detective O'Malley asked from the doorway behind Sam.

Rick was stunned to find the detectives standing behind Sam. He had been so focused on Sam that he had failed to notice anything else.

"If you don't mind, Professor Sampson, we would like to ask you a few questions," Detective O'Malley said.

The two police officers escorted Rick down the hall to his office for some additional questioning.

"Sam, since we are alone now. Why don't you spend a few more minutes with me," Arthur suggested, using his arm to indicate that Sam should return to his office.

"Oh, sure. What would you like to talk about?"

"I'm concerned about you, Sam. You have done so much to move your life forward over these past few months and I don't want you to slide back into a life that will bore you or cause you to stop writing," Arthur said.

"Thank you, Arthur, but I won't be getting back together with Rick. In fact, we have our last joint meeting before the divorce hearing next Monday morning," Sam said.

"Really, you have no idea how glad I am to hear that," Arthur replied.

Sam and Arthur talked a bit more about Sam's meeting with her agent and her trip to Florida. They also talked about the horror of Ariella's death and the fact that her body had been found on the roof this building. The police and the campus security officers had yet to find the location of her murder, if it happened on campus, or if not, where else the murder could have taken place. They also were not aware that Rick and Ariella had not been living together for the past week.

The University had done a good job of making sure that their campus wasn't obviously invaded by the police, at least while classes were taking place. Of course, most of the needed evidence had been taken over the weekend and Ariella's body was with the medical examiner's office waiting to be autopsied. More information was to be released on Tuesday night or Wednesday morning, pending notification of Ariella's family, which consisted of her mother, who would officially identify Ariella's body and then arrange for the funeral.

As Sam was heading down the hall after her conversation with Arthur, she ran into Rick once again. He was in the departmental office going through his mail box and quickly disposing of all of the unnecessary mail and memos.

"So, how's the romance novel coming along? I'm sure that a romance novel must be easier to write and sell than a novel of more depth and substance," Rick said.

"Oh, I don't know. They are pretty firm on what they want in a romance novel and they aren't very flexible with first time writers," Sam said. "How is your novel coming along?

"Really, I don't think that there is any comparison," Rick replied.

"Well, I guess we'll see each other at the meeting on Monday," Sam said, heading for the staircase.

"Yes, I guess we will. So what did you and Ariella talk about the night before you left?"

Like I said, we just talked about Ariella's work and a bit about my romance novel," Sam replied.

"I'll never know why she liked you so much. Ariella was so much more intellectual than you and certainly had a brilliant career in front of her."

"I guess we'll never know now that she's gone." Inside Sam was steaming. She did not appreciate being compared to Ariella and she particularly did not like being compared to Ariella by the man they had both once loved. "Well, I need to get going."

"Have a good day," Rick replied to Sam's back. Sam headed through the door and down the staircase as fast as possible.

Sam decided to walk home. It was still a beautiful day and Rick had made her so mad she needed to get her temper under control. She hoped that he would decide not to attend the dinner party on Wednesday night.

And the fact that Ariella had spent a whole evening with her and never once mentioned that she had left Rick also left her dumbfounded. Nothing about this was mentioned on the news. If anything, they all assumed that Ariella and Rick were together and that Rick was the grieving lover. Sam was deep in thought regarding all the information that she had picked up when she heard her name being called. She stopped to see who it was and was surprised to see Jimmy.

"Mrs. Sampson, it's good to run into you," Jimmy said.

"Hi Jimmy. I'd rather you called me Sam than Mrs. Sampson."

"Oh, sorry, I wasn't thinking. I'm sorry, I hope you aren't offended. I just always think of you as Mrs. . . . Well I guess I'll have to think of you as Sam now."

"It's ok. I'm using my maiden name and I never actually changed it. At work I was always Sam Monroe."

"Of course, I knew that you had never changed your name."

"Really, how did you know that?"

"Well, Professor Sampson used to say that you had never changed your name. But he used to refer to you as Mrs. Sampson so I guess that's how I always think of you, or thought of you, until now."

"Well, I bet you weren't looking for me to talk to me about my name. How are you feeling about everything that's happened?" Sam asked.

They walked and talked and discussed Ariella and her writing and her murder. Jimmy was having a hard time coming to terms with her murder. He and Ariella had been good friends and they had spent a lot of time together. Jimmy said that he had been in love with Ariella but she never even considered him as a romantic partner, which had broken his heart. Ariella had come to him to talk about her feeling that someone was stealing her work but she had never revealed who she thought it was to Jimmy. Sam let Jimmy know that she was sympathetic. She was hearing a lot now about how Ariella's concerns about plagiarism but had never talked with Ariella about her concerns. They hadn't really talked much about their personal lives with one another; it had all been about writing and critiquing each other's work. While Sam regretted that a little bit now, it was something that they might normally have developed over time, had they had more time.

They walked for quite a long time together. Sam's goal was to get to the Boston Police Department Bureau of Investigative Services to give her official statement about her whereabouts at the time of the murder and for the whole weekend. Jimmy walked with her so he could continue talking. Sam lent him a sympathetic ear while she knew she would take any information she gathered back to Mr. Fantini and Detective O'Malley. Funny, she hadn't thought about it that way until now. She would report back to each of them.

It wasn't long before they were in front of the Boston Police Department building where Sam was going to give her statement. She turned to Jimmy to say good-bye or at least so long until they had a chance to talk again. Jimmy let her know that he would be at Professor Churykian's party and Sam said she was glad that she would see a friendly face there. Jimmy smiled and waved good-bye and said that he was looking forward to it.

"By the way, Jimmy, do you have any idea where Ariella was staying for the past few weeks?" Sam asked.

"Oh, she didn't go anywhere. She stayed at the apartment and had one of her girlfriends move in with her," Jimmy replied.

"Oh, so where was Rick staying?"

"I'm not sure, but I think he was staying in a hotel somewhere nearby. At least that's what I heard," Jimmy replied. "I'm off to the library; I'll see you on Wednesday night."

Sam waved to him and he headed off. She turned to look at the building she needed to enter to give her statement. If she had ever been inside a police department, either this or any other, she couldn't remember when it might have been. She had always mailed in parking tickets and once completed a police report at the scene when their car had been broken into. This reminded her that she needed to think about getting a car. Once the condo was sold she anticipated living outside the city and a car would be a necessity.

"Ms. Monroe I sort of anticipated talking with you inside the building rather than out here." The voice startled her from her reverie. She looked up to see one of the detectives from the previous night standing on the sidewalk next to her holding a large coffee in his hands.

"You took me by surprise," Sam replied.

"I can see that. You now, it's warmer inside that it is out here. Why don't we finish your statement inside," Detective Girard said. "I started a statement for you this morning based on the information we got from you last night."

"Yes, I think that that will be a good idea. I was just thinking that I don't believe I've ever been inside a police station before," Sam said.

"Well, I'd be more than happy to show you around. It's not very exciting but we like to call it home." His jovial manner caused Sam to smile.

Detective Girard and Sam enter the building and headed up to the investigative unit. Detective Girard took off his coat and hung it on a coat rack and then led Sam to his desk. He noted that he had expected to see Sam sooner, based on a call Detective O'Malley made earlier when she left the campus. Sam let him know that she had decided to walk from campus to the police station and one of Ariella's friends had joined her so it took longer than expected. Plus she had been outside for a little while.

Detective Girard printed off the statement he had begun and had Sam review it. Sam made some edits and they finished off the statement regarding her whereabouts at the time of the murder and she signed it.

He made her a copy for her files and then asked her a few questions about the late night visit from Dominic Fantini as well as her thoughts about her conversation this morning with Professor Churykian, Derek and Rick. Sam went over what had happened while Detective Girard took notes. As they were finishing up, the Investigative Services bureau chief came over to introduce himself and chat about Dominic Fantini. The Bureau Chief also let Sam know that Ariella's mother was arriving that day to identify the body and would be staying until the funeral.

Sam expressed her sympathy for Ariella's mother, whom the Bureau Chief would be seeing soon, and asked him to pass on her sympathy to Ariella's mother. Sam also indicated that that she would be more than happy to talk with Ariella's mother at any time, should she want to talk with Sam. The Bureau Chief said he would pass along Sam sympathies and her offer and would let her know if that was needed.

By the time Sam left the police station, she realized it was 4pm and she had not had any lunch and very little breakfast. She was starving and tired so she decided to take a cab home. When she arrived home to her clean and shiny place she had a message from Kate and Ben saying they would be by with some Chinese take out for dinner and that she shouldn't do anything. Sam decided to lie down on her couch for a moment and was asleep almost immediately. She didn't wake until there was a knock on her door and Kate, Ben and the food arrived.

Chapter 20

Sam got out of the cab and looked up at the old, painstakingly restored Victorian mansion that was the home of the English department chair. Ruth had loved this house so and had worked hard to restore it. The mature trees, cascading over the house and lawn, captured and reflected the light back down, creating a lovely, glowing effect around the front of the house. It was both exciting and awful standing there. As always, she noted the uniqueness of the houses paint colors – they way they were put together always enthralled her.

She never really thought she'd be attending a party here ever again, and she wasn't sure she wanted to attend this one. She thought of leaving right now, but the cab was already down the street and around the corner. If it weren't for Kate and Ben, she wouldn't be dressed so glamorously in a black, spaghetti strapped, cocktail dress with a beaded, black silk jacketbut something old and too large for her. She doubted she would ever be a size 6 again, but her new size 10 body felt good. Of course, this was all hidden under her wool coat. She sighed, squared her shoulders and started up the front walk to the front door. She was so engrossed in her own thoughts she didn't hear others arrive behind her.

"Sam, is that really you?" The voice broke into her reverie about paint and dresses. Her head spun around quickly to see Henry and Mathilda Crowley coming up the walk behind her.

Henry, tall and thin, his shock of thick silver gray hair making him look very distinguished. Mathilda, Henry's third or fourth wife, an equally tall, elegant black woman smiled at Sam and said how wonderful it was to see her again. Sam now felt better that she wouldn't be entering the party alone.

"So, are you coming to keep Rick in line?" Henry asked mischievously, raising an eyebrow in her direction. He now had Sam on one arm and Mathilda on the other as they walked up the front stairs.

"Arthur invited me," she replied, smiling somewhat mischievously herself.

"Well, well, this should add some excitement to an otherwise dull party," Jonathan mused.

"It's always so sad when a couple gets divorced or separated and we get stuck with the boring half," Mathilda said. "We're happy to have the exciting half with us tonight."

"I don't really know if Rick is the boring half, but I do appreciate the compliment," Sam replied, a light laugh in her voice, though maybe it was a little too high-pitched.

The front door opened and Arthur greeted them with a booming voice. The party was in full swing. Arthur greeted them, told them where the food and drink were located and pushed off to join the party while he greeted the next group. Henry, Mathilda and Sam were surprised to find themselves not at a small gathering but at a much larger cocktail party. Besides the caterer, there was an open bar with a bartender and live music.

Sam soon found herself separated from Henry and Mathilda. She found herself greeted warmly as well as quizzically by a wide variety of guests, both those she knew and those she didn't know. Most had seen the news about the death of Ariella, as well as all the information on the news about Sam, alternately being wanted by the police and later removed as a suspect in Ariella's murder. Sam found herself in a conversation with two female assistant professors that she knew slightly.

"Sam, I just have to ask you about all this news about Ariella. Why did everyone think that you did it?" Asked the first woman.

"Yes, I just can't believe all this publicity around you?" suggested the second woman.

"I wasn't here at the time and everything has happened so fast that I'm not really sure how they connected me to the murder," Sam responded, lying mostly. "I guess it may be because Ariella visited me the night before she, ummm, died.

"Really, what did you talk about?" they asked, almost in unison.

"Well, not much really. Just this and that," Sam replied

"Wow, I can't wait to find out what's going to happen next. It's like our own little family murder mystery," said the first woman.

"Well, why exactly are you here?" asked the second.

"Arthur invited me," Sam replied. They looked at her blankly, waiting.

"He's been wonderfully supportive of my writing and helped me find an agent for my novel," Sam explained. "Now I have a contract for write three more."

"Really, you're having a novel published?" One of them asked.

"It's just a romance novel, but I'm very excited about getting it published."

"How did you find time to write, what with a full-time job and all?"

"I was laid off about six months ago. I used my severance money to pay the bills and write my novel. Well, my severance money and some help from my father." She figured the story would get around the party in about 5 minutes so she might as well spin it as much as possible. Hopefully before she left she would hear it repeated back to her with embellishments, and those embellishments would be fascinating, particularly with these two telling the story.

"Well, I need a refill," and with that both of them headed off.

Sam was standing in the library talking to a few former grad students that she had gotten to know in the past when Rick arrived, with Donna on his arm. Rick and Donna looked happy and cozy together, holding hands and at least Donna was looking at adoringly at Rick. Rick, on the other hand, was scanning the crowd. Sam was glad that they hadn't seen her yet. The confusing set of emotions going through her made her tongue tied. The small group of graduate students she was talking to stood by her and watched also.

"I've never seen Rick with her before. Boy, it didn't take him long to find someone new." She heard one of the students whisper.

"She doesn't look like a student," said another. "Not like him to date someone older than 21."

"Shhh, his ex-wife is here. She doesn't know about all this." Another said.

"I think it's a little late to worry about what I know and don't know," Sam replied dryly.

The students looked a little started at this comment. Mathilda came up and put her arm around Sam's shoulders in a show of comfort and support. Someone must have decided to tell Rick that she was there. Rick looked directly at Sam and Mathilda. Donna followed their gaze and showed visible surprise when she saw Sam. There was a moment of silence followed by a low buzz of conversation at the encounter.

"How dare you be here," Donna yelled across the room at Sam. "This is my moment, not yours."

"Sam, I'd like you to come with me to the kitchen," Mathilda spoke quietly to Sam. Mathilda led Sam back through the library, down the hall and into the kitchen. Sam heard lots of buzzing, mostly from her own head. She was having a hard time seeing Donna and Rick together. The caterers were all talking in the kitchen, but their eyes were not on Sam. She felt a moment of relief at that.

"Sam, I had no idea that he would be bringing your friend," Mathilda said.

""I know, I know. I'm not sure that it was a good idea for me to come here this evening," Sam was trying hard not to cry. Mathilda patted her shoulder.

"Sam, if you're ready to go, I'd be more than happy to give you a ride home." Derek Soper said. He and a few others had followed Mathilda and Sam to the kitchen.

"Thanks, I would really like a ride home. I was just about to call a cab. Didn't you come with Jimmy?" Sam said.

"Yeah, we came together but he's going to get a ride home from someone else. He's been hot for one of the new adjunct faculty members and she's offered to drive him home," Derek replied.

Henry brought Sam her coat and she and Derek headed out the kitchen door and up the side of the house to the street where cars were parked up and down the narrow street, along with the catering van. The rain had stopped and the lights peeping out of window up and down the street made everything seem dark and dreary.

"You know, I'm really glad that you and Rick broke up," Derek announced as they approached his car. "He's a lying, plagiarizing, son of a bitch."

"Really," Sam said. The word plagiarizing certainly got her attention, even through her tears.

Sam didn't know Derek very well, she'd met him only a few times at English department functions and now that he'd dropped out, she didn't run into him when she visited Arthur the same way she did his roommate Jimmy. He'd always been fun and entertaining with a glib and humorously sarcastic manner. He and Ariella had always seemed like good friends.

"Yeah, you were too nice to be with him."

"Wow, that's a lot to say about one of your advisors, sorry, former advisors. What makes you think I'm too nice for him?"

"You're kidding, right?" Derek said.

"No, I'd like to know why you think I'm too good for him. We don't know each other all that well and I suspect you don't know me as well as you think you do."

"Actually, you're an open book lady. You've held up your head while Rick was having all those affairs with students. And you've never complained about all the times he worked late, and all that stuff."

"Well, it's easy to hold up your head when you don't know about all the affairs. As a professor, I knew that Rick would have evening classes so nothing seemed that erratic to me. I was working a lot of hours too so it didn't surprise me. You know, I never knew anything about this until I came home that time in May."

"Yeah, I know. Ariella was so surprised when you were surprised. She couldn't figure out how you didn't know already."

"I've gathered that over the past few months. I imagine my reaction took her by surprise the day I found them in bed together."

"I'll say it did. She had a lot of respect for you after that. It must have been quite a moment. Wish I'd been there to see it." He chuckled as he said that.

"Do you miss her?" Sam asked.

"Yes," he replied as the smile and the humor drained from his face. "I had no idea how much I really loved her until she was gone."

146

They rode in silence for a while, each lost in their own thoughts.

"You know," Derek broke the silence first, "I figured she would get over Rick pretty quickly and she did. Did you know that they weren't living together anymore?"

"I just learned that on Monday. Ariella never told me. And I never knew about Rick and Donna until tonight."

"Yeah, she's quite some friend, isn't she? Did you know that he's been staying with Donna?"

"Ah, no, I didn't know that until tonight either," Sam replied. What a shocking night this has been, her best friend and her not quite ex-husband being together was just hard to believe.

"Donna was a good friend of mine but I've been avoiding her these last few months," Sam replied. "She's been so hard to get along with."

"Yeah, I bet."

"Well, here we are," Derek said, pulling his car up to the curb in front of Sam's building.

"Thanks," replied Sam. "I didn't know you knew where I lived?"

"Oh, ah, well. I remembered it from when I visited here before. You know, for the party," Derek said.

"Oh right, I forgot about that."

Derek breathed a sigh of relief. She didn't seem to remember that he had never been there when she was home.

"So, do you want to invite me in?" Derek asked.

"Ah, well, it's been a long night and all, I think I'd like to take a rain check on that," Sam said. She wondered if this night could get any weirder.

Sam put her hand on the door latch to leave the car and found that it didn't work. She was jiggling the handle when she realized that Derek was almost on top of her. He turned her head in his hands and started to kiss her. It took Sam a moment to gather her wit and push Derek away from her. She did so without screaming or creating a scene. She wanted him to know that she was in control and to not show any fear, no matter how fearful and scared she felt. At first he didn't move and his dark eyes continued to drill into hers, making her anxious but then he moved back to his side of the car and slumped behind the driver's wheel.

"Uh, Derek, I'm really grateful for the ride home but I think we should say goodnight here," Sam said. She wanted to be kind and get out of the car as fast as she could without causing alarm.

"You don't find me attractive, do you? Well, she didn't find me attractive either. Jimmy's the one who discovered he was plagiarizing her but you'd think she'd be more appreciative 'cause I'm the one who told her," Derek said.

"Ah, do you mean Ariella?" Sam asked.

Sam wanted to get out of the car as quickly as possible. First he attacked her and then he was rambling on about Ariella and possibly Rick. She pumped him for more information while she thought of ways to get out of the car. She couldn't help herself, she desperately wanted to get out as quickly as possible.

"Oh look, it's getting late and I've said way too much. Thanks for the talk, too. Here let me let you out of the car," Derek said. "I need to get that door fixed."

Derek jumped out of the car and walked around the back to the passenger's side door and opened the door for her. Sam stood up and found Derek standing right next to her. So close she could feel his breath on her cheek.

"Thanks for a wonderful evening," he said. "Maybe we can do this again sometime. Unless, of course, you want to invite me up."

Derek then bent down to kiss Sam. When she didn't respond he let her go.

"Well, I guess it's just not our night."

"No, I think not. Thank you for the ride home," Sam said. "And thanks for talking about Ariella. I hope it helped."

Sam turned and walked up to her front door. She unlocked the door, turned and waved to Derek who was still standing beside his car. She let herself into the building foyer and closed the door behind her. She let herself through the second door into the lobby and elevator area and turned to lean against the door as she breathed out a sigh. What a night.

"Jesus, did you see that," Wu said.

"Uh, do you think they're dating?" Martinelli replied.

"Be serious. I think he just tried to attack her," Wu replied.

"You don't think she wanted to be kissed?"

"Get real. She pushed him away in the car and she didn't invite him up. Plus it looks like the passenger has no control over the passenger's side door. I bet there's an assault complaint about him in the system," Wu said.

Martinelli made a call in to the dispatcher outlining their suspicions about Derek and provided his license number while Wu wrote up some notes. Larrabee was on duty and could look up the records and then get in touch with O'Malley. Wu and Martinelli then settled in for the remainder of their shift. The only excitement of the night was watching a drunk attempt to open his car door. He repeatedly tried to open his car door with his keys but couldn't find the lock and kept dropping his keys on the ground. They called the dispatcher to send someone to check on the drunk.

"Man, how the hell can she be a suspect? She has 8 alibis or something like that," said Martinelli.

"I don't think she's a suspect, I think O'Malley wants us to make sure she's OK," Wu replied evenly.

"Why? Has he got the hots for her or something," said Martinelli.

"Maybe. Maybe he thinks she's a target." Now that she was home their job was to keep the building under surveillance for the rest of the evening. Wu wished he had a more intelligent, interesting partner for this surveillance. As far as he could see, Martinelli was sure that Sam was the murderer and had trouble focusing on anything else, except his stomach. Someday Wu would be a detective or even a bureau chief and Martinelli would still be walking a beat, or so Wu fantacized.

"Do you have the camera ready?" Wu said, slowly and evenly as if explaining something to a child for the umpteenth time. His manner was not lost on Martinelli, who sat up a little straighter and pulled the camera out of the back seat.

"Yep, everything's ready," Martinelli replied.

They were about to get out and do a sobriety test on the drunk who still hadn't opened the car door. Dispatch had let them know that they didn't have anyone in the area to handle the call. That's when they got a call to check on Sam Monroe's place.

******

Sam took the elevator up to the 6th floor, walked down the hall and let herself into the condo. She turned on the lights, looked around, inhaled sharply and didn't move. Someone had definitely been here while she was gone. Books were knocked off the bookcase, dishes were on the kitchen floor and papers were strewn all around.

She slowly opened the door behind her and stepped back out into the hall. She stood for a moment, listening for sounds through the door and heard nothing. She then headed for the stairs and walked swiftly up one floor to the top floor. It was already one in the morning and she knew Ben was working nights at the hospital but hopefully Kate would be home. Sam knocked on Kate's door, rang the bell and knocked louder. She continued knocking until she heard Kate open the door.

"Sam, what is the matter?" Kate asked. Kate was cinching her robe and covering a yawn with her hand as she waved Sam into her place.

"I just got home and opened my door and my place has been ransacked," Sam said. "Can I use your phone to call the police?"

"Of course you can. Don't you have a cell phone?"

"Well, yes I do," Sam said, pulling the cell phone from her bag. "I just didn't want to be standing out in the hallway by myself making the call.

Sam dialed 911 from her cell phone and reported the break-in. She explained that she was not currently in her place but calling from a neighbor's upstairs. Kate could see that Sam's hands were shaking but her voice was firm and clear.

The 911 operator commended her for her quick thinking and kept her on the line while notifying the police dispatcher. Wu and Martinelli were alerted to the incident. They made a call to O'Malley to let him know what was happening and then headed to the front of the building. They rang Kate's intercom, identified themselves and were let into the building. They went to Kate's place first to pick up Sam and then headed down the one flight to Sam's place.

The door was intact and had not been forced. Inside the place looked just as Sam had left it 10 minutes before. Wu and Martinelli checked to make sure that no one was in the place and then called Detective O'Malley. O'Malley was already on his way and arrived just a few moments later.

Wu and Martinelli took Sam's statement. They noted that no doors or window had been forced in the break in and that most of the windows as well as the back door were still locked. Sam looked through each room carefully and noted that nothing seemed to be missing or to be broken. A few books had their bindings torn and the pages strewn around the living area. Her computer was on and the screen requesting a password was on the monitor. Papers and flash drives had been moved around but she wasn't at all sure if anything was missing.

O'Malley, who had arrived while Wu and Martinelli were taking Sam's statement, was concerned for Sam's safety and asked if she could stay with someone for the rest of the night. Kate, who had stayed quietly in the background through the whole thing, offered to put Sam up for the night. Kate had a second bedroom and wasn't taking no for an answer.

Officer Wu had just a few last questions to ask before Kate and Sam stepped out.

"How many people have keys to this place?" Wu asked.

"Oh, not many, I had the locks changed once my husband left," Sam replied. "My dad and my brother Andrew each have a key."

"And would any of them have a need to enter your place while you were out?"

"No."

"Is there anyone who might break in to look for something or just to be malicious?" Wu continued, while Martinelli took pictures.

"I did find out that my friend Donna and my husband Rick are sharing a place right now. I wouldn't be surprised if they broke in to harass me. They were suspiciously late for a party tonight. Or they maybe they were looking for something, or both. I think that Donna is far more malicious than I ever would have thought." Sam said.

"But they don't have keys, is that correct."

"They have a key to the outside door of the building but they don't have a key to this condo," Sam replied.

She winced at the thought that Donna and Rick might have been in her place. Donna and Rick being together made her stomach churn. She was still more connected to Rick than she wanted.

"Are you sure that no one else has a key?" Wu asked again.

"Yes, no one has a key that I know about."

Wu was about to ask more about Donna and Rick but O'Malley put his hand up to stop him. He then arranged to have Sam meet him for breakfast at 7am at a diner near the police precinct. Kate thought that that was fairly early, but O'Malley insisted. Sam agreed to join him for breakfast and the headed off to get some sleep at Kate's place. O'Malley, Wu and Martinelli left at the same time and Sam locked the door behind them. They let her know that it would be ok to clean up the next day. They did not anticipate finding anything of use.

Chapter 21

Detective O'Malley was already at the diner, along with Detective's Kelvin and Girard when Sam arrived the next morning. She was exhausted, she had gotten to bed at Kate's after 2am and it was now 7am. She had gotten up, dressed at her own place and realized that she would need to clean again today, which made her even more tired. She had not had much sleep lately.

She greeted the detectives and sat down in the empty chair at their table. As busy as it was, a waitress was standing next to her with a pot of coffee and ready to take her order as soon as her bottom hit the chair. Sam took coffee and asked for a few minutes before ordering, the detectives had already started to drink theirs, and they all ordered. As soon as the waitress left to place their orders, she was surprised to see Arthur walking towards them.

Detective O'Malley announced that he had called Arthur Churykian early that morning to join them for breakfast as well. Arthur pulled up a chair and joined the group. He hadn't shaved this morning and was wearing an overcoat over jeans and a t-shirt. He was looking considerably less dapper than the previous evening but then again, Sam thought, but she suspected she was looking a lot more the worse for wear too. The waitress was back to offer more coffee and to take Sam's and Arthur's order. She asked if anyone else would be joining them, giving the impression that they were disrupting her well-organized system. O'Malley indicated that this was it.

Sam noted that O'Malley looked rather casual and even a little disheveled with his 2-day growth of beard and dressed in jeans and a button down shirt. She wondered if this was how he looked in real life, rather than in his work life and then shook her head. Arthur was crazy

154

for suggesting that O'Malley was in any way interested in her, other than to help with the murder investigation. Kelvin was dressed in her usual outfit of tight-fitting dress pants, a jacket with a silk shirt underneath and low heeled shows. Sam was a bit jealous of how well this outfit accentuated Detective Kelvin's petite 5'2" frame and her toned figure. Girard was dressed in a suit but it looked like he might have slept in it and he kept looking at his BlackBerry.

"His wife's due any day now and he wants to make sure he doesn't miss the call," O'Malley said, explaining Girard's behavior. "I want to thank you both for joining us this morning. I know it's early after a fairly late night last night for both of you."

"Thanks, we are both glad to help as much as possible," Arthur replied, for both Sam and himself. While Sam was in agreement with the statement, she could have said it herself. Sometimes Arthur's paternalistic behavior, particularly to woman, was irritating, mostly because it was just a reaction. It was not deliberate and did not take into consideration anything Sam might have liked to say.

"I'd like to go over what happened at the party last night," O'Malley continued.

"Sam, I want to apologize for the way that you were treated by Rick and that girl," Arthur said. "I had no idea that Rick and Ariella had broken up and that Rick had found someone new. And someone that you know as well."

This was news to everyone at the table, except Sam. Sam explained how the party appeared to her, focusing on the arrival of Rick with her friend, or former friend, Donna, on his arm. It was been a dramatic entrance that hadn't been as well received as the couple had anticipated it would be but it made them the center of attention. Since everyone at the party was a part of the University and most of them were associated with the English Department, seeing Rick arrive with a new woman only days after the murder of his lover seemed audacious and rude and certainly constituted something to talk about. When Rick and Donna had seen Sam, things had gone downhill.

Since Sam had left soon after that with Derek, Arthur was able to fill them in on how things had gone after Sam's departure. The party had become less fun with Rick and Donna belittling Sam's romance novel, which Arthur felt belittled him and his party. He had then explained to most of those there how he had helped Sam by having her become part of a writing critique group of his, helped her find an agent and provided her with comments on her manuscript himself.

Once Arthur defended Sam, people broke into small groups to talk among themselves. Arthur and Rick then go into an argument and Arthur made a point of telling Rick, quite loudly how disturbed he was at Rick's behavior, both in relationship to Ariella and to Sam. The sense of joy and camaraderie left the gathering quickly. He also pointed out that this was his final department party and he did not appreciate it becoming a grandstand show for Rick. People started to leave soon after and only a loyal core of people remained.

Rick, in turn, had called him a stuffy old bag and hoped that he learned how to treat his guests better in the future. Arthur informed Rick that there might not be a future for Rick in the department. Rick accused Arthur of favoring Sam over Rick and Arthur in turn accused Rick of not being able to write, and who ever heard of a writing professor who was not published. Sam could just imagine the conversation going on in the English Department today.

Sam then told her story of getting a ride home from Derek, a former student, and how Derek had accused Rick of plagiarizing off the work of one or more of his students on his latest work in progress; the one Rick anticipated getting published and pushing him closer to tenure. She let them know that Derek had attacked her, that his car had a passenger side door handle that didn't work and that he tried to come up to her place. She also told them that Derek said he loved Ariella, all in a very short amount of time. Sam had been very uncomfortable with this encounter. O'Malley let them know that two plain clothes police officers, Wu and Martinelli, had been sitting in a car behind Sam and had seen the incident with Derek. They were looking into any other reported assaults that had involved Derek.

Sam then continued with the story of her place being broken into and how there had been no forced entry. Kelvin and Girard, having heard all of this for the first time, were taking it all in and wondering how either of them could get up and join them for breakfast the next morning.

O'Malley, Kelvin and Girard were wrapping things up and getting ready to walk across the street to the precinct station for their 8am briefing. The Bureau Chief would not let up on their morning meetings and, with luck, Larrabee would have some more information about Derek. The Bureau Chief had made it very clear that he would be displeased if they were late so they were always on time. As the three detectives paid their bills and gathered their things, a very pregnant woman stopped by their table.

"Well, well, look who's having breakfast here today," the woman said. Detectives Kelvin and Girard looked at the woman and then at Detective O'Malley.

"Good morning Siobhan, it's good to see you looking so well," Peter O'Malley replied. His tone was even and pleasant but his body seemed to stiffen and he stood up straighter than normal.

Sam and Arthur looked from Siobhan, to Detective O'Malley, to Kelvin and Girard and then at each other, wondering what might possibly be going on.

"Well, I'm fine. Due in just a few weeks you know," Siobhan said. She rubbed her stomach absently as she turned to smile and blow a kiss to a man standing by the door. "Edward is fine as well. He has an early meeting at the station so we thought we would stop here for breakfast, for old time's sake."

Edward waved back and looked at his watch deliberately. He then waved to Siobhan to join him. He tapped the glass front of his watch

157

with his left index finger which seemed to indicate that they were on a schedule, and Siobhan should be ready to go. Siobhan decided to stay where she was and continue talking.

"My wife is due in about three weeks," Girard said.

"How nice for you and Isa. What, this must be your 6th child now?" Siobhan said.

"Actually, it's our fifth. We're hoping for a girl this time. Do you know the sex of your child?" Girard continued.

"No, we've decided to be surprised. It won't matter to us so long as the baby is healthy and happy."

"Really, I thought you would be one of those who would want to know the sex of your child," Girard replied. While the detective had a smile on this face, Sam sensed that this was an obvious dig and one that caused a brief moment of anger to pass across Siobhan's face before she regained her composure.

"Darcy, I wonder if you will ever be able to experience of giving birth to your own child," Siobhan turned her attention Darcy Kelvin.

"I guess we'll just have to wait and see, won't we," Darcy replied evenly but without a smile.

"Peter, I see you're hanging out with celebrities these days," Siobhan turned her attention to Arthur and Sam.

"No, just a couple of people helping us with a murder case," O'Malley replied.

"Really, well they've both been on TV recently. This handsome older man was interviewed the other night on the news and this very pretty young woman has had her picture plastered all over the news for several days," Siobhan said.

Sam and Arthur looked at each other and then back at the detectives without responding. They had no idea who this woman was or why she seemed to know so much about each of the detectives. Siobhan didn't wait for a response from either Arthur or Sam but kept her attention focused on O'Malley.

"Well, Siobhan, it's always good to see you. I think Edward is really ready to go now," O'Malley said. Edward was now tapping his foot and rolling his eyes.

"You used to have such interesting stories to tell me when we were married. I do miss those. Well, I guess I really have to go now. Ta, ta all. Please give Isa my love." With a wave of her hand Siobhan headed over to Edward who held the door open for her. O'Malley, Kelvin and Girard waited for Siobhan to get into the parked car out front and leave. Edward talked briefly to his wife, closed the car door and headed across the street to the precinct station.

"Well, we better get to the meeting before we get our butts kicked," O'Malley said.

"I cannot believe that you were married to that bitch for almost 10 years," Kelvin said. She had her arms folded across her chest and was tapping her foot.

"Yeah, well, we all make mistakes," O'Malley replied. "I'm sorry she was so rotten to you Darcy."

"And to think that she could just wander over and throw her pregnancy in our faces like that," Kelvin said. "Particularly after telling you that she wasn't sure she wanted children."

"You know that woman never lacked for balls," Girard said. "It's time for us to get going. We don't want to be late for our meeting."

With that the three detectives did finally leave the diner. Arthur and Sam sat there for a few minutes more, finishing their coffee and talking about what had just happened.

"Well, it looks like Detective O'Malley has a reason to be so reticent around women. She must have done a job on him," Arthur said.

"I just thought he was just a detective focused on solving the case," Sam said.

"My, my, you have no idea how he looks at you, do you?" Arthur said.

Sam looked at Arthur and just shook her head. He was known to be a matchmaker, or at least try to be a matchmaker. His matchmaking had yet to produce any tangible results but that did not stop him from trying. The waitress dropped a check off at their table and topped off their coffee. Arthur took the check and gathered up the money from the table and then added some money of his own. He wouldn't let Sam add anything for her breakfast. He felt that she had done enough work on this case and that it was the least he could do after last night's fiasco.

Sam and Arthur headed out together. Arthur had taken a cab this morning and he hailed a cab on the street to take him home. He offered to drop Sam off but she declined, saying she preferred to walk. She needed some time to clear her head and put her thoughts in order.

The walk home was refreshing. She decided not to ponder the events of the night before or the past week and just get organized for the future. She and Rick had a joint meeting with their divorce attorneys on Monday morning to finalize the settlement and she needed to get to work on those re-writes before her agent was really breathing down her neck. Sam hoped her role in this investigation would soon be over, she had done more than enough already and it was time to get back to her own life.

She stopped at her mailbox on the first floor to retrieve her mail. She hadn't checked for a few days and the mail had begun to pile up. Not only was there junk mail, it looked like there was a manuscript she had agreed to review for one of the members of the writer's group, and it looked like she had a package to pick up at the post office. She thought it was most likely something she had forgotten in Florida which her mother had mailed to her.

When she got to the condo, she was not surprised to see that her place looked just as bad as it had last night. In the light of day it actually looked worse. She threw her mail and her bag onto the counter and went to the make herself some tea. She was startled to see Mr. Fantini sitting and Mr. Jones sitting on her couch. Mr. Jones was sipping from a coffee mug.

"Well, you have certainly been a busy girl these past few days," Mr. Fantini said. "And we see that someone wants you to stop whatever you're doing or they are looking for something you might have. Do you have any idea who might have done this?

In her musings she had forgotten all about Mr. Fantini. She decided that it might be wise not to mention that to him right now.

"No, I have absolutely no idea. The police assume it's someone with a key, since there was no forced entry. I'm inclined to agree with them, even though I changed the locks when I kicked Rick out and only 2 other people now have keys, my father and my brother. Unless, of course, you did this?"

"No, we did search your place but we did so without disturbing anything. You never seemed to notice."

"By the way, how do the two of you get in?" Sam asked.

"We have a key," Mr. Fantini replied.

Sam looked at him a bit dumbfounded. She thought she had been so good in changing the lock and keeping a limited distribution of the key to others. Obviously that hadn't worked out as she had anticipated.

"In case you are wondering, we obtained a copy of your key from the man at the hardware store who changed your locks for you. He is normally a very reputable person but almost anything can be had if you want something badly enough. The locksmith needed some help so we made an arrangement. I'm not sure, but he may have made other copies as well."

"Of course," Sam said

"Well, if you don't mind, I'd like to suggest that you allow me to arrange for someone else to change your lock this time. He will leave you enough copies to distribute and a number if you should need more. No other copies will be made. Also, I'd like to arrange to have the cleaning people I know come in and clean this mess up for you. As you know, they are quite reputable."

"Of course, how could I possibly disagree," Sam said. "Can I hire the cleaning people to come in regularly to clean?"

"Alas no, this is a onetime or in this case a two time arrangement for a special reason. They are not part of a for hire service," Mr. Fantini. "Besides, you're selling the condo soon."

"Yes, I was thinking of keeping the cleaning people on until the sale was completed so that it would always be clean for viewings," Sam said.

"Well, we'll see what I can do. Mr. Jones, would you make some green tea for Ms. Monroe here. I think she could use some while we talk." Mr. Fantini joined Sam at the kitchen bar seating area while Mr. Jones went behind the counter to start water for tea.

Sam thanked Mr. Fantini and Mr. Jones, which seemed a little strange since they were her guests without being invited. While Mr. Jones heated some water for tea, Mr. Fantini made a few phone calls. He moved across to the window on the other side of the living room and spoke quietly. Sam was not able to hear anything that was being said but she assumed that he was calling for the keys and the cleaning people. Of course, he could just as well have been calling for sports scores or to arrange a hit, she just couldn't tell.

Once Mr. Fantini was done with his calls and Sam had a perfect, steaming mug of green tea in front of her, she filled them in on the events of the past few days, since they had last talked and she had been convinced to help with the investigation. She told them about the detectives knowing that Mr. Fantini had visited her and requested her help in solving the murder. As they had discussed, she had visited Arthur the next morning, as they had agreed, and the detectives were there taking statements so she ended up telling them everything that had happened. She had been surprised that the detectives had agreed to have her do some investigating and that Arthur had invited her to his annual faculty bash.

She also let them know about the call from Misty Mustoe to be interviewed, which she hadn't decided whether or not to do yet, providing a statement to the police, attending the party, including the ride home with Derek, his semi-assault of her and then finding her place broken into and calling the police followed by having breakfast with the detectives. She even told him about the strange encounter with Detective O'Malley's ex-wife.

Mr. Fantini asked her to describe the events of the party in greater detail, particularly going over how Sam felt when she saw Rick arrive with Donna. Sam told them that Donna appeared to be in love with Rick but she wasn't sure how Rick felt. Donna was showing off at the party and she didn't particularly care who saw them together. Rick was enjoying the attention but he hardly looked at Donna. She knew that Donna felt that Sam didn't pay enough attention to Rick but she never thought that they had a relationship that she didn't know about. She could see where this fit a pattern with Rick, but she was still very surprised.

She also let them know that Rick's argument with Arthur in the middle of the party. Arthur's description had shocked her as she had never heard Rick raise his voice to the Department Chair before and didn't think he would get into such a public disagreement with the Department Chair. Arthur had her know that this argument had pretty much put an end to the party.

163

They asked a few questions about Derek and his advances on her. Sam indicated that Derek seemed confused between her and Ariella. He would talk about them interchangeably. First wanting to come up to Sam's apartment and then saying how much he loved Ariella. It had been a bit schizophrenic and Sam had been happy to get out of the car and into her building. Of course, finding her apartment ransacked had also been a surprise.

Mr. Fantini and Mr. Jones asked a few questions here and there for clarification but they also didn't seem too terribly surprised at all of the events that had taken place. Once she was done, Mr. Fantini suggested that Sam might want to stay with Kate again that night, while her locks were being changed and her place was being cleaned. Sam reluctantly agreed to ask Kate if she would like some company for one more night. Even while she was complaining about asking Kate to stay one more night, Sam knew she needed some sleep and she also knew that she wouldn't be able to sleep if she stayed at her own place, every little sound would wake her.

Mr. Fantini let them both know that he needed to leave for a little while but that he would be reachable by cell phone. When Sam asked him where he was going, he let her know that he was heading off to meet with his ex-wife to talk about the funeral arrangements and to comfort her since she had to identify the body alone. He neglected to mention to her that he would also be visiting with his police contacts.

Once Mr. Fantini had left, Mr. Jones let her know that her friend Donna had called. He suggested, quite firmly, that Sam return the call to Donna while he was still there and could deal with the locksmith and the cleaning people. Sam was surprised by the request but went ahead and listened to the message from Donna. If Mr. Fantini and Mr. Jones had not been there, she would have deleted the message and not returned Donna's. She didn't want to talk to Donna ever again after the previous night's episode. Mr. Jones pointed out that calling Donna might be a great way to get more information.

While Mr. Jones worked with the locksmith, Sam returned the call to Donna using her cell phone in the office. She didn't really want to talk to Donna and hoped that no one would answer. Donna picked up after the first ring. After a few pleasantries, Donna launched into her reason for calling.

"So, I just wanted to call and ask you what you thought of the party last night," Donna said.

"Oh, well, I was having a pleasant time until you and Rick showed up together. I was rather surprised to see Rick arrive with someone new so soon after Ariella's murder," Sam said.

"Well, you of all people know that Rick and I are just friends. I accompanied Rick to the party so he wouldn't be alone," Donna said.

"Really, because it looked to me and to the people standing around me that you two were more than friends," Sam replied. She could tell that her anger, however much it was suppressed on the phone she was causing her face to redden.

"Oh, are you jealous?" Donna said.

"No, actually I'm angry with the two of you for flaunting Ariella's death and the investigation by just showing up together like nothing had ever happened. And at Arthur's party. You know that it looks like you are either preying upon a man in mourning or that the two of you had something going on behind Ariella's back. Since she was murdered and they don't know who the murderer is yet, it might be a little suspicious to the police," Sam said.

"Well, who would be telling the police about the party, you?" Donna asked.

"I could since I'm still being questioned by the police. But then so are Arthur and Rick and you even," Sam said.

"Really, and why would they want to question me?"

"Well, haven't they questioned you already about the murder and your relationship with Ariella and Rick? You and Rick have been together a lot and Rick is most likely a strong suspect for the murder. I think they say that most women are murdered by someone they know."

"You're just jealous because Rick and I are friends and you and he are not," Donna replied. The pleasantness gone replaced with a certain, high-pitched nervousness that Sam hadn't heard since Tom had left Donna.

"I'm not jealous of you and Rick but I think that you are setting the wrong tone with the police, particularly with a police investigation still going on," Sam said.

"Yes, you are jealous. Rick is brilliant and you just got lucky selling your first novel," Donna replied. "How dare you think that you can compete with Rick in the writing world. And why in the world would anyone think that Rick would be involved in Ariella's murder?"

"You mean other than the fact that they lived together and she was a student of his and now there's some talk of possible plagiarism?."

"Oh, get real. Rick doesn't need to plagiarize anyone's work. Those stories are just the ravings of those who are jealous of Rick's work and his potential," Donna said.

"Well, if that's the case, then there is nothing to worry about," Sam said.

"So, how did you get home last night? You seemed to have disappeared very quickly," Donna asked.

"Strange that you should ask. I got a ride home with Derek, that student who's taken a sabbatical.

"How did that go?,

"Well, he alternately attacked me and then told me how much he loved Ariella, then he wanted to come up to my place and then he started to cry. It was really very strange," Sam replied.

So, how is your romance novel coming along?" Donna asked. The change in topic and tone took Sam by surprise but she rolled with it.

"Well, it's going to be out in July and I've been asked to write three more," Sam replied.

"Really, well I hope that it all works out for you," Donna said. "I hope that this doesn't cause us to lose our friendship as that would be very sad."

"Well, I think that under the circumstances, what with Rick and I getting divorced, and you and Rick being such good friends, I'm not sure what that does for our friendship," Sam said.

"Well, again, I hope that we can continue to be friends."

"All this drama around Ariella's murder has definitely taken its toll on our relationship. Maybe we should talk more after the murder is solved and everything settles down a bit."

Donna agreed that they should talk more once the murderer was found and the murder solved. Sam remembered to ask Donna about her new job. Donna spoke enthusiastically about her new job as a customer service rep at the bank. She enjoyed the people she was meeting and working with every day. She felt it was much better than their old job.

Sam blew out a huge sigh after she hung up with Donna. That was one strange conversation. She returned to the kitchen area and found Mr. Jones and Kate talking. She announced that she really didn't intend to ever talk with Donna again. Mr. Jones quietly pointed out that until the murder was solved, talking to Donna might be an important avenue to information, however strange it might seem to Sam right now. Sam thought it over and reluctantly agreed that Mr. Jones might have a good point.

Mr. Jones and Kate waited while Sam gathered some clothes for the night and for the next morning, along with her toothbrush, toothpaste and all the other items she needed for the stay at Kate's. Mr. Jones walked them both up the one flight of stairs to Kate's apartment. Kate opened the door and they both thanked Mr. Jones for the escort. Mr. Jones took the stairs back down and entered Sam's place using his key for the back entrance behind the kitchen.

"She seems like a very nice girl. Too bad she's caught up in this," Mr. Jones said to Mr. Fantini while standing at his now usual place at the kitchen counter. The locksmith and the cleaning people had already arrived and were busily doing their work.

"Yes, she is a nice girl. Ariella was right to like her and to try to confide in her. It's very sad that things turned out the way they did," Mr. Fantini replied.

"Have you seen Mrs. Fantini?" Mr. Jones asked.

"Yes, she wasn't up for discussing the funeral details yet so I came right back. We will have to do this soon but I'll give her until tomorrow morning. I've arranged for a suite so that we can stay together. She is, of course, devastated. Ariella was her only child."

"Have they released the body yet?"

"No, they are still doing some tests and such. I expect that they will release the body tomorrow," Mr. Fantini said. "Would you mind supervising the work here. I need to meet with my police contacts."

It was much more of a statement than a request and Mr. Jones agreed. With that, Mr. Fantini rang off and headed off to his next appointment. Mr. Jones absently sorted through her mail, tossing the junk mail, putting the bills on her desk and putting the Post Office package pick-up notice on the refrigerator.

Upstairs, Sam sat on Kate's couch, and told both her and Ben all that had happened in the past few days. There was so much to tell them, so much that had happened in the past few days and she needed to talk to get things straight in her own mind. It took most of the afternoon and into the evening to fill them on all the things that had happened. They decided to have an early dinner at their favorite local Italian restaurant so that Ben could get to the hospital on time.

On the way back from dinner, Kate asked Sam more about Detective O'Malley. Sam laughed and called her and Arthur both incurable romantics. Kate mentioned that she would like to meet Arthur sometime, since they had both Sam and incurable romanticism in common. Plus Kate needed a new gentleman friend to keep her entertained. They also talked about Mr. Jones, an intriguing character but far less of an incurable romantic.

Kate then filled in Sam on her latest ex-gentlemen friend, who, it turned out was married. Kate was less surprised than Sam at this turn of events. At her age, which was her mid-forties Sam estimated, this was not an uncommon occurrence. Sam wondered if Mr. Fantini might not be a better fit for Kate. He was quite charming and debonair. The drawback to a relationship being that he was wanted by the FBI and was a former mobster and possible murderer, which might put a crimp into dating. Sam realized she must be overtired to think of something so absurd as Kate and Mr. Fantini together. Besides, there seems to be a Mrs. Fantini and, well, Kate needs someone a bit stable and less dangerous than Mr. Fantini. Sam thought of all of this without ever saying a word to Kate, who continued to talk about meeting Arthur.

Chapter 22

Jimmy Reynolds made his way up the stairs of Baker Hall to the third floor and the English Department. He had decided that the only person who could help him was Dr. Churykian. Jimmy wanted to show the professor the journal that he had in his bag. Ariella had given it to him a week ago for safekeeping. Now Ariella was dead and Jimmy needed some advice to help him decide what to do with her journal.

Last Saturday, when the police had arrived to interview both he and Derek, Jimmy had decided not to tell the police about the journal. He wasn't sure why but he had wanted time to think about what to do with this information. He had thought about talking to Derek about it, but had hesitated. Derek and Ariella had once been an item. Although it was brief, before Ariella had taken up with Professor Sampson, he knew Derek had been angry.

Since Sunday night he had only seen Derek at Professor Churykian's party. What he saw of Derek's actions he did not like. He never talked about Ariella or the murder and acted as if nothing had happened. He hoped the professor would have some idea of what to do with the journal pages. Carrying the journal around, both the physical copy in his bag and the mental copy in his head, was wearing him down. He needed some help to understand how to deal with this.

Jimmy stepped through the door from the stairway to the activity of the English department. The floor was set up with the offices around the outside wall so that everyone would have a window and the center held the office for the department secretary, facing the staircase, with a large seminar room that was also used for faculty meetings and graduate seminars followed by a smaller meeting room and then a storage room. The seminar room had book cases all around and a locked, glass front cabinet that houses some rare editions of books that had been donated to the department over the years.

Jimmy waved to Mrs. Nancy Smythe-Brill, the department secretary, but didn't stop to talk. He turned swiftly to the right and then took an immediate left down the narrow hallway that ran the length of the floor. Professor Arthur Churykian had a corner office in the back, right-hand corner of the floor. His assistant had the office immediately to the right of the professor. Jimmy greeted the assistant and asked if Professor Churykian had a moment to see him. She pointed Jimmy to a seat to wait while she went into the Professor's office to let him know that Jimmy was there. The assistant came out with Arthur right behind her.

"How good to see you young man. I understand that you have been working feverishly on your dissertation. I hope that I am able to read it soon," Arthur said, escorting Jimmy into his office and closing the door behind them.

"Professor I want to thank you for seeing me without an appointment," Jimmy said.

"Of course, you are one of our star students and I was very intrigued by your voicemail message. Besides, I want to get your thoughts on the party last night."

"Thanks for inviting me. I'm not sure that I deserve it yet," Jimmy said. "I still have a lot of work to do."

"Well, I'm always happy to have students come and mix with their professor's in a social setting," Arthur replied. "So, tell me what you thought of the evening."

Jimmy hesitated only briefly before letting Professor Churykian know that the party had been a lot of fun, up until the time Professor Sampson had arrived with the red-haired woman. The party had definitely changed once they made their dramatic entrance and then the arguments had started, first with Sam and then with Arthur. It had seemed like they had arrived to deliberately start trouble.

Arthur nodded his agreement with Jimmy's statement about the arguments. "Well, only time will tell how these things will turn out for everyone. By the way, how has Professor Sampson been reacting to our work, as your advisor of course," Arthur said.

"Well, he's not been very helpful lately. Of course once he and Ariella broke up things became a bit strange between us. He knew that Ariella and I were friends and that seemed to cause a lot of friction," Jimmy replied.

"Hmm, well hopefully that will sort itself out. I need to have a long conversation with Professor Sampson and how he treats his students is one of them. I thought the party took an odd turn when Professor Sampson and his friend Donna arrived, too."

"Well, I have a problem with Professor Sampson acting like nothing happened to Ariella and then bringing this woman to the party. It made me very resentful. How could he be so, so cold? Jimmy asked.

"I have to say, the more I deal with the people the less and less I understand them. Anyway, let's talk about what brought you hear today," Arthur replied.

Jimmy launched into an explanation of the journal pages that Ariella had left with him. At first he had just ignored them and just stuffed them in his backpack. Then when Ariella was murdered and the police showed up to question both he and Derek, he had decided that it was time to read them. Once he read them in the library he had been so rattled that it took him a couple of days to decide what to do.

"Did you bring the journal with you?"

"Yes, I have it right here in my backpack," Jimmy replied.

Jimmy pulled Ariella's journal pages out of his backpack for the two of them to review together. Jimmy had marked some of the most important pages with pieces of paper to make everything easier to find. Professor Churykian swiftly read the entries, rereading some of the sections a second time.

Ariella, in her journal, had been concerned that somebody was looking for it and for her and they were making her nervous. She noted that she had found things moved around in her apartment and at her research cube both before and after Rick had left. Nothing dramatic, just enough to make her nervous and think that someone was following her and looking for something. The description reminded Jimmy a lot of what he had done to a sophomore student two years before.

Jimmy was concerned that it was Derek who was following Ariella. Derek and Ariella had been dating and everything seemed to be just fine between the two of them when Ariella announced that she wanted to break up with Derek because she had found someone new. She told everyone that they did not know who the new person was, but eventually it turned out to be Professor Sampson. Derek was angry but not so angry that he tried to do anything to Ariella, as far as Jimmy knew. It was not something that he and Derek had discussed.

Once Ariella and Professor Sampson broke up, Derek had tried to get Ariella to move in with them. They had a 3rd bedroom and would love to help her out, Derek had told Ariella. Jimmy had expressed his concerns about such an arrangement, knowing that Derek and Ariella's past plus Derek's continued attraction to Ariella would cause friction. In the end Ariella had decided to stay in her own place. Money didn't seem to have been a concern for Ariella.

Last Friday morning Ariella had arranged to meet Jimmy for coffee. Over coffee she had asked him to hold onto her journal plus photocopies of some of her journal pages. Jimmy had agreed, thinking that Ariella was being more paranoid than anything else. Ariella told him that the pages contained important information about how Professor Sampson was using student work, including hers and Jimmy's, as his own and then getting the students to update their Ph.D.

dissertations to remove the information he had borrowed. Jimmy had agreed to hold onto the pages and the journal for her for a few days. Ariella has said that she would take the journal back after the weekend and would ask Jimmy to hide the copies for her so that there was more than one copy. She asked him not to talk to Derek about it so he had kept it to himself.

A little more than 24 hours later he had learned that Ariella was dead. Jimmy had been so shocked he had initially forgotten that he had the journal in his possession. He didn't think of it when the police questioned him. By Wednesday he had read it all the way through and marked the most pertinent parts. He had wanted to tell Derek about the pages but had been reluctant since Ariella had asked him not to do so. After struggling with whether or not to tell the police what he had, he had decided to talk with Professor Churykian for advice.

After a few minutes Professor Churykian looked up at Jimmy and took off his reading glasses. Leaning back in his chair, why Ariella felt Jimmy only needed to hold the journal for a weekend. Jimmy had pondered the timing of the request and why Ariella had thought that everything would resolve itself on Monday. He had no idea why Ariella thought everything would be resolved by Monday morning.

Professor Churykian did not hesitate for a moment. He let Jimmy know that they needed to call Detective O'Malley immediately and let him review the journal and talk to Jimmy himself about how the pages had been received and why they hadn't come to light until now.

Professor Churykian asked Jimmy to go the small conference room while he called the Detective. Jimmy stepped into the hallway and saw his roommate, Derek, talking with Rick Sampson. He definitely did not want Derek or Rick to see him or to let them know that he was talking to Arthur. Rather than walk towards them, Jimmy turned to his right and continued down the opposite hallway to the stairs. Arthur had the journal with all the marked pages and would be able to handle the discussion with the detectives. Jimmy just needed to get out of there. He still had his own photocopies in his backpack and needed to hide them before he headed home.

Derek hadn't been home much in the past week but when he was home; he seemed to be searching for something. Jimmy had caught him going through his desk and Derek had said he was just looking for his favorite pen. Since then, Jimmy had made sure that the journal and the photocopies were always in his locker at school, safe from prying eyes.

Arthur made the call to Detective O'Malley's cell phone. The detective picked up the phone immediately and Arthur summarized what Jimmy had shown him that morning. Arthur then asked Detective O'Malley if he could join them in the conference room.

Detective O'Malley let Arthur know that he was actually on campus but would need an hour or more before he could join them. Arthur thought that someone needed to come now. O'Malley agreed to send Detective Kelvin to join Arthur and Jimmy immediately.

Arthur thanked O'Malley and when he went to the seminar room, he found it empty. He saw Derek and Rick still talking in the hallway. Arthur assumed that the sight of these two had scared Jimmy away. When they asked Arthur what he was looking for, Arthur feigned absent-mindedness and said he was looking for a book he had laid down somewhere and couldn't remember where. Nothing like using people's perceptions of old age to put them off with an easy explanation. Derek and Rick watched Arthur return to his office and then continued their conversation.

"So, no idea where she hid her journal?"

"I've checked her desk in the library, her apartment, Jimmy's room, your old apartment and your office. I didn't find anything. That bitch really went underground," Derek replied.

"Damn, I knew she would be more useful alive than dead," Rick replied.

"Well, too late now. She pushed the limit when she let us know that she had all the documentation and she was just waiting to present it to the Dean. We'll just have to keep looking. I'll see you later," Derek said.

Rick smiled, clapped Derek on the back and loudly wished him luck with his re-entry to the Ph.D program. Derek thanked him and ambled down the hallway to the elevator. It was only 3 flights but he hated stairs, particularly enclosed stairs. Plus Nancy couldn't see the elevator from her office. He hoped that his and Rick's ruse about re-entry would answer any questions others might have about why he was on the floor.

O'Malley didn't tell Arthur that he and Kelvin were in a cleaning supply room off of one of the underground tunnels that connected several of the older buildings together. The room was infrequently used and a cleaning person had found what looked like blood on the floor of the room. O'Malley needed to stay while the forensic team took samples and photographs and wrote up the scene. If it turned out to be blood, O'Malley wanted to have everything in order before the room was sealed. He knew that someone would leak information to the press as soon as they saw the crime tape so the most he could do was make sure that as much was done and out of the building before the news hit the media.

Detective O'Malley disconnected from his second conversation with Arthur. The first had been to let him know about the journal and the second to let him know that Jimmy had disappeared. Arthur suspected it was because he had seen Derek and Rick talking in the hallway and he was spooked.

"Darcy, would you go over to Baker Hall and talk to Arthur Churykian, he says he has Ariella's journal to show us and it's got some very incriminating evidence. I'll stay here with the team," O'Malley said. "He also said that Jimmy Reynolds was there and that Ariella gave him the journal and some photocopies a week ago, the day before she died. It looks like Jimmy disappeared while Arthur was calling but Arthur has the journal to show us."

"Sure, there isn't much for me to do here."

Thanks, I really appreciate it."

Hey, did you see that there's a security camera up there by the pipe. We should check and see if there's some video we can look at," Kelvin said.

"Damn, it's a good thing you're here. I never would have seen that camera," O'Malley replied, bending down to look behind the pipe to see the camera.

Kelvin smiled, being shorter sometimes paid off. She headed off to Baker Hall to meet with Arthur and take a look at the journal. If anyone asked, she would just say that they had some additional questions for Arthur. They would then go to the office to look at the journal. She would not tell them anything about the potential blood in the maintenance room.

After a few moments in his office, Rick decided it was time to talk with Arthur. He went down the hall and checked in with Arthur's assistant to see if he was available. Arthur was more than glad to talk with Rick.

"So, Arthur, how are things with you. It's been quite a while since we've had a chance to chat," Rick said.

"It's certainly been a hell of a week," Arthur replied.

"Yes, yes it has. I want you to know how devastated I am at the loss of Ariella."

"Really, you didn't seem that devastated on Wednesday night at my party."

"Well, it was a party and we've all been so jumpy, I think we all just wanted to have a good time and forget about everything that had happened," Rick replied.

"Well, I guess we weren't quite ready for that, were we," Arthur responded.

"No, I guess not. By the way, I was surprised that Sam was there. I didn't know that you had invited her."

"She's a part of a writer's critique group that I run. She and Ariella both, actually, and some of the other's at the party are or were also a part of the group," Arthur replied.

"Well, that explains it. You know that Sam and I will be divorced soon?" Rick asked.

"Yes, I do know that," Arthur replied.

"Well, I will have a completed manuscript for you to review by the end of the week. I just want to make sure that everything is perfect."

"That's great Rick, I'm looking forward to reading it."

Darcy arrived while Arthur and Rick were talking. Rick decided to use that as his queue to step out and let Arthur and Darcy talk. Darcy explained that she just had a few follow-up questions for Arthur and also for Rick. Rick let her know that he had a class shortly but would be back after lunchtime. Darcy let him know that she would be in touch with him, either after lunch or by phone to ask a few more questions.

****

Jimmy Houser left Baker Hall without the journal pages that Ariella had given him but with the photocopies of some of those pages. He stopped on the granite steps of Baker Hall to catch his breath. He knew what his next stop would be and he needed to get these photocopies there as soon as possible. Derek stepped out of the door a few minutes later and Jimmy was nowhere to be seen.

Chapter 23

Misty Mustoe was ready to appear before the cameras again with an exclusive news story. A nice young man that she knew had given her, just given her without any compensation of any sort, some photocopied pages from Ariella's journal.

"This is Misty Mustoe with an update on the Ariella Fantini murder investigation. In my hands I have some photocopied pages from Ariella Fantini's personal journal indicating that she was concerned about the use of her work for her Ph.D. dissertation by a faculty member at the University," Misty said, pausing for effect. "Our investigative team is researching this information as we speak and will keep you updated. Sarah and Frank, back to you," the focus of the broadcast switched back to the news anchors, Sarah and Frank, in the news room.

"Well, that is certainly some fascinating information," Frank Kercher, the lead evening news anchor said, turning to look at his co-anchor Sarah White.

"Yes, Frank, I'm looking forward to hearing more about this. It's been a very sad story," Sarah smiled and looked at the camera. "Now, back to our story on the Friday night traffic."

Ron turned off the light on his video camera and started to pack up his equipment while Misty helped to roll up the mike and the cords. They were standing on the sidewalk just outside the entrance to the University. It was a cold and blustery November evening and they wanted to get warm as soon as possible. Only a few people were on the streets at this time.

"So, Ron, what did you think?" Misty asked.

"Pretty good. You weren't too overly dramatic and the information could be explosive or it could be anti-climactic. You didn't telegraph any expectations, so that's good," Ron replied.

"Yeah, I know. Have you read this stuff? She doesn't name the person but I think it's pretty obvious who it was," Misty said.

"It's the boyfriend, right?" Ron replied.

"Yeah, I think it is. He had the most access to her stuff and she indicates that it was someone close to her, very close to her," Misty said.

"The kid didn't give you any pages that said who it was?"

"No, he doesn't have the full journal, he left that with Professor Churykian. These are just photocopies of some of those pages," Misty said, stuffing the pages she had used for the broadcast into her bag.

Ron and Misty finished wrapping things up and got into their van to head back to the station. It would be a long night of talking about all this information with the news director and the producer as well as Frank and Sarah. Misty was feeling good about this. She really wanted Ariella's murderer brought to justice and she really wanted to help her childhood friend Derek.

Back at the news station Frank and Sarah signed off with the promise to be back at 11pm with even more news. They gathered in the conference room with the news director and the news producer to wait for Misty and Ron. They each had copies of the information from the journal that Jimmy had left with Misty to continue their discussion about what to do with the information, particularly when the police and the University attorneys called. They had not vetted the information through these sources before the 5:30pm news broadcast where Misty made the announcement.

It wasn't long before the call from the University attorney came into the station. The news director decided to take the call in the conference room so that everyone could hear what was being said. The conversation was restrained and the University did not like the implication that the University was responsible since no one was named. They would be taking what had already been said into consideration. The news director agreed to fax the pages to the attorney's office.

Misty and Ron arrived at the conference room as the agreement to fax the pages was being reached. Misty was vigorously shaking her head no to indicate that they should not do this, but the new director put his hand up to indicate that this was not up for discussion.

Once off the phone with the attorneys the news director explained his discussion with the station attorneys. Since no discussion about the pages had happened prior to the news cast, the attorneys were very concerned. The journal belonged to someone who had been murdered and murdered on the University campus. Jimmy was nowhere to be found to talk to them about how and where he had obtained the journal. They wanted to proceed very cautiously and they wanted to know if Misty received any new information before it hit the news again. The news director had to agree to this or lose his job, so he agreed.

The news director told them all that this situation was being monitored closely. Since Misty presented the pages to them for use on the news, she would be watched most closely. While they had all agreed to air the brief story, both because it was a great story and because they hoped to find Jimmy to interview him, they all knew they were now on a short leash and would need to consult the attorney's before any other information was released. The attorney's were most concerned that by the time Misty had told all about her conversation and showed her the pages on Friday evening, they hadn't been able to find Jimmy for confirmation. They wanted to talk to Jimmy directly and he seemed to have disappeared.

Detectives O'Malley, Kelvin and Larrabee decided to come directly to the station rather than call the news director after the 6pm news broadcast. Detective Girard was not with them. He had received a call that afternoon that his wife was in labor and had headed to the hospital. The detectives arrived at the station conference room soon after the call with the attorney's was completed and were escorted to the conference room to talk with the whole team.

"Interesting broadcast this evening," Detective O'Malley said while they were all seated around the conference table.

"Yes, yes it was," the news director replied.

"We would like to know where you got the pages from the journal," Larrabee said.

"Misty, would you like to explain how we got those pages," the news director said.

"Jimmy Houser visited the station early this afternoon. Once he explained to me what he had, I agreed to look at the pages to see if it was at all useful. It was good stuff and I convinced the news director to let me use it," Misty said.

"We don't have the full journal," the news director said. "Here are copies of what we do have." The news director passed copies the pages to Detective O'Malley in a folder.

"Thanks for the copies. We actually do have the original journal pages in our possession. Jimmy left it with the Arthur Churykian this morning and then disappeared. Arthur called us in as soon as Jimmy disappeared and gave us the journal. We're glad to hear that you saw him this morning as we haven't been able to find Jimmy either," O'Malley said.

"Are you concerned that something may have happened to Jimmy?" the news director asked.

"Yes," O'Malley replied.

"Have you talked with Professor Sampson?" Misty asked.

"No, we haven't talked with him yet. Since no one is directly named in the journal, we are proceeding as if it could be anyone in the English department and questioning all the professors. We've even brought in a specialist to compare texts of various documents, both published and unpublished, to identify who may have written what," O'Malley said. "Of course, I'm telling you this all off of the record."

The news director and O'Malley did most of the talking while the others watched and listened. They all agreed to not reveal anything on the news until such a time as the case was resolved or they had they had the direct permission of the attorneys. The news director agreed to pass information along to the detectives if they learned anything on their own. For this, the news team would receive an exclusive on the story and would be first to make any results public. The detectives would also talk with Arthur Churykian so that he knew about the arrangement as well. No one could force Arthur to talk with the news people, but they could ask him to consider an interview once this was all resolved.

The conference ended with a round of hand shaking. Misty was encouraged to contact the detectives if she heard anything more from Jimmy or from anyone else for that matter. They news station and the police both expected to hear from lots of people now that Misty had talked about the journal and its revelations, however non-corroborated or downright crazy the information might be.

The meeting broke up with the two anchors heading home to their families for dinner.. There would be no update on the journal or the murder or Ariella Fantini so they anticipated a quiet evening. Misty and Ron stayed behind to chat with the news director and the news producer while the three detectives were heading back to the station house. The detectives needed to write up their report for a 6:30am meeting with the Bureau Chief and it was now 7pm. They also expected to have phone calls generated from the broadcast.

As they were leaving the news building, Detective O'Malley's cell phone rang. He recognized the number and answered immediately. Generally, he would have muted it for the discussion with the news people but he wanted to make sure he was available for any calls from Detective Girard. Detective Girard announced that Isa gave birth to a girl, finally. O'Malley congratulates him and sends along the congratulations of Kelvin and Larrabee as well. They wish him well and update him briefly on the case. They will fill him in on everything once Girard is back in the office, which wouldn't be for a week or two, depending on how everything worked out with Isa, the baby and her 4 brothers.

Back at the station, several phone calls had already been received in reference to the news broadcast ranging from sympathy to outrage to those with more information to share. The detectives picked up the messages and separated those tagged as possibly being serious from those that the operators knew to be total crack-pots or recognized people who called them constantly with unfounded information.

Calls to the news station regarding this story were all being forwarded directly to the police station for review as well. They weren't telling the callers who they were holding for but indicated that someone would be with them momentarily. It was going to be a long night, but O'Malley and Kelvin had nowhere to go and Larrabee wanted to make sure he made a good impression because he wanted to become a part of the team, no matter what had happened in the past when he was a beat cop.

Sam, Kate and Ben were watching the news from Kate's apartment. Sam hadn't really moved back into her own home yet. It was easier to stay at Kate's and hang out and have other people around than it was to face being alone and wondering who was going to break into her place next, even though she knew that Mr. Fantini and Mr. Jones had someone watching her place.

Staying with Kate allowed Sam to put off thinking about things, such as the murder, Mr. Fantini and Mr. Jones, and making a list of everything that is missing or broken or even the meeting with her attorneys and Rick and his attorneys on Sunday regarding the divorce. She really did need to look over those divorce documents but she could put it off until Saturday when there was light and Andrew would be here to accompany her to the meeting. And she owed her agent the latest round of edits on her novel, which were going to be late as well.

"So Sam, when do you think you'll move back to your own place?" Ben asked.

"I don't know," Sam replied while munching on their favorite Chinese takeout.

"I'm not trying to be pushing but I think you might need to get back to your life pretty soon."

He wasn't trying to be pushy or to point out that Sam was cramping Kate's rather free-ranging style, but he was concerned that Sam would retreat and stay at Kate's too long, or at least much longer than was good for Sam.

"Like I said, I have no idea," Sam replied. "Kate, are you looking to get rid of me?"

"No sweetie, I'm not, but I think that you need to take the plunge and move back to your place sometime soon. Definitely before it's sold," Kate said.

Sam munched on her moshi pork and egg foo yung in silence. While her friends made perfect sense, she resented them for being right and for having her best interests at heart. Plus, she probably was cramping Kate's style.

"OK, OK, I'll move back tomorrow. I can't imagine anything else could happen that would scare me away from this decision." Sam said. "Plus Andrew is coming up tomorrow evening to accompany me to the meeting with the attorney's on Sunday.

186

Chapter 24

O'Malley and Kelvin left the station at about 1am, when most of the leads that might have any semblance of truth associated with them had been called and their stories investigated. Larrabee had lasted until 11pm but had pulled too many double shifts to stay awake any longer.

All three knew that they needed to be back at 6:30am for a meeting with the Bureau Chief. O'Malley, Kelvin and Larrabee were all at their desks at 6am waiting for the 6:30am meeting. The Bureau Chief was already there, crisply dressed and looked as if he had never left the building.

At precisely 6:30am the Bureau Chief invited the three of them into his office. The Bureau Chief was the first to tell them that Jimmy's body had been found during the night on the roof of Baker Hall. This time the roof was considered to be the murder site. Jimmy's throat had been slit, just like Ariella's and the Chief would not be surprised if it turned out to be by the same knife. There was blood all around the body and his clothing was also soaked with blood. Of course, forensics would determine with more veracity what had happened, whether the blood was all Jimmy's or if some belonged to someone else and if the same knife had been used on both bodies in both murders.

The chief stressed to them the need to be circumspect and cautious at all times moving forward. Everyone in the city, including the chief, felt that this murder was related to the broadcast from the night before. Two murders in a week at the same building at the same University were attracting the attention of the mayor, the city council and University Trustees as well as administration. It wouldn't be long before the national media and all the local news outlets got wind of this. They needed to make sure they were thorough before any more information hit the news, whether leaked or as part of an official statement.

O'Malley thought back to the night before and could kick himself. As much as he wanted to flush out the murderer, he had not wanted to cause another murder. If he could have found a way to stop this murder, he would have done anything to make it happen.

O'Malley, Kelvin and Larrabee were tasked with going to the University, checking out the murder site and talking to Arthur Churykian, Sam Monroe, Rick Sampson, Donna Sussman and Derek Soper, if they could find him. The chief would take care of Jimmy's parents, Ariella's mother and keep the mayor's office appraised of any new information or developments. He would hold down the office, monitor forensics and assign anyone willing to work on this case with them to help out as needed. He would also keep the lines of communication open with the news director and the news producer at Channel 8 news.

O'Malley and Kelvin asked if any blood analysis had come back from the work they had done the previous morning on what was found in the maintenance room in the underground hallway or if there had been any tape retrieved from the camera that was in the underground hallway. The chief knew nothing of any results being received yet but would keep them up to date on that information as well. The chief then dismissed them with a nod of his head and sent them on their way.

It was Saturday morning, which would be a slower day both in the city and on campus. There weren't as many people coming into the city to work and there would be far fewer classes taking place on campus than during the week. This provided them with some sense of being able to move around without running into too many people, at least in the early part of the day. The downside was that it was the second murder in a week at the same location with a similar methodology. It was going to attract attention and news of the murder would spread quickly. They would need to get as much done as possible as early as possible.

A small crowd had already gathered in front of Baker Hall when they arrived. O'Malley immediately spotted Misty and Ron in the small crowd. Misty looked red-eyed, like she had been crying. Ron looked like he always did, 3-days growth of fine gray beard, gray to almost white hair sticking out of his watch cap, glasses and a perpetually calm gaze. O'Malley, Kelvin and Larrabee showed their badges to the two officers doing crowd control. O'Malley headed for the door to the building while Kelvin and Larrabee went over to grab Misty and Ron and take them up to the English Department conference room, which they were using as a command center until such a time as the body was removed and everyone they needed to interview on site had been interviewed. This had already been arranged with campus security, the bureau chief and the Dean's Office.

Arthur Churykian, as department chair and at the request of University administration, was waiting for them when they arrived on the third floor. He and a couple of campus police and security officers were the only people present on the floor. The Boston police were making sure that they kept the campus police in the loop and did not talk to the reporters. Arthur looked old, much older than he had looked at his party or even at breakfast on Thursday morning. The first murder had been sad, the second much more personal and painful because he felt it could have been prevented. If Jimmy hadn't left the small conference room or if they had been able to find Jimmy and protect him he would be alive today.

Kelvin and Larrabee arrived with Misty, Ron and a student reporter for the school newspaper. "Hey boss, I thought it would be best to bring the student along. She was taking pictures and talking to people about what was going on and she seemed to know that Jimmy was the person found murdered on the roof," Kelvin said.

O'Malley looked at the trio appraisingly before responding. He asked all three of them to stay in the small conference room together while the three detectives and Arthur went into Arthur's office to talk. O'Malley wanted to know how the three of them found out about the murder and the location of the body. Arthur had not told them. He had

189

been alerted to what was going on by a campus police officer. He assumed these three had found out in a similar manner. When asked, none of the three of them responded quickly, indicating that they didn't want to reveal how they had found out about Jimmy's murder.

O'Malley pulled the campus police officer who had called Arthur into the large conference room and lectured him loudly in front of the Boston police officers and the campus police officers on duty in the room about never calling anyone regarding this or any other murder without first consulting the Boston PD. He hoped it would teach them all to keep whatever they heard that day to themselves. Any campus police or security officer found to have talked to the reporters or anyone else about the murders would lose their jobs. It was embarrassing but it was better to have a full-time job than a one-time payoff for information.

They then moved on to what needed to be done that day. Larrabee was sent out to find Rick Sampson and Donna Sussman. No one had been able to reach them by phone so they would do an on-site visit to see if they were at home but not answering their phones or if they had fled. Larrabee took Officer Martinelli with him. He liked Martinelli and was a little bit intimidated by the meticulousness of Officer Wu. Their plan was to visit Rick at his hotel, then visit Donna and lastly to visit Derek and Jimmy's apartment in the hopes of finding Derek.

Kelvin was assigned to take Arthur's statement and then the statements of the reporters or other faculty members who showed up, depending on how things went with the initial interviews. O'Malley went up to the roof to view the body and talk with the medical examiner.

In addition to having his throat slit, someone had tried to remove his testicles but had been stopped. Jimmy was found with his pants and underwear pulled down around his knees. And he was found by the same cleaning crew that had found Ariella. The two-man cleaning crew was once again huddled on the roof of the building, both fiercely determined to give up smoking or to enter this building again. With 2 bodies in 8 days on the same roof, no one blamed them.

After talking with the Medical Examiner and viewing Jimmy's body, O'Malley let the photographers and the ME get back to work on evidence collection. He took the two cleaning people with him down to the 3rd floor larger conference room to have their statements taken and then have them taken home with instructions to speak to no one but the police. He didn't think the two cleaning people would have any problems with those instructions.

O'Malley joined Kelvin in Arthurs' office. Arthur had not heard from Jimmy since he had left so abruptly on Friday morning. Arthur had been surprised to hear about the journal pages on the news the previous evening, he thought the journal was the only copy. Arthur had been shocked to hear about Jimmy's murder from the campus police early Saturday morning. He was concerned about everything that had happened in the previous week and how this affected the reputation of the department and the University.

O'Malley and Kelvin were both concerned about Arthur and how he was handling all this stress caused by the two murders and the suspicion of plagiarism about a faculty member or members. They asked if they could contact anyone in his family. After a few minutes of insisting that he had no family who lived nearby, Arthur produced a phone number for his daughter, Anastasia, who lived in Northampton. He hadn't wanted to disturb her and her family but by now she may have heard about what was going on at the University. O'Malley called her and asked her or someone in the family to come and stay with her father.

Done with Arthur, Kelvin went to talk with Misty, Ron and the young campus newspaper reporter. She and a police took each of their statements, letting them know that no information was to be revealed by them to anyone and particularly anyone in the media. Misty and Ron had already heard and agreed to this the previous evening. The young student reporter started to protest, until she realized that she would be kept in the conference room all day if she continued. She then asked to make a phone call. They let her know that she wasn't being charged with anything, only questioned and that she would be able to make a phone call soon but for now she would wait. The police temporarily confiscated their cell phones so that they would not be able to make phone calls or text messages from the conference room.

O'Malley and Kelvin then decided to question each of them alone to find out how they had received information regarding this murder. When questioned alone, Misty let them know that she had had a phone call from Jimmy during their meeting with the detectives the previous evening. She had had her cell phone on mute and didn't realize he had called until much later that night. On her voicemail, Jimmy had sounded concerned and scared. Misty had spent a time trying to track him down but had never found him.

She had kept the voicemail message so the detectives were able to listen to it and Kelvin then arranged to have the voicemail message from Misty's phone forwarded to the police department system so that it could be kept as part of the evidence for this case. Misty had also received a call from a campus security officer around the time a call had been made to the Boston PD at 5am letting her know of the second murder. She said that she had contacted Ron to join her this morning after she had received the call from the campus security officer. Misty didn't know who, exactly, had called her and she hadn't asked for a name.

Ron's story was pretty much the same as Misty's. He had gone home to his wife and daughter after the meeting the night before; he'd then stayed home until the early morning call from Misty. His wife and daughter were used to his coming and going at all hours so dinner was waiting for him when he got home. His wife would be able to corroborate all his whereabouts for the night and his daughter was up and had gone for a run when he had left this morning.

The young student reporter had also received a call from campus security and she was able to provide the name of the person who had called. She was also listening to the police scanner so she knew that the Boston PD had been called to Baker Hall. She was sure that they were holding her illegally and she let them know that. She was also sure that she should be allowed to leave and to work on a special edition of the school newspaper. O'Malley pointed out to her that she might have a much better story if she waited until there was more information. She reluctantly agreed to stay until released.

Because all the calls had been received on cell phones, the police were able to gather information regarding the phone number used to send the message. The campus security officer who made all of the calls had used his own personal cell phone rather than a University phone but he was easy to track. The security officer was hoping to make some money as an informant. Now he was suspended without pay pending further investigation. If he talked to anyone else, he would be immediately fired.

On the road, Larrabee and Martinelli were not meeting with much success. They had found that Rick had checked out of the Holiday Inn and left no forwarding information. Calls to his cell phone were not being answered. They found no one at Donna's apartment in the South End. One of the neighbors let them know that they hadn't seen Donna much since the Thursday evening. Since the neighbor was so talkative and seemed to be observant, Larrabee asked if he had seen anyone else around the apartment. The neighbors described a young man who had been looking for Donna and/or Rick on Friday. The neighbor had not taken much notice of the person so didn't have any description to provide. Martinelli noted that Donna definitely had some very nosy neighbors in this building.

Their next stop was a second address they had on Donna Sussman. It turned out to be a business address in South Boston with what looked like an apartment above. No one named Donna Sussman lived there, according to the mailbox and to the neighbors. The only person known to live there was a Tom West but he hadn't been seen frequently for over a year. Larrabee and Martinelli were taken by surprise by this information and immediately called it in to dispatch to find out more about this address which turned out to be a reference in Donna's file. Someone would need to do some research and call them back. They made a call to O'Malley to find out what to do next. O'Malley had them head over to Derek and Jimmy's apartment to see what they could find out.

They arrived at the apartment in Andrew's Square to find Jimmy's parents and the Bureau Chief about to enter the apartment. Derek was not there. Jimmy's parents had been informed of their son's death and had viewed pictures of the body but had not yet identified the body yet. The medical examiner and the forensics team were still working with the body. The Bureau Chief called O'Malley to let him know that he had the parents and that he was at the apartment to see if there was anything they could identify as being unusual or out of place. The parents had a key to the apartment so there was no need to force the lock.

Larrabee and Martinelli were asked by the Bureau Chief to join them in looking around the apartment. None of them was prepared for what faced them when they opened the door. The apartment was a disheveled mess of clothes, food, papers, books and dishes strewn everywhere. The parents had visited before and while they didn't think either Jimmy or Derek was especially neat, they had never seen anything like this. The mother started to cry and the father took her in his arms and stepped back out of the apartment.

The Bureau Chief followed Jimmy's parents and indicated to Larrabee and Martinelli that they should continue to look around the apartment but to not touch or move anything, if at all possible. The chief would have the forensics team come in and see if there was anything they could do with this mess. Larrabee and Martinelli moved through the areas of the apartment where they felt they would move the least amount of stuff and not disturb anything important. It didn't take them long to determine that the apartment consisted of an eat-in kitchen with a back door to a porch, a living room with a front door to the hallway, and three bedrooms, one of which was used as an office or computer room. While this room had two desks, only one of the desks had been trashed. They surmised that this must be Jimmy's desk. There had once been an Apple computer on the desk but that appeared to be smashed on the floor. Derek's desk had all the cords for a computer but no computer was in sight.

Of the two bedrooms, it was fairly easy to determine which room was Derek's and which Jimmy's just based on the materials in each room. Derek had his name on several items in the room, and raised letters spelling out his name on the wall. His room was messy but not overly disturbed. Jimmy had a desk, bed and dresser but the dresser had been pulled apart and clothes strewn around the room. The mattress was ripped apart and the stuffing was lying around the room. Someone had really wanted to find something.

After completing their review they realized they would get nothing from this mess until someone came in to organize and review all the materials. They hoped a computer forensics team would be able to retrieve something from the smashed computer but that would have to wait and see as well. Larrabee and Martinelli waited at the apartment until a team came to relieve them.

The Bureau Chief took Jimmy's parents back to the station to help them arrange for a hotel room and to talk with them as more questions were raised. The parents were able to confirm that Jimmy had an Apple laptop as well as an iPhone. With Jimmy's phone number, police officers arranged to monitor all calls to this phone with the carrier. And they were monitoring any calls that came in to the land line at Jimmy's and Derek's apartment. They were looking into getting access to Jimmy's university email account too. They were working on identifying if he had Facebook and Twitter accounts.

Soon after sending Larrabee and Martinelli on their way to do fieldwork, O'Malley called Sam. It was early and he woke her but he wanted to break the news of Jimmy's death before she heard it on the news. He also wanted Sam to come down to Baker Hall to keep an eye on Arthur until his daughter arrived and while they interviewed the various reporters and went through all of the English Department offices, particularly Rick's office. O'Malley hoped she could help identify anything unusual in Rick's office. It was a long shot since neither of them knew what unusual might be in this instance.

The chief had obtained a search warrant for this search and had worked with the University attorney's to allow just one other person, besides Arthur, to be on the floor representing the English Department. They had all agreed that the second person should be the departmental secretary, Nancy. Nancy had been with the department nearly 30 years, having started their right out of secretarial school. She enjoyed the work and the department members and was having a hard time thinking about what would happen once she retired. That was still 10 years away, but it was on her mind. She also had keys to everything on the floor plus a few other spaces in the building.

Sam showered, dressed, grabbed a cab and was at the building in 45 minutes. Before she left, Sam told Kate where she was going, just in case anything happened or someone was looking for her. She didn't have time to call anyone else, particularly Andrew, but at least one person knew where she was going but not what had happened and Kate didn't ask for details. As soon as Ben returned back from his night shift at the hospital, he and Ben would go down to Sam's apartment to make sure that everything was locked up and that nothing unusual had happened during the night. Sam thanked Kate for her concern and for all her help.

Once she got to Baker Hall, Sam was held outside while calls were made to clear her through to the third floor command center. Officer Wu went down the elevator to escort Sam up to the floor. O'Malley greeted her as the elevator doors opened up and escorted Arthur's office. He told Sam that Arthur's daughter was on her way but she wouldn't be there for another two hours. She was driving in from Northampton, MA, and had had to get things at home organized before she left. She would be taking her father back to Northampton with her. O'Malley felt that that would be best. Arthur was sitting in his swivel chair with his back to the desk and looking out his window. He didn't move as Sam entered and he waited a few moments before he spoke.

"Do you think I've been a fool?" he asked.

"A fool about what?" Sam asked.

"About everything. Should I have known more about what was going on in this department? There's always some drama or other, it is academia after all, but we've never had a murder, let alone two murders, before. I somehow feel that I could have done something so that this didn't happen. I feel like there is something important eluding me and I can't put my finger on what it is."

"Arthur, you have been with the department a long time. This department, this University and your scholarship have been your entire working life. Not many people have murder mixed up in their lives and I don't think you should judge your entire career by what has happened this past week. I've spent a lot of time over the past few days thinking I could have done something to prevent Ariella's murder. I feel that I let her down somehow and yet, I had no idea that this would happen. There is no way I could have stopped this chain of events," Sam said.

"Yes, Ariella's murder is particularly disturbing. It just seems so senseless. Why would anyone kill her over a small bit of plagiarism," Arthur said.

Arthur turned around and looked directly at Sam. He was pale and his brow was furrowed. The skin around his mouth and his eyes was more lined than she remembered having seen before. He seemed to have aged overnight. She wondered how she looked right now. Kate kept saying that she never smiled anymore. She couldn't think of anything she had had reason to smile about lately. Other than her mother's birthday party, it had been the worst week of her life.

"You know that they are going to go through all of the offices. Nancy should be here soon to monitor what they do," Arthur said.

"Yes, they think I might be able to help with Rick's office but I'm not so sure about that. I understand that Anastasia is coming to get you," Sam said.

"Yes, they think I should have someone watching over me. As much as I resent it, I have to say it seems appealing to me right now. I don't want to go home tonight and being at Anastasia's for a while might help be put everything into perspective," Arthur said.

"I think it's a good idea too. There's not much that either of us can do except to get out of the way and let the police do their job."

"You know, I'm going to put the house on the market. That was my last party Wednesday night and now it will be a more memorable than anything I could ever have imagined."

"You'll stay on with the department, won't you?" Sam asked.

"I'm not so sure now. I've let the Dean and the President I'm ready to move to emeritus status. They promised me I could do that when I was ready. They'll need to find a new department chair quickly," Arthur said.

"It will be sad day when you leave," Nancy said from the doorway.

Neither Arthur nor Sam had heard Nancy at the door. From the look on her face, it was apparent that she had overheard Arthur's plans. O'Malley came into the office to let Nancy know that they were ready to begin and that they wanted to begin with Rick's office. Rick had known both victims very well and for that reason, plus the fact that they couldn't find him, they wanted to make sure to go through his office first. He asked Arthur and Sam to wait until he was ready for them.

Nancy had already helped O'Malley and Kelvin put together a list of all the offices and the faculty associated with those offices. She had helped the detectives determine in what order they should do their search. Nancy was happy to be helpful but saddened by the reasons for all this activity. Nancy was also saddened by the news that Arthur would be leaving.

While they waited, Sam asked Arthur if he had had any breakfast and he indicated that no, he had not had any breakfast yet. Sam asked one of the police officers if some food and coffee could be delivered, even if it came from one of the cafeterias. Arthur provided a credit card to pay for the food for themselves and everyone else on the floor, including the police, Misty, Ron and the student reporter. It would make the work go a little bit faster.

Arthur returned to his window gazing and Sam started to dose off on his couch. She was surprised when the food arrived quickly. They all adjourned to the conference room for breakfast and Sam was surprised to see Misty in the room. Sam had only seen Misty on TV before, except for the night that Misty had been yelling to her outside of her condo building. Sam was stunned to realize that that had been just this past Sunday.

"Hi Sam, my name is Misty," Misty said.

"Hi Misty, good to meet you," Sam said.

"I know that this is not the right time or the place, but someday I would like to interview you," Misty said.

"What would we talk about?" Sam asked.

"Oh well, most likely about these two murders but maybe we can get something about your book in there too."

"The book part would be good," Sam said. "But the murders are a bit gruesome."

"That's ok, people like gruesome. Since you've been accused and then cleared of committing a murder, it would make an interesting discussion for our audience. Well, anyway, it's been good meeting you. They are going to take us back to the other room now so that we don't talk to each other," Misty said.

O'Malley and Wu asked Sam to stay in the conference room to talk. They wanted to ask her some questions about her friend Donna.

"Donna isn't really a friend any more, but once she was my very best friend," Sam said.

"Well, we've been having a hard time finding her," Wu said.

"Really, she hasn't been at her apartment?" Sam asked.

"We haven't been able to find her at her apartment in the South End. We have another address for her in South Boston but no one seems to have heard of Donna Sussman there," Wu said.

"I think it must be her ex-husbands business. He used to run a computer repair shop and he owned the whole building. He doesn't live there any more, he moved to Attleboro when he remarried a few years ago. I think they have two kids now."

"And his name is Sussman?" Wu asked.

"No, his name is West, Tom West," Sam said.

"Thank you," Wu replied. He got up swiftly and left the room.

"I'm surprised she gave you that old address. She hasn't lived there in years," Sam said to O'Malley.

"When was the last time you talked with Donna?" O'Malley asked.

"Oh, she called me on Thursday evening. She wanted to talk about the party, she said," Sam replied.

O'Malley waited a few moments before continuing, allowing Sam the time and space to add anything. When Sam didn't offer any more information, O'Malley decided it was time to push her.

"So, what did you end up talking about?" he asked.

"Oh, we talked about Rick. She went into a tirade about how I had not been paying attention to him and how everything that happened was my fault," she said. "And he was a good person who was misunderstood and my writing a novel had only added to the misunderstandings."

"What did she mean?" he asked.

"Now that you ask, I don't really know what she meant. At the time, I thought she meant that it was my fault that Rick left me for Ariella because I wasn't paying enough attention to him."

"Do you feel you weren't paying enough attention to Rick?"

"Well, we had drifted apart. I had been working more and more and Rick was working on getting published. Our schedules were not the same so we weren't seeing each other too much. I thought we were developing our careers," Sam said.

"I understand that you put Rick through college?" O'Malley asked.

"Well, yes I did work while Rick finished his Ph.D."

"Did you feel angry with Rick about that?"

"Sometimes, I had wanted to continue my education. Are you creating some sort of psych profile on me?"

"I'm mostly trying to see what was going on between you and your husband."

Sam let O'Malley know that she had never felt angry enough to kill anyone. Sure she was sad and depressed but she had moved on with her life after he left her. If anything, she felt she had moved on rather quickly with her novel and not really looked back at what might have been with Rick.

"How did Donna feel about your writing?" O'Malley asked.

"When we talked about it, she was quite negative. She always said I wasn't a professional writer," Sam said.

"When did the relationship between the two of you start to change?"

"I always thought it was as soon as I was laid off from the bank. But now that I've had more time to think about it, it started to change as soon as she and Tom divorced. She was jealous that I was married and she was not and that I didn't want to go out partying with her," Sam said.

"Were she and Rick friendly?" O'Malley asked.

"Well, yes. When we were all married we used to go out as couples. After that, we went out a few times as a threesome. Apparently they had developed a relationship that didn't include me."

"Did you go out partying with her after her divorce?"

"I went a few times with Donna and others from work. I was always the first to go home. I was never much of a drinker and I wasn't looking to pick anyone up," Sam said.

"So, when do you think Rick and Donna became so friendly?" O'Malley asked.

"You know, I've given this a lot of thought and I just don't know how this happened. I've been getting so irritated with Donna recently, with all her comments about my not being a 'real' writer and why I had been ignoring Rick. They should have set some bells off in my head, but they just didn't. And this whole thing with Rick and Ariella and then Rick and Donna happening so quickly afterwards, it's really, really creepy," Sam said.

"You know, I agree with you Samantha," Arthur said from the doorway of the conference room. "This whole thing is creepy and I don't understand much about it either."

Sam and O'Malley were both surprised to see Arthur at the door. O'Malley asked him to take a seat. The conversation continued with O'Malley asking them both about their recollections of what happened at the party on Wednesday. While their stories differed on some details they were essentially the same. Sam had arrived with Henry and Mathilda and Rick had arrived late with Donna on his arm. They had both been surprised to see Sam at the party. Some words were exchanged and Sam had left with Derek.

Then Rick and Arthur exchanged some words. Arthur remembered more the reaction of everyone else. He was disappointed to see Rick show up so happy and with a new woman on his arm. Arthur also noted that several of the graduate students immediately left the room when Rick arrived. At the time he had chalked it up their dismay over Ariella's death and Rick's lack of mourning, but now he wasn't so sure.

Back at Sam's building, Kate and Ben decided to go into Sam's condo to check up on things. In just a week, they had seen their friend's life be turned upside down again and her apartment ransacked twice. They weren't sure there was anything they could do, but they could check to see. As they entered the apartment, they were greeted by two men, one sitting at the breakfast bar and the other standing behind the counter. The man at the breakfast bar was dressed well in a dark overcoat and a gray suite while the man behind the counter had jeans, a turtleneck and a tweed jacket. It was a moment before anyone spoke. The one behind the counter was Mr. Jones, who had been there when Kate dropped in the other day and he had escorted them both to Kate's apartment.

"You must be Kate and Ben. Sam has mentioned you before. I'm not sure that she has mentioned me before, I'm Dominic Fantini," the man in the dark overcoat said. He got up from his seat and walked over to shake their hands and close the front door. "I'm Ariella's father."

Kate and Ben introduced themselves and Mr. Fantini introduced them all to Mr. Jones behind the counter. Kate and Mr. Jones said hello. Mr. Jones asked them if they would like some coffee. Kate and Ben accepted the coffee and took seats at the other two seats at the breakfast bar. Leaving didn't seem to be an option.

"So, tell me, have you seen Sam today?" Mr. Fantini asked.

"Well, yes, I saw her early this morning. She said she had been asked to go down to the University and she asked me to check on her plants," Kate said.

"And I just got out of work at the hospital," Ben replied.

Mr. Jones had taken most of Sam's plants and watered them in the kitchen sink and placed them on the counter. "She has definitely not been taking care of her plants," Mr. Jones said. "I've given them a good soaking and hopefully that will help. And she hasn't picked up her package yet."

"Well, I'm concerned about Sam and I suspect that she hasn't called her parents yet. Actually I know she hasn't called her parents yet because she has been getting calls all morning from people looking for her," Mr. Fantini said.

Kate and Ben looked at one another and at Mr. Fantini and Mr. Jones. They had no idea what to say and doubted that they were expected to say anything.

"I think that we need to go down to Baker Hall and make sure that everything is ok," Mr. Jones said.

"I agree with you Mr. Jones. My car and driver are outside. Would you care to join us for a ride down to the University," Mr. Fantini said. It seemed more like a direction than a request.

They locked up Sam's condo and headed down the elevator to the first floor. The driver was waiting by the car and quickly got them settled. Mr. Jones instructed the driver to head to the post office first. He then handed the package stub to Kate and asked her to go in and pick up Sam's package. Once that was done, Kate let them know that she was picking the package up for her friend. With the package in hand, they headed for the University. The streets were much busier than when Sam had taken a cab earlier. The Saturday shoppers were out and about.

At the University, Mr. Fantini let the police guarding the door to the building know that he was there to see Detective O'Malley. He let them know that he was Ariella's father and that he needed to talk about the current case. The Boston PD officer was surprised when O'Malley said to let all four of the up to the third floor. The maintenance men had adjusted the elevator settings so that the elevator would only stop at the third floor. It provided a sense of control and didn't encourage people to wander through the building.

O'Malley was waiting for them as the elevator doors opened. Kate and Ben greeted him as they exited the elevator. They had met him at their initial interviews. Mr. Fantini and Mr. Jones introduced themselves. O'Malley asked Kate and Ben to join Sam and Arthur and Anastasia in the seminar room. Anastasia had arrived just about 10 minutes earlier. Anastasia had decided to stay and see what was going on because her father was way too interested to leave at this point.

While Kate, Ben, Sam, Arthur and Anastasia made small talk in the seminar room O'Malley took Mr. Fantini and Mr. Jones into the department office, Nancy's office really, that faced the elevators to talk.

"Mr. Fantini, you do realize that I could arrest you and let the FBI take you away," O'Malley said.

"Yes, I do know that. I think you'll wait on that in case I can help you with this murder. Am I right about that?" Mr. Fantini replied.

"Yes, you are right. The chief has requested that we not arrest you or inform anyone of your whereabouts should we run into you, as we just have. I don't know why he has requested that but he has and I'll do as he has requested. What made you decide to come down here and talk with me today?" O'Malley asked.

"As you know, Ariella is not my only child. She is, though, my only daughter and what has happed to her has devastated both her mother and me. We want a resolution to this case so we can bury our daughter in peace and with the knowledge that her killer has met his or her justice," Mr. Fantini said.

"We're also concerned about Sam," Mr. Jones said.

"Is there any way that you can be traced here today?" O'Malley asked.

"We don't think so," Mr. Fantini replied. "The car is a leased car and it and the driver is on his way back to Rhode Island as we speak. With different license plates than the ones used to drive here. And I don't think Sam, Kate or Ben will do anything to reveal our presence."

"I assume you used one of your own companies?" O'Malley asked.

"As you know, Detective O'Malley, a man in my position has no companies. I am a man without a country and with very few friends. But the friends I do have are very helpful to me."

"Really, well than it should be easy to discuss this arrangement with you. Our Chief is willing to work with you on the information you can provide. He will tell the FBI about the arrangement after you have had some time to do whatever you need to do to," O'Malley said.

"That's a rather generous offer. What would prompt him to be so generous," Mr. Jones asked.

"I suspect it has something to do with the murder of his son," O'Malley replied.

"Yes, you are right about that. I seem to have joined that rather exclusive club of parents of murdered children. I assure you, it's not one you will ever want to join willingly. How are the parents of this boy Jimmy doing?"

"How did you know about Jimmy?" O'Malley asked. He was surprised to hear that Dominic Fantini knew about this murder. They had been working hard to make sure that nothing had hit the news outlets yet.

"As you may have noticed, I do have many, many sources in the city. Several of them are in the Boston Police Department as well as here at the University. You may not know that this, but I am a graduate of this University," Mr. Fantini replied. "I have a degree in chemistry."

"Well, I can honestly say that I did not know that," O'Malley said.

"And I studied here as well," Mr. Jones said. "I left after two years."

"Mr. Jones was a mechanical engineering student. Someday he would like to finish his studies," Mr. Fantini said.

"Well, I hope that you are able to do so," O'Malley said. "Now, let's get down to business while we still have time."

O'Malley let them know that he had to let Misty, Ron, Arthur and Anastasia go. Kate and Ben most likely did not need to stay either. He also wanted them gone while he talked with Mr. Fantini and Mr. Jones as he felt that they might compromise the case too much if they were still around. Sam would be staying around to go through Rick's office with Detective Kelvin.

Mr. Fantini and Mr. Jones agreed to wait in the office while O'Malley made the arrangements to let the others leave. O'Malley also let them know that a University attorney was in with Arthur, asking Arthur to sign a letter letting the Dean know that he was taking a short leave of absence to rest at his daughter Anastasia's house in Northampton with she and her family. The University attorney was then meeting with a young student newspaper reporter. The young woman would not agree to suppress any information about Jimmy's murder unless she got something in return. In this case, she wanted to interview with Mr. Fantini. She had researched Ariella well and knew that Mr. Fantini was a graduate of the University as well as a sometime police informant and, of course, a known mob boss.

"Well, the young woman has certainly done her homework," Mr. Fantini said. "I'd be more than happy to talk with her while you do what you need to do. If you don't mind, I'd like to have Mr. Jones observe what's going on, just as my eyes and ears."

"That would be fine."

"And I think Kate and Ben should stay for a while. They can escort Sam home and it will look a little less suspicious. We'll want to take a look at the package Sam had waiting for her at the post office."

"Do you think that someone is following Sam?" O'Malley asked. "And what package?"

"Yes, I think she is being watched closely. I don't know why, but I'm not sure that it will matter if things don't go well," Mr. Fantini replied.

"Sam had a receipt for a package at the post office. We picked it up for her on our way here," Mr. Jones said.

O'Malley thought about that for a moment but decided not to pursue how they had picked up a package at the post office that was not addressed to any of them. With that, O'Malley brought Misty and Ron into the conference room and let them know that they were free to leave but that they should report anything suspicious to him immediately. He gave them each his card with both the station house number and his own cell phone number that they could call at any time.

O'Malley then let Arthur and Anastasia leave. He encouraged Arthur to call him if he heard or thought of anything. Arthur had already signed the letter for the University attorney and identified the faculty member who he felt should be the Acting Department Chair in his absence. O'Malley gave Arthur and Anastasia the same card and the same instructions as he had given to Misty and Ron with all of his contact information. He wished Anastasia and Arthur a safe drive. They would be stopping at Arthur's house first to pick up some clothes and then would be heading to Anastasia's home. They were also told that they should not speak to anyone about this case or anything they had heard today except Detective O'Malley or, in his absence, Detective Kelvin.

Kelvin took Sam into Rick's office to look around, leaving Kate and Ben in the large seminar room. O'Malley moved them to the small conference room and brought the young reporter to the large seminar room. The University attorney was there to talk with the young reporter prior to her interview of Mr. Fantini. The University attorney reviewed the letter with the young reporter regarding her knowledge of the murder and her interview with Mr. Fantini and then asked her to also sign a letter. The letter stated that that she would not reveal any information until expressly told that she could by the University attorney. In return, she would be allowed to interview Mr. Fantini for 30 minutes. This interview would also not be released for a couple of weeks or until the murder was either solved or became a cold case.

When all letters were signed, the attorney made copies for each of the recipients. He then packed up his things and headed out of the building. He was dressed relatively casually and was using a backpack so he would blend in with the Saturday crowd in the neighborhood. The University had no desire to be more obvious that was necessary.

O'Malley then brought Mr. Fantini and Mr. Jones into the conference room for their interview with the young reporter. Mr. Fantini took off his overcoat and removed his tie to appear slightly more casual. Mr. Jones did not have to go to such efforts to look casual. O'Malley left them to join Nancy, Kelvin and Sam in Rick's office.

"Is there anything out of place or unusual, that you notice?" O'Malley asked Sam and Nancy while all of them were standing close together in Rick's faculty office.

"I can say that it looks neater than the last time I was here, but that was more than 10 months ago. My sense was that he had papers in piles all around the office, even on the couch, but now everything looks neat and there are lot fewer piles around," Sam said.

"I agree with Sam. This is much neater than Rick traditionally has kept his office," Nancy said. "I've been in his office more recently and don't remember it being this neat."

"What about the drawers in his desk and the file cabinet. Do you notice anything unusual about them?"

"No, I don't think I've been into the drawers before," Sam said. Nancy also agreed. Each faculty member is responsible for their own office. There wasn't anybody around to help except the grad fellows.

"Who was Rick's grad fellow?" O'Malley asked.

"This year, Jimmy Houser," Nancy said.

"And last year?"

"That was Ariella," Nancy said.

"Are there any other of Rick's former grad fellows around or anyone for whom he was a grad fellow?" Kelvin asked.

"Well, there is Professor Whitworth," Nancy said. "She's an adjunct faculty member now. Professor Sampson was her grad fellow about 8 years ago. I can give you her home phone number, if that would help. The other two grad fellows that Rick had have graduated. I can look them up for you."

O'Malley agreed that that would be a tremendous help to get both Professor Whitworth's information as well as the names and contact information for the other two grad fellows. After Nancy returned, O'Malley let Nancy know that she could head home. He asked her know to talk about the events of the day to anyone, except the police. And to call him with anything suspicious or curious or which otherwise might cause concern.

"And Jimmy's body, is it still up there?" Nancy asked.

"No, it's been removed by the medical examiner. We are rushing an autopsy in case to gather any evidence that might be helpful to the investigation."

"Very good. Well, if you see them, please tell his parents that he was a wonderful boy and that I will miss him," Nancy said. She left right after that, with tears in her eyes.

Sam and O'Malley joined Kate and Ben in the small conference room. Kate and Ben were looked like they wanted to leave as soon as possible. Which was understandable since they hadn't really known what they were getting into when they had come with Sam earlier..

"Oh, you know, I'm supposed to see Rick tomorrow morning at our divorce meeting with our attorney's" Sam said.

"Can you tell us where that would be and what time?" Kelvin asked.

Sam provided the information. She and Kelvin discussed how unusual it was to have a divorce meeting on a Sunday. Sam explained that it was in preparation for a hearing with the judge on Monday morning. Sam wondered if Rick would actually show up. Sam, Kate and Ben left soon afterwards. Sam was surprised to see Mr. Fantini and Mr. Jones in the conference room. Sam noticed that Mr. Fantini spent some time looking at Kate and wondered, once again, if they would be good for one another.

"Sam, now that everyone else has gone, would you take a look at the package that we picked up from the post office today," Mr. Fantini said. The attorney and the young reporter had both left and it was now just Mr. Fantini, Mr. Jones, Detectives O'Malley and Kelvin, Officer Wu, Kate, Ben and Sam left.

"What package?" Sam asked.

"Oh, this one," Kate said, pulling a large manila envelope out of her bag and handing it to Sam.

Sam took a look at the envelope and noted that it did not have a sender's name. She opened the package carefully and removed the contents onto the seminar room table. She smiled as she looked at it. It was a set of handwritten comments on her manuscript from Walter, one of her writing group partners. Walter was a retired doctor who wanted to write novels and who was challenged by technology. He much preferred writing his comments in pencil on a manuscript and mailing them to his writing group partners. And his penmanship was atrocious so his comments were always hard to decipher. Sam's story caused everyone in the group to smile except Mr. Fantini and Mr. Jones, both of whom looked very disappointed.

"Is there a problem?" Sam asked.

"No, not at all. We're glad you received your comments, we were just hoping the package was from Ariella," Mr. Jones replied.

"Ah, yes. It would be nice to have a package from Ariella," Sam replied.

O'Malley thanked them all for being so patient and asked Mr. Fantini and Mr. Jones if they would stay a little longer. The chief was on his way down and would like to speak with them. Kelvin and Wu were staying as well.

Sam, Kate and Ben strolled out of the building and off of the campus onto the busy street as if they had not a care in the world. The sun was shining and it was getting warmer. After a few blocks they grabbed a cab and headed home. Ben needed to sleep, Kate to get ready for a date that night and Sam just needed time to think and absorb everything and she needed to find out if her brother Andrew was coming into town to go to the meeting with her and her attorneys.

Andrew had accompanied Sam to most of the meetings and this time she would really need him. It was a Sunday meeting as that was the only day they could all agree to for this meeting. Sunday meetings were a little unusual and would most likely cost a fortune. She was now glad that her Dad had agreed to pick up the tab for the divorce.

She wondered how much she should tell him and Andrew about the events of the day. She was definitely not telling her mother too much, especially if she was going to talk to reporters again.

Chapter 25

Sunday morning arrived clear and cold. Andrew had come up from New York City the night before and Sam, Ben and Andrew had all had dinner together. They had braved being seen out in public with Sam and hardly anyone had noticed her. The news about Jimmy's murder still had not been released and so there had been no fresh Ariella murder news for a couple of days. Ben left from the restaurant and headed directly to work while Sam and Andrew walked back to her condo.

Sam spent the rest of Saturday night filling Andrew in on all the things that had gone on that week. She had hardly had time to tell anyone what was happening and she had deliberately not told either her mother or her father many of the details. She didn't want to see her mother on TV again or to have her father calling regularly for updates on the investigation of Ariella's murder. While her parents are loving people who have only her best interests at heart, it would be better to tell them all about the details once it was all solved.

On Sunday morning, Sam and Rick were scheduled for a joint meeting with both sets of attorneys to finalize the divorce agreement prior to meeting with the judge on Monday morning. Andrew was there to support Sam and to provide guidance without drama that each of her parents might cause, if they were there, and their Dad might have a hard time with the divorce agreement. Andrew and Sam both know that their father had provided the deposit on the condo and had had to co-sign the mortgage with Sam since Rick had such a poor credit rating. He would protest the splitting of the proceeds between Sam and Rick, even though Rick and his attorneys had agreed that Rick's portion of the proceedings would go to student loans that have Sam's name associated with them so that Sam's name would be cleared of those debts as much as possible.

Of course, the condo needed to be sold first and the mortgage paid off and all other expenses paid off before they can split the proceeds. The condo was purchased ten years earlier at a lower price that it would sell for today and Philip Monroe had put down a generous down payment. In addition, Sam had been a frugal family financial planner and had bought down the mortgage enough for there to be a tidy profit now.

Sam and Andrew walk to the downtown office building for the meeting. It was early on Sunday afternoon and their stroll was short but pleasant. They strolled through Post Office Square Park and enjoyed the holiday decorations beginning to go up on the buildings around the square.

They were surprised to see Rick pull up to the building in a cab and they were even more surprised to see Donna get out of the cab as well. Sam had been pretty sure that neither of them would show up, given the inability of the police to find them the day before. They greeted one another pleasantly but without too much emotion and entered the building together. The security guard confirmed their appointment and escorted them to the elevators, setting the elevator to stop only at the pre-designated floor for the meeting. On the weekend the building is basically shut down with only limited, pre-arranged access to specific floors.

The ride up the elevator was filled with discussion about the weather and the quietness of the day. No talk of murder took place. Their attorneys are waiting for them in the conference room just off of the elevators. The typed agreement was ready for their review and they all read it through silently.

Rick then asks to speak with his attorneys privately. They excused themselves to a smaller conference room and Donna went with them. After a half-hour or so, one of Rick's attorneys stepped into the large conference room and asked to speak privately with Sam's attorneys. Sam and Andrew are left alone in the conference room.

"I bet he wants to change the agreement. He wants all the proceeds from the sale of the condo again," Sam said. "He makes me so angry about that. He's only contributed to the mortgage for a few years and even then, it's been pretty spotty."

"I agree, he's always wanted all the proceeds. He even wanted you to move out so that he could live in the condo with Ariella, but that's not going to happen. Your attorney's will never agree to that," Andrew said. "That's one reason I'm here, to provide you support while you go through this discussion one last time."

Sam was frustrated and jumpy while waiting for her attorneys to return to talk with them. It took over an hour, but her attorneys finally returned to the conference room, without Rick, Donna and Rick's attorneys. After much discussion Rick and his attorneys agreed to and signed the document that was presented today and which all parties had agreed to preliminarily. They had decided to stay in a separate conference room to reduce any arguments that might arise from seeing one another until the documents were signed by both parties.

All parties were brought back into the conference room once Sam had signed the agreement. Rick never once looked directly at Sam, only at his own attorneys. This attitude angered Sam, she would really have liked to have an amicable discussion about the divorce, but realized that that would most likely never happen. Donna smiled at her briefly but tended to look at everything in the room but the people. The room definitely had some nice artwork and a spectacular view of Boston and the harbor out of the 24th floor window.

Rick, Donna and Rick's attorneys all exited the conference room as soon as they had copies of the signed agreement in hand. The copies were made by a secretary who was in for the afternoon, just for this purpose. Rick, Donna and their attorneys headed directly to the elevator and left as quickly as possible.

Sam and Andrew waited in the conference room with her attorneys until the first group was on the elevator and out of the range of hearing any conversation.

"So, Rick did come in with a proposal to take all of the proceeds from the sale of the condo for himself. The argument this time is that you made more money than he did while you were married and that you were profligate with spending on yourself so he had to make all the mortgage payments. Because he struggled so to get his degree and keep you in the style to which you had become accustomed, he deserved the proceeds. We went through all the numbers again and it just didn't add up. In the end, we convinced him to stay with the original agreement. We also noted that any delay in an agreement would mean that we would have to reschedule the court date and that might mean another 6 months. And then there is the 120 waiting period after the court date before the divorce is final."

"So he decided to agree to everything because he didn't want to wait?" Sam asked.

"Essentially, yes, he decided it was better to proceed than to delay. He seemed quite antsy. Of course, he doesn't know that the police will be waiting for him downstairs."

"Thank you for telling me." Sam said.

"You're welcome. It's my job to tell you everything that happens. So, we'll see you in court on Tuesday morning. Here are your copies of the signed agreement," her attorney said. "By the way, I know that you are involved in this murder investigation and that Rick is still considered a suspect and you are considered a person of interest. I would like to arrange to have one of our criminal attorneys be on call for you, in case something comes up. I particularly don't want anything to come up before Tuesday morning."

"Yes, I'd be happy to talk with one of the criminal attorney's here. So much has happened this week, I haven't really had a chance to think about an attorney," Sam said.

"Great I'll have someone get in touch with you tomorrow. And congratulations on the book and the contract for the additional books, that's great. By the way, Andrew will you be in court on Tuesday?

"Yes, I'm leaving to head back to New York tonight and I'll be flying in on Tuesday morning," Andrew replied.

"Great, we'll see you both then," Sam's attorney said.

The meeting was concluded. They shook hands with the attorney, said good-bye to the secretary who was waiting outside the conference room and headed for the elevator. "Boy, he talks so fast," Andrew said on the elevator.

"Yes, which is good since he charges by the hour," Sam replied.

As they were leaving the building, they noticed that Detectives O'Malley, Kelvin and Larrabee were talking with Rick, Donna and Rick's divorce attorney's across the street. The detectives seem to have been waiting for Rick. Sam decided not to stop and she and Andrew continued on their way across the park and back to the condo to pick up Andrew's bag and walk over to South Station so he could catch the train to New York. When he had the choice between taking the train and flying, Andrew generally chose the train. On the way, Sam explained that she had told the detectives about the meeting and let them know that Rick was scheduled to be there. She had not known that Donna would also attend, so that was a double-bonus. She explained that the detectives had not been able to find Rick or Donna the day before.

"So now that they had agreed to the sale, and everything but the hearing has taken place, how do you feel?" Andrew asked.

"I feel great. I didn't think I would be so elated but it's been a long time coming and I'm happy to be free," Sam replied.

"Almost free, there's still the hearing, selling the condo and the 120 day waiting period."

"Yes, but now there is a plan and a schedule for selling the condo and settling everything. I'll be able move ahead with my life and that will feel good too. I'll miss the condo but a fresh start seems to be in order," Sam replied.

"You have certainly made quite a few fresh starts in the past few months, why not moving too."

They said good-bye at the train station and Sam headed back to her condo. It was raw with a freezing rain, snow combination coming down on the city. With the low clouds, it made everything seem so dark. She would be glad to be home sleeping in her own bed tonight. She would definitely miss the ability to walk anywhere in the city from her condo when she moved because she was fairly sure she would not be able to afford anything in the city. But she decided not to worry about that today.

The detectives escorted Rick and Donna into the station house to take their statements regarding Jimmy Houser. They indicated that they had been looking for Rick and Donna since Saturday morning but had not reached them at either of Donna's their apartments, at the University, at Rick's hotel or by cell phone. Rick let them know that he and Donna had gone to the Cape on Friday night for a getaway and had just returned this morning. They had decided to turn their cell phones off and just decompress from the week.

"I thought the two of you were just friends with no romantic attachments?" Detective O'Malley asked.

"We are. We went to the Cape as friends," Rick replied. Donna did not look particularly happy with this response but she didn't say anything.

"That's good because if you were romantically attached, that might shed a bit of a different light on Ariella's relationship with you and with her murder," O'Malley said.

"Why would that be?" Donna asked.

"Well, until now, you have been considered just a friend of both Rick and Sam Monroe's, particularly Sam. If the relationship was different and Rick here is a suspect in the murder you could be considered a person of interest."

"Oh, I didn't know that," Donna replied.

"Did either of you know that Ariella was pregnant at the time of her murder? About three months along the report says," Kelvin said.

Both Rick and Donna were visibly surprised by this news. "Uh, no, I didn't know that she was pregnant. Who was the father?" Rick asked.

"We won't know until we take a DNA sample for testing," Kelvin replied. "Would you be agreeable to allowing us to take a swab?"

"I would like to do that," Rick replied.

Kelvin produced a DNA swab kit and took a swab of saliva from Rick's mouth. She quickly labeled everything and handed it to Larrabee to send off to the lab. Larrabee wasn't happy to go, he really wanted to be there for the interview but being low man on the team didn't provide him with the opportunity to protest.

"So, now that that's done, let's talk about why we brought you here. Did you know that Jimmy Houser was murdered early Saturday morning and found in the exact same spot that Ariella was found?" O'Malley asked.

Rick and Donna looked at each other and at the detectives in amazement. They had not watched any TV or listened to the news so they were completely unaware of Jimmy's murder. O'Malley explained to them that it hadn't been released yet but would be announced by Misty Mustoe on the Sunday night news at 6pm. Because Misty and her bosses had agreed to suppress the story to allow the beginning part of the investigation to go on unhampered, she had been given an exclusive on the story.

Rick and Donna stuck to their story that they were on the Cape and they had the hotel receipt to prove it, just like Sam had her receipts to prove her trip to Florida. Kelvin noted that Sam's case wasn't quite the same as she had people who had seen her or been with her over the entire weekend. Rick and Donna didn't really have anyone who had seen them, just the hotel receipt and possibly the hotel clerks. The restaurants they had gone to were takeout. They had had a very quiet weekend and they hadn't really interacted with anyone.

Their statements were taken and they were released but told to let the detectives know if they were planning any other trips out of town. Donna's current address and name were confirmed for the record. She apologized for any confusion she had caused with two names and two addresses; it had just been a slip on her part. Rick provided the detectives with his current hotel location. He too apologized for any confusion that he may have caused by moving and not providing updated information.

Once outside the police station, Rick and Donna decided it was time to part company. They had provided the police with too much of a reason to put them together as more than just friends. Rick grabbed a cab to his hotel and Donna decided to walk to her apartment. O'Malley had been prepared for this separation and he had two unmarked cars outside, waiting to follow each of them.

Misty and Ron were ready for her Sunday evening at 6pm broadcast. They were stationed at the main gate to the University. This time the content and tone of the broadcast had been reviewed by the station attorneys, the University attorneys as well as the news director and the news producer. The parents also knew what would be said.

"This is Misty Mustoe for Channel 8 news. This evening I have the sad news to report to you that the young man who provided me with the pages from Ariella Fantini's journal indicating that someone what stealing her work, has been found murdered.

"Jimmy Houser was found on the same rooftop as Ariella had been discovered. He was found early Saturday morning. His throat was cut in a manner very similar to Ariella's. The only difference, in this case, was that Jimmy was murdered on the roof and not in a different location.

"The police asked us to hold onto this story while they conducted their investigation. They have not yet identified the murderer but they do believe that the same person or persons murdered both Ariella and Jimmy. The police want to stress that these murders are not a threat to the general population of the University and that no students should be concerned for their safety while on campus. The target of these two murders have been very deliberate.

"We will keep you advised of any updates in this case. Students and their parents who have any concerns should contact the University at the number that appears at the bottom of your screen. This is a hotline set up to handle these concerns. Should you have any information for the police regarding these two crimes, please contact the police tip line at the second number that appears on this screen.

"This tragedy must be resolved soon. Back to you Sarah and Jim."

With that the news cut back to the anchor desk where Sarah and Jim expressed their concerns and their sympathies for the families of Ariella Fantini and Jimmy Houser. The assured the public that they would keep them updated on these two cases and they reiterated.

Sam and Kate were watching the news together, this time from Sam's place. She was relieved to find that her face did not appear on the newscast this time as a person of interest. The parents of Ariella and Jimmy watched the newscast together from their hotel and did their best to comfort each other. The president of the University and the Dean of the College watched the newscast together in the Dean's Office. They knew that class attendance would be light on Monday and probably for most of the week, until either the perpetrators were caught or the students forgot about the murders. The second scenario might happen sooner than the first.

The University call center lit up as soon as the number appears on the news. Mostly with calls from students asking for school to be cancelled or parents calling to express their concerns that the University wasn't doing enough to protect the safety of their children. All calls were recorded and each operator noted the name of the person they were talking to and the time that they called. The goal was to flag anyone who might be calling with a lead to more information.

The police hotline number also received immediate call activity as well. Many of these calls were parents as well as neighbors concerned about the safety of the neighborhood and the University. Again, all calls were recorded and notes taken by each operator regarding the name of each caller. Nothing of any significance arose from any of the calls received.

Chapter 26

"Ok, folks, can I have your attention," O'Malley announced in the Detectives Briefing Room. He didn't wait very long for things to quiet down before he began.

"Welcome to Monday morning. For those of you who actually had the weekend off, ee have a lot of things to discuss this morning. We'll start with the Fantini and Houser murders. As you know, Officers Wu and Martinelli spent the night watching Sam Monroe's condo building. In particular they were keeping an eye on the people coming in and out of the building. Our main suspects, Rick Sampson, Donna West and Derek Soper were not seen in the area. On Sunday afternoon, we had Officers Wu and Martinelli waiting outside the attorney's office, where the preliminary divorce meeting was taking place, and Rick and Donna both showed. We were able to grab him and get another statement from both Rick and Donna, who seem to be quite friendly with one another these days. Apparently Rick and Donna had been on the Cape from Friday night until Sunday morning and did not listen to any news, read any newspaper or go to any restaurants other than to pick up some take-out. We're looking into their alibis."

"Once we released them from custody, we had unmarked cars follow each of them. Rick Sampson returned to his new hotel and did not leave for the rest of the night. Donna Sussman-West returned to her apartment and remained for the rest of the night. We have no idea where Derek Soper may be. Derek has not been to the University or reported for any of his scheduled work rotation. So far, Rick has not returned to the University. He has scheduled classes this afternoon, so we'll have to see if he decides to show up or not."

"Are there any updates from forensics on either Ariella or on Jimmy Houser?" the Bureau Chief asked.

"Yes, we have the complete report and autopsy on Ariella Fantini and she was pregnant at the time of her murder. About three months along. It would have been a boy. And it appears that she had been given or had somehow ingested the date rape drug GbH. That might well explain how she was murdered without much of a struggle. We have taken a DNA swab from Rick Sampson to determine if he was the father.

"Some preliminary testing on Jimmy Reynolds indicates that he was given the same date rape drug, which would also explain the lack of struggle."

"Damn, there goes our one good suspect," Det. Dawson said after letting out a low whistle.

"Who would that be?" the Bureau Chief asked.

"Don Fantini or someone out to get Don Fantini," Detective Dawson replied.

"Yes, it does seem to eliminate Don Fantini and his associates but we haven't fully determined that yet. We know where Don Fantini was when Jimmy was murdered and when Ariella was murdered so we can eliminate him personally for those two. They have never been known to use drugs or to slit throats, particularly of their own children. Plus, we have had the opportunity to talk with both Mr. Fantini and Mrs. Fantini. At this time we do not feel that either of them had anything to do with this" O'Malley continued.

"You don't mean to tell me that you think Sam Monroe is still the murder suspect, do you?" one of the older detectives said loudly from the back of the room.

"No, we really do not consider Sam Monroe a suspect any longer. She has a very solid alibi. We are definitely focusing all of our attention on Rick Sampson, Donna Sussman and Derek Soper. The three people, whom we cannot currently locate," O'Malley responded crisply and professionally.

"Sam Monroe did receive a package last week. At first it looked like it might be something from Ariella but it turned out to be comments on her manuscript from one of her writing group members. An older gentleman who doesn't like technology so he hand writes all of his comments. He also has terrible penmanship, so his comments are extremely hard to read," O'Malley continued.

Some of the detectives noted, under their breaths, that they hated computers too.

"Are we sure it wasn't something from Ariella that was disguised to look like it came from someone else?" A detective asked.

"But we're not even sure that a manuscript by Ariella ever existed?" Kelvin responded. "And besides, these comments were on Sam's manuscript."

"No, but we do know that Ariella wanted to leave something with Sam and Sam declined to accept it since she was going away for a few days. We just don't know at 'it' was that Ariella wanted to leave behind. Possibly it was the journal pages that she ended up leaving with Jimmy. Possibly it was something else," Detective O'Malley said.

The Bureau Chief dismissed the meeting and indicated that they would get together again on Tuesday morning at 8am for their daily briefing. He thanked them all for their time and attention to this case and let them know that he felt this would all be over soon.

Chapter 27

On Monday morning, while working on her much delayed and much promised revisions for her novel, Sam hears her phone ring. She decides to let the call go to voice mail. If it's her editor, she's already late and she will call her later. If it's anyone else, she'll deal with it later. In a few minutes, Sam's cell phone rings. Against her better judgment Sam looks at the number and sees that it's Rick. She hopes that it has nothing to do with the divorce hearing on Tuesday but it's probably better to find out now rather than find out later. Rick is actually calling to let her know how upset and saddened he is by the Jimmy's murder.

Sam is a bit surprised that he is calling her, particularly since she didn't really know Jimmy very well. She'd met him but they were separated most of the time he was Rick's grad assistant so she hadn't spent much time with him. Rick then wanted to know how Arthur was doing and why he was taking leave, particularly before the end of the semester. And why at his daughter's house. Sam decides to let Rick know that Arthur has been devastated about the deaths of Ariella and Jimmy and all the attention their murders have brought to the English department and to the University. Arthur needed to get away for a while and this was how he chose to do it.

Sam and Rick also talk about the condo and she lets Rick know that she has arranged for a realtor to come to the condo that evening to assess its condition and to provide an asking price for the sale. She hasn't engaged the realtor yet. The realtor was recommended to her by Kate and Sam wants to make sure that she can work with the realtor before hiring him. Rick lets her know that he will be there as well to meet the realtor. Sam isn't too happy about this but she agrees that they can do this together.

Sam is surprised that the conversation with Rick went so well. Their conversations for the past year have been terse or even non-existent, the run-in at the English department an example of the former and the meeting at the attorneys yesterday an example of the latter. Sam knows that someone will need to be at the meeting this evening and hopefully someone will be around and able to support her, possibly Kate. The court hearing is on Tuesday morning and Andrew is flying in on Tuesday morning to be with her so he won't be available on Monday evening. Sam doesn't want anything to interfere with the finalization of their divorce.

Sam has been struggling with whether or not Rick is the murderer. For all of their problems, she just can't convince herself that Rick could or would murder another human being. He could certainly be haughty and condescending verbally but not physically aggressive. She can believe that he is a plagiarist. Rick was never one to let opportunity to pass by without grabbing it, even if the opportunity was someone else's work.

Sam calls Kate to join her that evening to talk with the real estate agent. Kate is reluctant as she doesn't want to be there with Rick and anyone that Rick might bring along with him, such as Donna. Nor does she want it to appear that she is being provided any material advantage for having recommended the real estate agent to Sam but she also doesn't want leave Sam alone. In the end, Kate agrees to be there for the meeting with the agent and with Rick.

Once Kate agrees to help, she goes all out. She enlists Sam to spend the day helping Sam to stage the condo to present it as well as possible. Having the cleaning people in to clean up after the break in has helped considerably. The windows are clean and the place is generally picked up. The amount of time spent arranging and rearranging furniture does cut into Sam's writing time. Sam knows that it will be painful to get all the work she needs to get done by the end of the week but she goes along, knowing that selling the condo and attending the divorce hearing are both major goals of hers. They bake some cookies so that the place smells homey and comfortable.

Outside of Sam's building, Officers Wu and Martinelli are once again parked for the evening to observe those coming and going. Detective O'Malley doesn't think that Rick is as innocent as he claims and he suspects that Sam might be in more danger than any of them anticipate. She is the only other person that Ariella tried to leave something with and while it hasn't been found yet and Sam doesn't didn't accept anything from Ariella, doesn't mean that it, whatever it might be, isn't somewhere near or around Sam. It would have been so much easier if it had been the manuscript at the post office.

The detectives have worked enough cases to know that just about anyone can commit a murder under the right circumstances and those circumstances do not need to be very complex or even make sense to an outsider. There is an element of emotion and cruelty to these murders along with the need to hide something that concerns the detectives. The fact that it is obvious that Sam was set up to take the blame for Ariella's murder make them even more concerned for her safety. The detectives feel fairly certain that Rick was the one to set up Sam but there isn't enough evidence yet to place Rick in that position.

Mr. Fantini and Mr. Jones are also certain that Sam was set up to take the blame for Ariella's murder. They are also having the condo building watched and the same crew is also keeping an eye on Officers Wu and Martinelli. They know the two officers will receive a call before they do so they want to make sure that they are in a position to follow the officer's if something comes up. Mr. Fantini's crew is monitoring the police band but know that any call Wu and Martinelli receive will be over a secure band or via cell phone.

All of them observe Rick and Donna as they enter the condo building hand in hand with their own key. While the lock to Sam's place had been replaced, there was no way to change the lock to the common entrance used by all the tenants and owners. They all make note of this closeness and familiarity, Wu and Martinelli call it into the detectives and Mr. Jones calls it in to Mr. Fantini at the hotel. Mr. Fantini is spending time with his ex-wife, who has not been handling the news that their daughter was pregnant at the time of her murder well. Not only did she lose her only daughter, she has now lost her first grandchild and she is devastated.

As Sam and Kate are getting ready to go out for dinner, there is a knock on her door. Sam is a bit surprised since that assumes that someone has a key to the outside door. She looks through the peephole in the door and it's Rick with Donna in tow. It's only 5:30pm and Rick is early, much earlier than expected. She lets Kate know who it is and opens the door to let Rick and Donna into the condo. Rick and Donna greet Sam warmly, as if nothing unusual has happened and they express surprise to find Kate there but they greet Kate in a friendly manner.

"So, did you use your building key to get in?" Sam asked.

"Yes. It felt familiar to use that old key again. I've always liked this place, I'll be sorry to see it go," Rick replied.

"You know, it doesn't have to be sold. I could buy out your share in this place," Donna said.

"Actually, the sale of the condo is a part of the divorce agreement that Rick and I signed yesterday. If we changed anything now, it would delay the divorce proceedings we have for tomorrow morning. I'm not sure either of us wants to wait another six months or so for the court hearing and then the 120 days after that to finalize the divorce in case either one of us changes our minds," Sam said.

"No, you are right; I'm sure neither of you wants to delay the divorce any longer. It's just an offer. I guess it's something we should have talked about prior to the meeting yesterday," Donna said.

Sam was surprised to hear the 'we' part of that statement. It both indicated that Donna was involved in the sudden change of heart regarding the agreement and desire to come here this evening to talk with her and that she and Rick were close, closer than they indicated to the police on Sunday.

"I see you've cleaned this place up really well," Donna said.

"What do you mean? It's always been relatively clean hasn't it?" Sam said.

"Well, I didn't mean to imply it was dirty. I guess I just like the way you've rearranged the furniture and the new bookshelf you've added," Donna said.

"Oh thanks. It was pretty ripped apart by someone earlier this week and I had some cleaning people come in to go through and clean everything, even the windows. I guess I'm just a little jumpy about that," Sam said.

"Oh, yes, I can quite understand why you would be jumpy," Rick said. "Did the cleaning people find anything unusual?"

Sam was about to speak when the buzzer went off indicating that someone was downstairs. If it was the real estate agent, he was certainly early. They were scheduled to meet at 6:30pm not 5:45. The real estate agent apologized for being so early. He was in the neighborhood and took a chance to see if anyone was home. Sam buzzed him in and they all waited for him to arrive at the front door. Sam let him into the condo and he stood at the front door taking in the space with an appraising look. He was a young guy, younger than Sam thought he would be. The real estate agent and Kate smiled and nodded to one another but made no signs of having met previously.

"Well, well, you have a very nice condo here. Are you sure you want to sell?" the real estate agent asked.

"Yes, we are in the process of getting a divorce and the sale is a part of the divorce agreement," Sam replied.

"That's too bad. I see from my notes that you got this place at a really good price. Well, let's see what we can do to sell this place and help you settle your divorce agreement. Can you give me the 10 cent tour?"

Sam showed him around the condo with Rick and Donna also following which took a bit longer than she anticipated. He asked a lot of questions and took a lot of notes. Kate stayed in the living room, sitting quietly on the couch and observing everyone. Rick and made a few comments about new items but otherwise they were less involved in the discussions. Rick checked is Blackberry a few times and sent a few messages while Donna wandered around, looking at the rooms as if seeing them for the first time. Sam tried to ignore them both as having them in the condo made her skin crawl.

"Well the good news is that this place looks to be in pretty good shape. I'm going to suggest that you reduce the amount of clutter in the second bedroom that you are using as an office. Get a bed in there along with the computer and desk and put everything else in storage. It will look more like a 2-bedroom that way. It would be great if you could reduce the number of books you have in the living room and in the office as well. Not everyone will be interested in books. The living area will look more spacious if you could remove at least one full bookcase," the real estate agent said.

"Some of those are mine. If you don't mind, I'd like a chance to go through them before they get packed away," Rick said.

"Of course. We'll arrange a time when we can both be here to go through the books. It will be easier if you can box and take yours away," Sam replied.

"Thank you," the real estate agent said.

"I think we'll be able to remove one and possibly two of the three bookcases," Sam said to the real estate agent.

"That would be fantastic," the real estate agent said. "We want to highlight the space and just provide some hints as to what can be done without overwhelming the potential buyers.

"When do you think you will have some numbers on what this place can be listed for?" Kate asked. She was looking directly at the real estate agent and avoiding the exchange between Sam and Rick.

"I'll need to crunch some numbers. I would like to get them to you before the court hearing tomorrow but I doubt I'll be able to do so. I understand the divorce is not contingent upon the final sale price of the condo. Is that correct?"

Both Sam and Rick nodded their heads.

"Well then, I'll leave you with two copies of my standard contract and I'll do my best to get those figures to you by Wednesday night, at the latest. You have a great view here and that will add to that final figure," he replied. He handed each of them a contract, said good-bye, thanked them for allowing him to come through early and headed out to his next appointment.

"Well, I was hoping he'd have all the figures for us tonight," Donna said. Again, Sam was surprised at the 'we' reference.

"Would you reconsider having me buy you out, Sam?"

"No, I'm going to move forward with the sale of the condo and the divorce agreement as Rick and I have agreed to," Sam replied.

"You know Sam; you have never treated Rick well. He is a brilliant man and you have thrown him away like yesterday's news," Donna said. She was perusing the books on the book case and not looking at anyone in particular.

"What do you mean that I have never treated Rick well? I worked while he was a full-time student. I made sure there was a food on the table and a roof over our heads," Sam said. She could feel her face grow hot and red while her temper rose. She did her best to keep her voice steady.

"Oh, you know what I mean. You didn't support his work, what he was striving to achieve. You went out and wrote you own book," Donna said.

"So we're back on the track of my writing a book detrimentally affects Rick's success in producing his own masterpiece. Even though we have different names and are writing totally different things?" Sam said.

"Yes, as a matter of fact we are. You could have worked with Rick to help him achieve success rather than achieving it on your own. Of course, we don't know what kind of success you will achieve," Donna said. "And the he might not have left you for Ariella."

"Or any of several other students," Derek Soper said. He was standing behind the kitchen counter leading against refrigerator in a black, hooded sweatshirt and dark jeans.

"Jesus Christ, I've been texting you for the past few minutes to not come in here tonight. We have it all under control," Rick said. He was looking at Derek and Derek was ignoring him.

"Well, I ignore all texts from you as a matter of course," Derek replied. "Well, well, we have quite a crew here, don't we Sam. Oh, and the place is looking very nice and cleaned up now."

Outside, Officers Wu and Martinelli were calling for back-up. While walking around the building, Officer Wu had noticed someone in dark clothing entering the condo building through a small half-door in the basement. Wu had called Martinelli on his radio to let him know and Martinelli had called it in to the dispatcher. If Wu hadn't been patrolling on foot at that moment, they would not have seen this person entering the building. Mr. Jones and his crew were able to pick up the police call. It was not made on a secure channel but on the general channel. He sent out two men to follow Wu as quietly as possible.

"Great, there is a basement door that allows the meter readers in to a small space with all the meters," Wu radioed back. "It looks like there's a door from this room that leads into the basement. From there he can probably go anywhere."

"Damn," Wu said.

"Officer Wu, might I have a very quick word with you," Mr. Jones had walked up quietly to Officer Wu. He didn't wait for a response before he continued. "I would like to suggest that my men accompany you into the building. I don't believe we have much time to wait. The person or people who killed Ariella and then Jimmy are looking for something and they think that Sam has that something. We need to act now."

"I agree," Wu said, with only a brief hesitation. He would process all the reasons why this was wrong from a police officer perspective later. For now he needed backup and it was here.

"Great, I've sent two of my men to follow you into the basement. Some of us will accompany Martinelli into the building. We have keys."

"Great, let's do it. Martinelli, did you hear all that," Wu said.

Martinelli replied affirmatively and indicated that the two men were with him already.

"I heard that as well and we are on our way. Don't wait for us," O'Malley's voice was clearly heard over the radio.

Officer Martinelli, Mr. Jones and the third man entered the front of the building with the Mr. Jones keys while Wu and two men entered through the basement. Martinelli, Mr. Jones and the third man grabbed an elevator to Sam's floor. Wu and the other two men took the back stairs, aiming for the back entrance of the condo that accessed through the kitchen.

Inside the condo, the conversation was ongoing.

"What do you mean by cleaned up?" Sam asked.

"You do realize that I'm the one who 'broke-in' and trashed your place," Derek said.

"No, I didn't know that. Why would you break in and trash everything?" Sam asked.

"Because we believe that Ariella left you something that we need?"

"Oh, and what would that be?"

"The files and documentation that she put regarding plagiarism in the English Department," Rick replied.

"You mean her journal?"

"No, we're talking about more extensive documentation; exact analysis and comparisons of certain documents with some commentary from Ariella," Rick replied. "She did a lot of work on those documents. It's too bad no one will ever see them."

"Oh, I had no idea. I thought it was the journal that everyone was looking for," Sam said. She was scared and had no idea what to say. She hoped to keep them talking while she figured out what to do next. Out of the corner of her eye she saw Kate with a cell phone. If she could keep them focused on her hopefully Kate could text someone for help.

"Well, do you really think we would kill someone, two people even, over a journal?" Derek asked.

"We?" Rick asked.

"Yes, we, meaning you, Donna and I. You don't really think I decided to do this all by myself do you?" Derek replied.

"Now, Derek, we agreed to keep Rick out of this so he could concentrate on his work and not worry about the messy details," Donna said. She was still standing next to the bookcase with her back to Kate. Kate was still sitting quietly in the corner, behind Donna and not as visible to Derek who was still in the kitchen area. Rick was sitting in a chair by the front door and Sam was standing between Rick and Derek.

"Oh, give me a break. Rick hasn't done anything original in years. He's been borrowing and using and sleeping with students for as long as I've known him," Derek said.

Sam turned to look at Derek as he spoke and noticed that he was now brandishing a knife, a particularly nasty looking hunting knife. He must have had it hidden somewhere when he came in, she thought. She turned back to look at Donna and Rick. Rick was looking at his Blackberry, which had just buzzed, and Donna was glaring at Rick.

"So, why kill Ariella for the information. Wouldn't it have been easier to have her give you the information?" Sam asked.

All eyes turned suddenly toSam. She hoped that by having everyone focus on her, Kate would be able to send a text message without drawing any attention. Certainly Derek, Rick and Donna were focused mostly on each other.

"Yes, it would have been easier to get it from her directly. Donna here thought it would be a good idea to give her the drugs to confuse her and have her give up the information. But, no, Ariella went into the bathroom, fell and hit her head in the bathtub and we couldn't wake her. So, I slit her throat to make it look more gruesome," Derek said.

"Why? If you had waited, she might have woken up and given you what you wanted."

"I'm pretty sure that the blow to her head would have killed her or left her in a coma. I was hoping that the way we did it, the police would

237

look for someone with more of a motive to kill her," Derek replied. "Like you."

"You thought the police would be so confused by the murder they would not look at the people closest to her?" Sam asked. "You thought you would convince them that I murdered her out of a jealous rage?"

"Yeah, that was Donna's big idea. She said they wouldn't look any further than you if you had no alibi."

"Shouldn't you have checked to make sure that I was an abili first?" Sam asked.

"Yes, that was a detail that I overlooked. You didn't tell me you were leaving town," Donna replied. "Anyway, where's the package you picked up Saturday morning at the post office?"

"It's in the office. It was comments from one of my writing partners in the writer's group," Sam replied.

"Look, we know that Ariella visited you the night before you left and that she had a package she wanted to leave with you. You said you didn't accept it, but it isn't anywhere that we looked," Rick said. "Can you show it to us?"

"It's still in my bag," Sam said pointing to her bag sitting in one of the chairs at the breakfast bar. She didn't make a move for it because it would bring her closer to Derek and Derek had the knife and was obviously crazy. Rick walked over to her bag, pulled out the manila envelope, opened it, turned it upside down and let the manuscript pages slide out onto the counter. They had a rubber band around them but still the pages fell all over the counter.

"Well, this is obviously your manuscript with some comments written in the margins. I don't think you or anyone else will ever be able to read this handwriting," Rick said. He looked at Donna and said. "She obviously didn't mail it to Sam. I say we leave now before we get into more trouble than this is worth."

Derek snorted in derision and Donna smiled and shook her head. Donna said they had come too far now to give up plus they couldn't leave Sam to talk to the police or even worse, Mr. Fantini. The police would have to follow procedures; Mr. Fantini would not need to follow the same rules. Derek let them all know that he felt Sam knew too much and needed to be killed, along with the nice woman on the couch, to make sure that there was no one who could point a finger at them.

Sam was very worried when Derek started to raise the knife and was heading for her. She was frozen to her spot and couldn't think of anything else to say to keep the conversation going when both the front door and the back door burst open at the same time.

The police were coming in both directions. Donna pulled a gun from behind her back and started to move forward when Kate tackled her. Sam turned to see Rick running towards her, blocking a knife throw from Derek. The knife hit Rick in the back and he collapsed just as he reached Sam, taking Sam to the floor with him. She heard Rick whisper 'I'm sorry' in her ear. His unconscious weight on top of her was both comforting and distressing at the same time. The knife sticking out of his back and the blood caused her to start screaming.

Office Wu from the front door and Officer Martinelli from the back door all fired at Derek. Derek had crouched in front of the breakfast bar after throwing the knife at Rick. Derek wasn't bleeding nearly as much as Rick. Donna broke free from Kate and ran to Rick, sobbing.

"What did he say?" Donna asked. She was kneeling next to Rick and Sam.

"I'm sorry," Sam replied.

Donna looked at Sam in shock and then at Rick. Officer Martinelli came up behind Donna to restrain her and Mr. Jones helped Sam up off the floor. One of Mr. Jones men helped Kate up. Officer Wu checked Derek's pulse.

"Officer Wu, I think we will be on our way now. It sounds like reinforcements have arrived," Mr. Jones said as sirens approached. He signaled to his men and they all headed towards the back stairs.

"Thank you," Officer Wu replied. "Is there any way I can get in touch with you?"

"I'll call you tomorrow," Mr. Jones replied and then they were gone.

It was just a few eternal minutes before Detectives O'Malley, Kelvin and Larrabee came through the front door, weapons drawn. With a quick scan, they put their weapons away and surveyed the scene. Rick and Derek were down and bleeding and it didn't look like either of them would survive. Donna was physically unharmed. Sam and Kate both looked to be in shock. O'Malley had called for ambulances as soon as he heard shots fired from both Wu's and Martinelli's guns over the radio.

The EMT's arrived quickly and began to work on Derek and Rick. Derek was pronounced dead but would need to be transported to the hospital for the official call to be made. Rick was still alive. Although he had lost a lot of blood in a very short time, the knife hadn't hit the heart or lungs so there was a possibility of survival.

Once Rick and Derek had been taken care of and removed, they turned their attention to Donna. She was sitting on the floor covered in Rick's blood, rocking back and forth and letting out a high-pitched sound. The EMT's had had to remove Donna from clutching Rick to work on him. Sam suspected that this is what they referred to when someone was making a keening sound. Donna was totally unaware of any activity taking place around her.

O'Malley took Sam by the shoulders and placed her in the chair by the front door, the one that Rick, until recently, had been sitting in. Larrabee escorted Kate back to the couch. Kelvin gave direction to the police officers, forensics team members and medical personnel as they arrived. Ben Gunn made it through the crowd of police in the hallway with his medical bag and his hospital tag. He took a quick look at Sam, shook his head and then went to check on Kate. He spoke quietly to her and then had her taken out of the room by a paramedic. O'Malley protested this move but Ben explained that as far as he could see, both Kate and Sam were in shock and would need some medical treatment before they could or should speak.

Mr. Fantini stepped quietly through the back entrance and walked over to Sam to see if she was ok. He completely ignored Rick and Derek and all the other activity going on around them. He asked Sam if she was alright and Sam was able to nod her head. Ben Gunn joined them and explained that Sam was in shock and most likely unable to talk. He was arranging to have her transported to McLean Hospital, along with Kate, for observation. Ben expected that in a few days or even a few hours, she would be able to speak but she would get better faster if she was not in this place. He gave Mr. Fantini his card should he care to call.

Mr. Fantini thanked Ben and for his kindness and concern. He patted Sam's hand and then stepped aside as two EMT's escorted her out of the condo and to a waiting ambulance. Mr. Fantini nodded to Kate as she was escorted out as well but Kate didn't seem to see him or anything else.

O'Malley stops them out in the hallway. He asks Ben if it would be OK to speak with Sam briefly. Ben nodded to the two EMT's to step aside for a moment and Ben stayed with Sam while O'Malley asked his question.

"Sam, I know that you have just witnessed a horrific scene. But I want you think back to the night that Ariella visited you before you left for Florida. Can you tell me everything that Ariella did while she was here?"

It seemed like an eternity before Sam spoke. "Ariella used the bathroom, made tea and took some ice cubes out of the freezer."

"Thank you. Ben's here and he will be taking good care of you," O'Malley said.

Outside, Misty Mustoe was recording for a news break. Misty turned in time to see Sam being escorted to the ambulance. Sam looked dazed and was covered in blood. Ronnie decided to film it and if the station didn't want to use it, that would be ok. At any rate, it was now on film.

Sam felt suddenly very, very tired and just wanted to lie down. She could think about everything tomorrow or the next day. The paramedics helped her into the ambulance and had her lie down on the gurney. They gave her a sedative and she soon drifted off.

The two ambulances, one with Kate and one with Sam, pulled away and headed for McLean Hospital, a psychiatric hospital that provided private care, security and seclusion. It was also used for those who just needed a few days of rest and solitude.

Misty began her broadcast as the ambulances were pulling away.

"This is Misty Mustoe for Channel 8 news. We are outside the condo of Sam Monroe, until recently a person of interest in the Ariella Fantini murder. We understand that shots have been fired and we have just seen a woman who appears to be Sam Monroe escorted to an ambulance. She appears to have been covered in blood. We'll keep you updated on any further developments from here, Sarah and Frank.

Sarah and Frank acknowledged Misty and quickly turned it back to the regularly televised programming with the promise to return as more details become available.

In the condo, the police and forensics teams worked carefully together. O'Malley patiently waited for them to finish with Derek's body. Once he is moved and the area around him is documented, they will be able to get into the freezer. Larrabee's role is to check out the bathroom for anything that Ariella might have left behind the night she was there.

242

Kelvin attempted to take a statement from Donna but she doesn't respond to any questions. It's as if she doesn't see or hear anything at all. When Ben Gunn returns, they ask him to do an assessment of her as well. Ben indicates that Donna seems to be near comatose and suggests that she be transported for observation as well. O'Malley agrees and Donna is taken out to an ambulance and transported to McLean Hospital for observation.

Ben asks O'Malley if he might be allowed into Sam's bedroom so that he can get some clothes for her. The clothing she is wearing will need to be bagged for testing by forensics and he lets them know that she will be much more comfortable and responsive if she has her own clothes rather than having to wear hospital issued garments. Detective Kelvin accompanies him to the bedroom. He quickly throws some jeans, shirts and underwear into a bag. Kelvin suggests that he also take some shoes or sneakers as there was blood on her shoes as well along with a sweater or two and she might want a nightgown and robe as well. Ben thanks Kelvin for her thoughtfulness and help.

Ben then asks O'Malley if he can do the same for Kate. Kelvin and a uniformed policeman follow him up to Kate's place and observe him making clothing selections. Kelvin again makes some helpful suggestions and Ben is happy to follow them. Ben is asked to sign a form for what he has taken from each condo, for recordkeeping purposes, and he does so. Kelvin has done most of the work on listing the clothing taken and Ben is happy to just sign.

Ben stops by Sam's place to let the detectives know how to reach him and how to reach Sam and Kate at the hospital. Ben heads out with the clothing for Kate and Sam. Mr. Fantini says good-bye to Detective O'Malley and quietly leaves. He leaves by the front door but he is hardly noticed by anyone. He is very good at changing his body language to that of one who has no reason to be noticed.

Misty Mustoe and Ron are still outside waiting to hear what the detectives will have to say to the press. They notice a non-descript man leaving the building without being stopped by the police. They assume that he is a resident who is not connected to the events of the evening.

Chapter 28

On Tuesday morning Sam wakes up and realizes that she has a court appointment to attend that day, after a few moments of though she realizes that it is most likely not necessary now. If Rick has survived, he'll definitely be unable to attend. She is rested and alert and she remembers what happened the night before. While she isn't sure she can face the world just yet, she does need to call her attorney to let him know what's going on and to call her brother Andrew and let him know what happened. She looks at the clock and realizes that he is most likely already in Boston.

She is in a private room that looks relatively pleasant. There is a window with sun shining through and she can't find a phone, either a land line or a cell phone. She sees her own clean clothes and decides to get dressed. There is at least a shower in the bathroom attached to her room. She checks the room's door and realizes that she is locked in.

She quickly takes a shower and gets dressed. A nurse pops in to see how she is doing and to let her know that she has some visitors. The nurse explains that she doesn't need to see any visitors if she doesn't want to, but that her father and her brother Andrew are here. Also, her attorney called to say that she doesn't need to worry about anything; he's informed the court of the events of last night and will handle all inquiries about the divorce and any other matters.

Sam takes it all in and decides to ask for breakfast, if that's possible and to see her father and brother. The nurse suggests that she might want to join her father and her brother in the solarium. The nurse assures her that no one will bother her in the solarium and it will be a more genial place to talk with her family.

While having breakfast and talking with her father and brother, Sam sees that Detectives O'Malley and Kelvin have arrived. They are with the nurse and with Ben Gunn obviously asking to talk with Sam. Ben has them wait for a moment and enters the solarium to talk to Sam. Andrew immediately gets up meet Ben before Ben reaches their table to see if there is anything that should be discussed without Sam.

Philip does his best to keep Sam focused on him and her breakfast but it's a lost cause. Sam is curious and wants to know what is going on. Andrew reluctantly agrees to let the detectives talk to Sam.

"Hello Sam, how are you feeling today," O'Malley asks.

"It's ok, I'm not crazy and you can talk to me like I'm a normal person," Sam replies. She smiles and there is a smile in her eyes, which O'Malley notes with a sigh of relief. Kelvin quietly observes the two of them.

"Great. We are here to officially inform you that you are not quite a widow yet. "And Rick is still in a coma at the hospital. They didn't hold out much hope but for now, he's alive. We are sorry for everything that happened to you yesterday," O'Malley continued.

"Interesting, I think that means I'm not a widow and I'm not divorced either. Did you find anything in my condo that belonged to Ariella?"

"Yes, we found a flash drive in a plastic baggie taped to the underside of the toilet tank. Ariella must have been prepared to hide something should you or anyone else she talked with not be able to hold this for her," O'Malley said.

"Is there anything on it?" Sam asked.

"We don't know yet, and once we do we may not be able to tell you anything until the trial," O'Malley replied.

"If Rick and Derek are both dead, what trial will there be?"

"Donna is certainly an accomplice and right now she is claiming that she knew nothing about this," Kelvin said.

"That's not what she said last night," Sam said.

"Yes, we imagine that you heard quite a few things. We are going to need to take a statement from both you and Kate on what happened last night. Dr. Gunn will be keeping you here one more night so we would like to do this tomorrow," O'Malley said.

"My daughter will be leaving with me for Long Island tomorrow," Philip said.

"Thank you, Dad, I really appreciate it. But I'm going to stay with Kate for a few days. We will both need the support and once my condo is cleared, I'll need to go through everything and pack it up. I won't be living there anymore," Sam said.

Sam noticed the frown on her father's face and knew he was coming up with a plan to get her to Long Island. "Once Ariella's funeral is over and I've made arrangements for my things and we know if Rick will survive, I'm going to come and stay with you and Vittoria for a week or two.

"Well, I'm not sure I'm comfortable with that," Philip replied. "I think you should come with me now."

"I've been on my own for quite a few years now and while I really appreciate your concern,, I have to get through this in my own way," Sam said.

"Besides, Miranda will be here tonight and is going to stay at least until Saturday. I'll be back on Saturday to take Sam to Ariella's funeral and to help get things packed up," Andrew said.

"Well, if you are insistent, I guess you'll have to stay," Philip said.

The detectives pointed out that they would need Sam to stay to complete her statement or statements over the next few days. Andrew said his good-byes, let Sam know that her attorney would be waiting for her call when she was ready and headed for the airport.

Philip had a car and driver and decided that he would stay one more day, even if Miranda was going to be there. He then stepped out to call Vittoria and let her know what was happening. The detectives also headed out and Ben encouraged Sam to finish her breakfast. Sam asked where Kate might be and Ben let her know that Kate was having breakfast in bed this morning but would be down in the solarium for lunch.

Chapter 29

Misty stood off to the side as Ariella's funeral service was ending. She was near a tree, under a dull November sky and she looked directly into the camera that Ronnie held.

"This is Misty Mustoe, coming to you live from Ariella Fantini's funeral. What an amazing two weeks this has been. We started off with the murder of a graduate student and ended with her funeral. The events in between have been the stuff of fiction; a love triangle, the murder of another student, the death of one of the murderers and the near death of one of the other culprits, and the attempted framing of an innocent party, all in the name of love and plagiarism and deadlines not met. The suspect still clinging to life is Rick Sampson, Ariella's lover and the man who may have been stealing her work. Two other deaths are those of Ariella's friend and confidante, Jimmy Reynolds, and Jimmy's roommate, Derek Soper, the suspected murderer of both Ariella and Jimmy. And the woman initially accused of the murder, Sam Monroe, estranged wife of Rick Sampson, is here today to attend the funeral. She is accompanied by her brother, Andrew Monroe, and her mother and step-father, Miranda and Joe Johnson."

"For those of you who may have been following the story during the past week, Sam Monroe has been working closely with local police to help solve the murder and is one of the witnesses to the death of Derek Soper.

"Ariella's mother, Mrs. Sophia Fantini, is also in attendance at her daughter's funeral along with her two sons and Ariella's two half-brothers, Antonio and Carlos. Ariella's father, Dominic Fantini, is still wanted by the FBI and did not make an appearance today although it is rumored that he has been in the area during the past week. It appears that the FBI is here today just in case Dominic Fantini does make an appearance.

"This is Misty Mustoe for Channel 8 news. Back to you Sarah and Frank."

With that the news cuts back to Sarah and Frank at the anchor desk.

"Well Frank, what a sad ending to such a turbulent week. I understand that the funeral was quite moving. And it was interesting that her mother decided to have Ariella buried here in Boston, where she was born, rather than taking her back to Italy where her mother and step-brothers now live."

"Yes, Sarah, it was a moving day. We look forward to the updates to this case as they happen. Such a sad, sad ending for Ariella and for Jimmy Reynolds, who will be buried by his family in Connecticut later this week." Frank turns to look directly at the camera. "Thank you for joining us today. Now we return you to our regularly scheduled programming."

"Thanks, guys, for coming in on a Saturday morning to do this," the news director says through the microphone to Sarah and Frank at the news desk.

"Not a problem," Frank replied. "How could we miss the latest update on this case? Well, I'm off to Maine for the remainder of the weekend, call me if anything comes up."

"Thanks, I wouldn't miss this for the world. I'm off to a 10 year olds birthday party," Sarah said.

With that Sarah and Frank were gone. The news director and the news producer were still in the control room, getting themselves ready to go. It had been a long, grueling week for them as well and, so far, no one had sued them or threatened them bodily harm.

Misty and Ron were breaking down the camera and sound equipment as the limousine with Ariella's mother and the step-brothers leads the procession of mourners out of the cemetery.

"How sad for her, she's lost her only daughter and the daughter's only child," Ronnie said.

"True, but she does have the satisfaction of knowing that her daughter's murder is resolved, at least in some fashion," Misty said.

"Well, that's true, but if I lost my daughter, there's nothing that would stop me from finding and punishing her killer," Ron said.

Misty had never heard Ron be so emphatic before. It both startled her and made her aware that Ron was very much a family man.

Mr. Jones drove the limousine that held Sophia, Antonio and Carlos. He had stayed with them constantly since Monday night, when everything had happened at Sam's condo, at the request of Mr. Fantini.

"Mr. Jones, I want to thank you for all of your help these past few days. You have been a rock for us, how can we ever repay you?" Sophia said. Her English was impeccable, but more heavily accented than he remembered. It had been a long time since she had lived in the Boston area.

"There's no need to repay me. Your thanks is all that I need," Mr. Jones said. The boys smiled at this gracious response.

"Ah, you have been well trained Mr. Jones. Well, again, our sincerest thanks. Will you be taking us to the airport this afternoon?"

"Yes, I will. What time would be you like to leave?"

"Around 3pm. Tell me, Mr. Jones, what will you do after we leave?" Sophia asked.

"I'm thinking of staying in Boston and returning to school. I have two more years on my degree," Mr. Jones said. The two boys raised their eyebrows in surprise but said nothing.

"Very good Mr. Jones. What will you study?"

"I think I'll finish my mechanical engineering degree," Mr. Jones replied.

"Do you know where my husband is today?" Sophia asked.

"I'm not sure but I think he mentioned visiting Professor Churykian in Northampton before leaving for his next stop," Mr. Jones replied.

They were already at the hotel and Mr. Jones got out, opened the door and let everyone out. Sophia reminded him to pick them up at 3pm and then entered the hotel in an elegant flourish of black.

A visitor appeared at the door of an elegant home in Northampton. Certainly more substantial than he expected. Professor Churykian's daughter had done very well for herself. A maid answered the door and Mr. Fantini asked to speak with Arthur Churykian. The maid asked him to wait outside while she went to check.

Anastasia opened the door within a minute. "Why do you want to see my father? He's supposed to be resting and not be disturbed."

"I've come only to thank him for his kindness to my daughter," Mr. Fantini said.

Anastasia looked at him, deciding whether or not to let him in. After some internal debate, she stepped aside and let him into the house. She then pointed to the back of the house and let Mr. Fantini know that her father was in the solarium reading.

He smiled his thanks and headed to the solarium as directed where he found Arthur sitting in a chair, reading a book and dozing. Mr. Fantini took the chair next to him.

"Well, so I have some company. Tell me the news from the big city, if you don't mind," Arthur said. He closed his book and focused on his visitor.

"I just wanted to stop by and thank you for your kindness to my daughter," Mr. Fantini said. "She was buried today and I need to be on my way."

"Well thank you and thank you for stopping by. I haven't really heard from anyone, except Sam of course," Arthur replied. "And I can honestly say that I don't miss the place that much, at least not yet."

"That's good. I think you deserve a good, long rest," Mr. Fantini replied. They talked a bit more about the case and then Mr. Fantini departed. He thanked Anastasia for letting him talk to her father and then he was on his way. He planned to be over the border in Canada by nightfall.

Chapter 30

"Well, everyone lets drink a toast to surviving the preliminary hearings and the grand jury investigation," Arthur said. Arthur, Sam, Kate, Ben, and Andrew were gathered for a dinner together. It had been a while since they had all been together for something other than a funeral or in the confines of a courtroom.

"So, Sam, have they decided yet if you are officially a divorcée?" Arthur asked.

"They have officially decided that Rick and I will still need to be divorced in a court. All the work we had done and our signed agreements were not accepted by the judge. We have a date for 6 months from now. Until then, I am still a married woman, unless Rick either doesn't come out of the coma or he dies," Sam replied.

"Sam, I'm so sorry to hear that. It's time you were free of that bastard, even if he's still in a coma," Arthur said vehemently. They all nodded in agreement.

"Who gets to pull the plug on life support?" Arthur asked.

"I do, as his next of kin," Sam replied.

"And?"

"That decision will be made on the advice of doctor's and with the consent of Rick's mother and father. I'm not doing that on my own."

"Too bad," Arthur said.

"By the way, I sold the condo. I've sold it to the real estate agent who came by that evening to check it out that night," Sam said.

"That's wonderful. Where will you be moving to?" Kate asked.

"I don't know yet. I'm wondering if I can stay with you for a few weeks until I figure out what I will do next. I promise I'll go to my father's every weekend," Sam said, crossing her heart in mock honesty.

Kate agreed to let her stay. The conversation ebbed and flowed around everyone's lives. Arthur had decided to retire and move to a retirement home near Anastasia, Eric and the boys. Andrew was continuing to work as an investment banker in New York City. Ben had accepted a position in the emergency room at Maine Medical Center. It would be a little slower paced but allow him all the outdoor activity he could possibly want. Kate had found a new position at the hospital as a volunteer coordinator on a part-time basis.

"So, Sam, we're all dying to find out. Has Detective O'Malley ever called you and asked you out," Arthur finally asked.

"No, well we do talk about the case from time to time but he's never asked me out," Sam replied.

"Why not?"

"I suspect because neither one of us is ready for that yet."

They raised their glasses in a toast to being survivors. Mr. Jones watched them, unnoticed, from across the room.

###

Proof

Made in the USA
Charleston, SC
17 February 2012